OLAF

By Rudy Thompson

Introduction

This novel is about a young man named Olaf Peterson leaving Sweden at age 18. He had no thoughts other than getting a job as a logger in Canada. What that simple event brought about is the basis for this story. Even though characters are fictional most locations mentioned are real and can be located on maps.

2-12-16

To
Jowell and Deborah
with Love.
Rudy

OLAF

Chapter 1
Olaf and Minnie Peterson

Olaf Peterson didn't know if he was Swedish or Norwegian. It depended on which side of his parents' home the authorities placed the Swedish Norwegian line at the moment. It was always in dispute.

When Olaf was 18 years old and finished with school he went to work in the woods. Logging was about the only kind of work available where he lived and too much of the time even that had no work for him. He had learned to speak some English in school and he had a plan. He had saved some money and when there was enough he would book passage to Canada. He knew that there would be work available in the Ontario forests.

His father had been killed in a logging accident and his mother had remarried. He had been very close to his dad, more so than to his mother and now with his dad gone there seemed no good reason to stop him from heading out to a new country; little did he know the chain of events that this decision would make happen.

Olaf's stepfather was fairly well off and when he learned of Olaf's plan, he offered to loan Olaf what he still needed for passage to Canada. When Olaf started making money in Canada he could send money to repay the loan.

Olaf thought that to be a generous offer and accepted it. Now, two months later Olaf had found a job in an Ontario logging camp. A timber faller needed a partner at the other end of his falling saw. When he saw that big strong blond Scandinavian he was pretty certain that the guy would be a good partner, it was Olaf that got picked from the job applicants. He knew that he had a good partner when he found that Olaf had learned timber falling in Sweden.

These timber faller teams got paid an hourly wage but they got a bonus for all the trees they put on the ground over a given number of board feet. Naturally too, there was competition between the teams. Olaf and Henry McKenzie were usually the top team.

Hank, as Henry was usually called, was half and half Scotch and Chipewyan, members of an American Indian people of subarctic Canada. Their language was known as Athabasca.

What became of interest to Olaf was that Hank had a sister named Minnie who worked in the camp mess hall. Olaf thought she was the most beautiful young lady he had ever known. Minnie knew that Olaf worked with her brother and was quite impressed with the husky young Swede.

Minnie and Henry's Scottish father was working for the Hudson Bay Company when he met a young lady member of the Chipewyan tribe during a fur trade. He was impressed not only with her beauty but by her skill with language interpretation between her tribal language and his Scottish accented English. He realized that if he could hire her to work for Hudson Bay Co. she would be an asset as they engaged in the fur trade. The members of her tribal family were reluctant to let her do that but a deal was finally worked out for her to work for the company. Her tribe would get a number of guns with powder and shot and he would be responsible for her wellbeing.

This was an arrangement that worked well, so well that he fell in love with her. When he asked her to marry him she said that before she could do that she would have to get permission from her family. In the Chipewyan tribe marriages were usually arranged by the family. The family would often pick an older person who was a good hunter and trapper, in other words a person who had in some way achieved success and would be an asset to the family.

With more guns with powder and shot, the family agreed to a marriage. In the past Cree and Chipewyan had for a long time been at war with each other. For a time the Cree had an advantage. In their trading they had obtained guns while the Chipewyan had only bows and arrows. When the Chipewyan began to acquire a few guns and then even more guns they were no longer attacked by the Cree and the two tribes maintained a fairly friendly relationship.

The grownup Minnie and Henry had found their way to an Ontario logging camp where they found work. They had lost both their parents in an epidemic of some sort. Henry became a tree faller and Minnie worked with food preparation to feed hungry loggers.

The upshot of all this was that within a year Olaf was in love with Minnie and had asked her to marry him. She had been wishing that Olaf would hurry up and do that and was ready with a "yes." She knew the story of her parents marriage and was happy that she didn't have to get permission from anyone, Minnie's last name became Peterson and Hank was happy to know that his sister had married just about the best person she could have found for a husband.

Hank and Olaf had been hearing much talk about logging in British Columbia. The area where they had been working in Ontario was getting near logged out. Perhaps it was time for them to move on to greener pastures.

They read about extensive logging in the coastal forests of British Columbia and that was where they decided to go.

Six weeks later Hank and Olaf were felling timber for a large logging operation in the Powell River area. Logging here was in some ways quite different from the logging in Ontario. Railroad spurs extended into the forest. Wood burning steam donkeys with a system of spar trees and cables yarded logs from the woods and in the area where Olaf and Hank worked, to the banks of a salt water cove. Here they became part of a raft capable of being towed to mills in the vicinity of Vancouver. Cedar and spruce logs were used to build these rafts. There was some Douglas fir in this area too but most of that was a little further inland. Cedar, spruce and hemlock were the predominant trees in this area. Hemlock at this time was of little value for lumber, there was a use for the bark which was high in tannin and was used in leather tanneries. Later a very large paper manufacturing plant was built in this vicinity and hemlock was probably the source for the pulp,

Hemlock logs had such a high water content that if they were dumped in a mill pond they would likely sink. A freshly milled two by four left out in the sun would tend to almost twist itself into a corkscrew. In later years ways were developed to better handle and dry lumber as it was milled and much of the wood went into dimensions such as two by four or two by six used in home construction. For a period of time vertical grain hemlock flooring became popular. One good thing about hemlock was that the wood didn't tend to sliver as did fir.

After almost a year of timber falling they learned that there was a need for saw filers. All those falling and bucking saws had to be kept sharp. This was a technique that both Olaf and Hank knew very well. In fact they had been doing their own saw sharpening, they thought that they did it better than the company sharpeners.

Now hired by the company to keep all the saws sharp they were working in the shop complex, they no longer worked in the woods. A gasoline powered drag saw was used to cut the blocks of wood to be split as fuel for the donkeys and the heavy drag saw blade had to be kept sharp. The best straight grain knotless logs were picked for this purpose. The easier the blocks could be split the less time would be spent doing it.

There was a bunkhouse for singles and rooms, some with cooking facilities, for married couples. Minnie had a job in the cook house and mess hall complex. She and Olaf had their meals in the mess hall.

The maintenance shop complex included a blacksmith shop as well as machine shop and a general repair shop that took care of the broken axe and shovel handles as well as broken pike poles. The steam locomotive shops were further inland. The tracks here were temporary and were moved around to where needed. Caterpillars were coming into use for clearing the way for rail roadbeds. There was a use for hemlock logs in these roadbeds.

Olaf and Minnie often talked about the huge number of skills required to run a large logging complex as was this. Minnie was a part of the many it took to feed the hard working crews. Welders and blacksmiths were kept busy repairing broken equipment.

Logging was a sometimes dangerous occupation. There were broken bones, sprains, cuts and bruises, and to care for those a sick bay with a doctor and nurse was available. On the water logs for the rafts were moved around by nimble young guys who wore lightweight calked boots as they rode rolling logs. But nimble and good at what they did, sometimes one would fall in what was very cold water. Their clothing was not designed for swimming so sometimes there was a drowning but other times the guy was fished out of the water quickly enough for him to be revived.

Another year had gone by when Minnie realized that she was pregnant. She told Olaf that she didn't much like having her baby here. They discussed their options, they could go to a more civilized part of British Columbia where he might or might not find work. Olaf knew that wherever there was logging he could find a job but logging wasn't everywhere.

They talked about going to the United States, perhaps Washington. Perhaps Hoquiam would be good as any as a destination, they knew that there was logging activity there. They talked to Minnie's brother about their plans, and would he like to go with them? His answer to that was no, he liked his work and didn't wish to move to some other place. Minnie knew the real reason he didn't want to leave. One of her coworkers had confided to her that she and Hank were becoming romantically attracted to each other.

One of Olaf's coworkers suggested that he and Minnie talk to the skipper of the big tugboat that was almost ready to tow a raft of logs to a mill in the Vancouver vicinity. Olaf did that and found that the tug was short handed and could use a little temporary help. Sven Johnson, the tug's captain, realized that Olaf had no tugboat experience but could find his help useful. When he learned that Minnie had been working with the camp cooks she could help in the galley.

The distance to Vancouver was not great but these large rafts made for slow towing. Bad weather might make for a three day trip instead of the usual two. Olaf and Minnie had drawn their pay and now they were saying goodbye to Hank. With all their belongings aboard they were now underway. They had come to Powell River on a ferry and now they were leaving on a tugboat.

This tug normally had a crew of five, the skipper, two deck hands, a cook and the engineer to care for the big diesel engine. At the moment the tug was short a deckhand. There had to be someone at the wheel in the pilot house at all times they were underway to keep the tug on course. Olaf and the deckhand would take turns at the wheel. Sven explained to Olaf that all he had to do was watch the compass and keep the tug on course. In this area there were tidal currents that would throw the tug off course, when this happened Olaf would tend to over correct but he quickly learned to avoid doing that. Sven complimented him on his quickness to learn.

It was into the third day that they arrived at Vancouver and late in the day by the time the log raft had been delivered to the saw mill and the tug was on its way to its home dock. Sven really liked Olaf and Minnie and he realized that they were strangers to Vancouver. Minnie had quickly learned how she could help in the galley. He had a big home and guest bedroom, why not invite them to spend the night at his home?

When he did that, their response was that they didn't wish to impose on his hospitality. When he pointed out that they were strangers and didn't have the faintest idea how to find their way around what was a very large city Olaf and Minnie accepted Sven's invitation.

Sven phoned his wife to let her know that he was bringing company for the night. To his wife Anna this was not a big surprise. Sven frequently did things like this. They loaded Olaf and Minnie's bags in his car and as they travelled Sven talked about Vancouver and its beautiful parks. They could see everything from the show a small variety of penguins put on with their under water swimming antics to a display of ancient totem poles made by the coastal natives.

At his home Anna welcomed her husband home with a hug and kiss then turned to Minnie and Olaf with a warm greeting. Anna announced that the main dish for dinner would be sturgeon and hoped that Olaf and Minnie liked fish. Minnie said that she had never eaten sturgeon but she and Olaf always liked fish. Anna explained that sturgeon from the Fraser River was a favorite food in Vancouver. She showed Minnie and

Olaf the guest room and bath where they might like to freshen up.

Minnie wanted to help Anna in the kitchen and she especially wanted to see how Anna cooked the sturgeon. After Sven showed Olaf his little work shop they both sat down in front of a fire in the fireplace to enjoy a glass of Canadian Whisky with soda.

Anna and Minnie had food on the table before Anna called the guys away from their seat by the fireplace. At dinner Sven said he would look up bus schedules. He planned to take them to the bus station in time to catch a bus to Seattle. There they could go by rail or bus to their final destination.

Olaf and Minnie wondered about what papers if any they would have to show to cross the border? Sven explained that people from Washington and people from Canada both travelled back and forth continually with no problems. They might be questioned as to where they were born and about certain items they might have with them. That was about the same for anyone crossing in either direction.

Minnie and Olaf commented on how much they liked the sturgeon and the way it was prepared. As the ladies worked together in the kitchen Minnie had told Anna that she was almost two months pregnant and she didn't want to start caring for a baby in a remote place such as the logging camp at Powell River. Anna said that she could understand that. She told Minnie that twice she had become pregnant and both aborted, in fact it was lucky that she was near a hospital because she had some sort of problem. Her doctor had told her that he didn't think she would ever again become pregnant.

Later the four sat in the living room watching the flickering flames in the big fireplace as they talked of many things. Naturally the subject of logging on the Washington coast came up. When Olaf mentioned that he had heard of much logging in the Hoquiam - Aberdeen part of the Washington coast, Sven spoke up. He explained why that would not be a good place for a couple to start a family.

While there was plenty logging in the area, it was an area with a bad reputation. The loggers were single men who spent most of their free time in the saloons or whore houses. Along with all the drinking and fighting there were many murders.

Sven went on to say that when the United States entered the war against Germany the U.S. Army created what was known as the Spruce Division. The aircraft industry needed the lightweight but strong wood from the Sitka Spruce that was abundant on the Oregon Coast. Construction was started on a large mill at Toledo, Oregon and Spruce Division soldiers who in civilian life had never worked in the woods were learning how to fall and buck the large Spruce timber.

Existing logging railroads were extended to the north and to the south with new locomotives to bring the logs to the mill. A member of the Canadian Military was sent to observe and report on this whole operation. Included in his report was a description of the area. He later returned to marry and bring back to British Columbia a lady he had met at a farm near one of these Spruce logging operations.

At wars end the mill and logging operations were sold to civilian interests. After the available old growth

Spruce was gone the extensive old growth Douglas fir forest became the source for logs.

Sven went on to say that at the present time a modern logging operation existed in the area around Siletz to the north of Toledo. As well as logging there was considerable farming in the area which made for a stable community much different from that of Hoquiam and Aberdeen. Siletz had been the site of an Indian Reservation which no longer existed as such. All government buildings and property had been turned over to a tribal council.

The logging camp itself was known as Camp 12 and was located across the Siletz River from the town of Siletz. There were upkeep and repair facilities such as machine and blacksmith shops. One shop devoted its facilities to replacing broken axe and shovel handles, sharpening axes and saws as well as splicing cables. Locomotives were based at Camp 12. There were cabins for married couples and those with families. A dormitory was provided for single men.

This was information that Olaf and Minnie found interesting. Of course a question arose as to how did Sven learn all these details about the logging there. Sven explained that a couple years ago his tug had been sent to Yaquina Bay with a barge that would be loaded with sawmill machinery for a new mill in British Columbia. While the barge was being loaded at Toledo he had time to rent a car and drive to Siletz and Camp 12. He was impressed with the way the logging company ran their operation. He saw the huge number of old growth fir logs coming by rail to the big mill at Toledo.

By now Olaf and Minnie had changed their mind about going to the Washington coast. Instead, their destination would be Oregon. Sven recommended that they buy a bus ticket to Seattle then from there a bus ticket to Toledo. He felt that they should take lodging in Toledo. Olaf could take local transportation to Camp 12 to learn about job opportunities. Sven found out when a bus would be leaving Vancouver to Seattle. In the morning he would take them there in time for buying their tickets.

After a good night's sleep and a hearty breakfast Olaf and Minnie were at the bus station with tickets in hand and their luggage loaded on the waiting bus. They were thanking Sven and Anna for their generous hospitality when the time came for a final goodbye as they boarded the bus. They had Sven's mailing address and had promised to write after they reached their destination.

Chapter 2

Crossing the border proved to be no problem. A U.S. Border Official came aboard the bus to ask a few questions and that was about the extent of it. In Seattle they found that it was best to buy tickets to Portland where they might wish to spend the night before taking a Greyhound bus to Toledo. They were going to Portland on a Pickwick bus.

There was a hotel fairly close to the bus station. They learned that they could take a trolley that had a stop close by the hotel where they wanted to go. They had all their belongings in two large suitcases which they had no trouble carrying with them on the trolley and before nightfall they were checked in at the hotel.

Aboard the Greyhound Bus and travelling down Oregon's Willamette valley, they were impressed by the fields alongside the highway with their signs telling the name of the crop they were seeing. The evening before, they had explored the shops in downtown Portland. They had stopped for dinner at a restaurant specializing in seafood to enjoy a meal of fried oysters. They expected to be in Toledo by early afternoon. Somewhere along the way they knew that they would stop to leave this bus to transfer to a more local bus to Toledo, it turned out to be Albany.

When they checked in at the hotel in Toledo the clerk advised them to get their money changed to U.S. currency. He would accept Canadian money but because exchange rates were continually changing it would be much simpler for them to be using U.S.

money even though so far wherever they had been, their Canadian money had been accepted. The hotel clerk pointed to a bank on the opposite corner on the street where their money could be exchanged.

At the bank the teller had to look up the current exchange rate. He explained that sometimes the Canadian dollar was worth more than the U.S. dollar and at other times it was the other way around. At this time the Canadian dollar was worth slightly more than the U.S. dollar, which might explain why they had not experienced any trouble using their Canadian money.

Back to the hotel they paid for their room with U.S. money and thanked the clerk for his advice. When Olaf enquired about transportation to Camp 12, the clerk said that frequently there was someone going back and forth between the sawmill and Camp 12. He offered to call the mill for information. Olaf said that he would appreciate that. The clerk called someone he knew at the mill office and found out that yes, there would be a person going to Camp 12 in the morning who would stop by the hotel at nine the next morning. Again Olaf was thanking the clerk for all the help he was getting.

Next morning as Olaf rode with the C. D. Johnson mill official on the way to Camp 12 he was asked about his purpose in going to Camp 12. He explained that he had worked for a large logging company in British Columbia and that his wife was pregnant. His wife wanted to raise their child in a more civilized place than where he had been working. He mentioned the tugboat captain being in Toledo with a barge to pick up some sawmill equipment and while he was there he had observed the logging company's operation and the surrounding community. His recommendation was that Camp 12 would be a place that could use his skills.

The mill official remembered selling a large amount of sawmill machinery and assorted equipment to someone in British Columbia and asked about Olaf's logging experience. Olaf explained that he had worked with logging in Sweden before coming to Canada. He had worked in the woods in eastern Canada before going to a large logging camp near Powell River. He had extensive experience with timber falling while working as a team with his wife's brother. He had kept his own saws sharp and later been employed in the shops to maintain all company saws.

The mill official commented that with those skills Camp 12 could probably have a use for him. He would take him to the Camp 12 office and introduce him to the right person to see about a job.

When they entered the camp office several people spoke up to say. "Good morning, Bob." What Olaf didn't know was that Bob was the company official in charge of the railroad and who made certain that after the logging company got the trees to the railroad everything went smoothly in getting the logs to the mill.

Bob took Olaf to the office of the person in charge of personnel. Bob introduced Olaf by saying, "Olaf Peterson and his wife are from Canada. He's looking for a job, please hear his qualifications. I think Camp 12 could make use of him." Bob left to take care of other matters but letting Olaf know that he would look for him later to give him a ride back to Toledo.

When asked about his qualifications Olaf pretty much told about his timber falling experience and saw sharpening as he had told Bob. The interviewer was particularly interested in his saw sharpening skills. It so happened that at the moment there was a backlog of falling and bucking saws in the maintenance shop.

The end result of the interview was that Olaf would be hired on a temporary basis as a saw sharpener. He would be given a chance to demonstrate his skills. He was shown a cabin where he could live. It was furnished with everything needed for taking up housekeeping except occupants must furnish their own bedding. However, until they had time to buy their own they could borrow bedding from the dormitory. The kitchen had the basic necessities such as silverware, pots and pans, etc. They could get their meals at the camp cafeteria until they got their kitchen stocked with food.

Olaf rode back to Toledo, with Bob who dropped him off at the hotel. As he rode with Bob, Olaf let Bob know how much he appreciated his help. Olaf was confident that he could successfully demonstrate his saw sharpening skill. He mentioned that he had his own gauges, etc., all he needed were the proper files. Bob assured him that there were plenty files at the Camp 12 saw shop. Also he said that there was almost every day someone with a car or truck going from the mill to the camp. When he knew when that would be he would have word sent to the hotel as to when Olaf and his wife should be ready to be picked up.

Olaf was beginning to realize that in some parts of the state there was no public transportation. He would need to purchase an automobile. He and Minnie had saved a fair amount of money since their marriage and now with a job he felt that he could afford to do that. However, there were a couple problems. He had never driven a car. He didn't think that would be too much of a problem. He had driven tractors so didn't think he would have trouble learning to drive a car. Another thing, he didn't have a driver's license and to get one he would have to pass a test which he knew he couldn't pass. There were rules that he didn't know.

In Toledo there were two car dealers, Ford and Chevrolet. The two cars were quite comparable in price and he liked the looks of both. People he had talked with had their likes and dislikes as to which were best so deciding which to buy would just have to be a personal choice.

At the Chevrolet dealers there was a new 1936 sedan on which they would make a good deal. The '37 models were out even though this was still 1936. When he explained that he had never driven, they offered to not only teach him how to drive but also coach him to the extent that he could pass a test for an Oregon Driver's license. He and Minnie thought that it was a deal that they shouldn't pass up, besides she liked the car. It was so comfortable when she sat in it.

Olaf had only been driving their new car for a few weeks when he suddenly had a need for it. He had no trouble learning how to drive it and he also had his driver's license. Minnie's time to go to the hospital in Toledo had come.

When Olaf started his work at Camp 12 Minnie lost no time before she found work. She just couldn't put up with sitting around doing nothing. She made her experience with food preparation known to the ladies who worked with the cooks and in the cafeteria. It wasn't long before she was working with them. She had been working until a little over a week ago but felt that she should stop working because she had a feeling that her time to give birth was near.

Minnie had found a doctor in Toledo who she liked and had made arrangements at the local hospital. They would be ready for her when her time arrived. Now she and Olaf were on the road to Toledo.

The way Minnie felt, she was ready to have her baby at any moment. But, in the hospital nothing was happening even though it was time. She was feeling miserable. Her doctor was concerned. He knew that labor pains should have begun. Perhaps a Caesarian procedure was the answer to the problem.

There were drugs available that might induce labor and it was worth a try. On the morning of the fourth day her water broke and that afternoon an eight and a half pound baby boy was in the arms of a totally exhausted new mother. Her doctor let Minnie know that he wanted her to be under observation in the hospital for a time.

Olaf had been spending the days at the hospital, going home at night for a little sleep. Taking time off from his work was not a problem, his superiors understood the situation. He and Minnie had shopped for all the things they would need for a new baby. A crib was in the bedroom, this was a one bedroom cabin which had been adequate for their needs.

It was normal in late October for stormy weather to occur on the Oregon coast. Their new little baby boy had been born on October 24th, 1936 and now three days later in the midst of a howling gale Olaf was bringing his wife and baby home.

Chapter 3
Larry Joe Peterson

Larry was the name Olaf and Minnie had decided for a first name if their baby was a boy, for a girl it would be Lisa. After going through a list of boy names, Joe seemed to sound right when all three names were spoken. Joe was the name picked as Larry's middle name.

Minnie had quit her work at the cookhouse and cafeteria a month ago but as soon as she could she took little Larry to show off to her friends at the cookhouse and there was the usual admiring "oh what a beautiful baby." Minnie really was proud of him. And too, he was a United States citizen which she and Olaf were not. They for sure must get started on becoming citizens.

Officially, Olaf was a Swede. He had no Canadian citizenship papers. Minnie being born in Canada was a Canadian. There was a problem. They had no idea how to start the process. They would just have to ask around for information. It was sometime later that they were disappointed to learn that they had to be in the United States continually for five years before they could apply for citizenship. In the meantime they would just have to go along with their daily tasks.

The big Fall storm with all its rain had not raised the Siletz River to flood stage but high enough to bring a fresh run of Fall Chinook salmon into the river. Jim, one of Olaf's friends in the shop where he worked invited Olaf to go salmon fishing with him. He had a boat and planned to troll on the lower river just upstream from Kernville. All Olaf had to do was get an Oregon fishing license. Jim had extra tackle for Olaf to use.

Olaf had no fishing experience but was ready to learn about something new. He accepted the invitation.

It was early Saturday forenoon when they were on the river. Jim had a twelve foot aluminum boat with a five hp Johnson motor. They had launched at Kernville and were trolling upstream a mile or so when a salmon hit Olaf's lure.

Jim had explained to Olaf what to do when this happened but when it did happen it caught him by surprise. He was surprised how strong that salmon was and started to lower his rod. Jim had to remind him to keep his rod up so the springy rod could absorb the sudden runs that the salmon was taking. Jim had set the drag on the reel just tight enough to let the fish run with a little line on sudden surges but tight enough to work the salmon to the boat. "Don't be in a hurry" Jim said and added, "just take your time and play that fish carefully, I know it's a big one."

Jim had his landing net ready and when Olaf finally had the tired Chinook alongside the boat. Jim netted it and lifted it into the boat. "About thirty pounds, I think." Jim said as he put it into a wet burlap sack. He complimented Olaf on how well he had followed instructions and gave him a "high five."

Olaf was in good physical shape but he felt a bit "pooped." It wasn't so much from his physical effort but from the excitement of catching that salmon.

Even before Olaf had his line back in the water, Jim had a fish on. He let it take a little line out but as soon as he started working it towards the boat, it broke free. Jim reeled in his line to find that his lure was still there. That salmon had not broken his leader but just hadn't been solidly hooked. Jim explained that sometimes when that happened the hook would have a bit of flesh on it indicating that the hook had been only in a soft part of the lip.

They continued trolling upstream past Coyote Rock. Jim pointed out a boat launch and said that he sometimes launched his boat here. There was a small resort store here that sold some fishing supplies and fishing licenses.

At Coyote Rock the stream narrowed and current was faster. Above the rock the stream widened again. This was tide water and as the time came for a tidal change and as water started rising Jim had a hit. This time it was a solid hookup and when he had the fish alongside Olaf was ready with the net. He had seen how Jim netted his fish and now he was lifting Jim's salmon into the boat. It was a little smaller than Olaf's but not much so.

It was lunch time. Jim had turned off the motor when his salmon hit and Olaf had reeled in his line. They were just letting the boat drift as they got out their Thermos bottles for coffee and sandwiches. It was quiet and peaceful, a very nice fall day. Other boats that had been on the river earlier had turned downstream. Silence was only broken by a kingfisher and its distinctive voice as it flew past and Jim's voice as he started to talk.

"Maybe you noticed that your salmon had a sort of hooked jaw whereas mine did not. That's because your fish was a male and mine a female. As the fish work their way to the spawning grounds that hooked jaw on the male gets even more pronounced. My fish will have a couple rolls of eggs that I'll save for steelhead bait. It won't be long before the winter steelhead run will be in the river. When that time comes I'll introduce you to steelhead fishing."

Back in camp Jim filleted the salmon. They both put aside enough for their dinners and the remainder would go in the camp freezer room for use later. Jim's fish produced two egg rolls that would later become steelhead bait. Jim commented that some people liked to fry the milt strips from the male salmon but it was not something he liked.

Minnie was happy to have fresh salmon on the table. Little Larry was now old enough to start eating solid food and he seemed happy with the bites that Minnie gave him.

It hardly seemed possible that a year could pass by so quickly but in his high chair Larry had in front of him a little cake with one candle. The candle had a flame that Minnie was trying to get Larry to blow out. He finally got the idea and blew out the flame. Every one cheered and clapped their hands. Jim and his wife Julie along with their two year old daughter Marie were members of Larry's birthday party.

There were two things that Minnie was especially proud of and that was that she had learned to drive their car and had a driver's license. Now while Olaf was at work she could take Larry with her as she went shopping in Toledo.

Olaf sometimes ran out of saws to sharpen and when that happened there were repairs to other equipment that he could do. He had learned arc and gas welding, but there were other things that he wanted to learn about. He watched as a machinist operated a very large metal lathe. He saw the machinist use instruments to get his turnings within thousandths of an inch of a desired size. He realized that was not something he could learn with a lesson or two. Sometime in the future perhaps he could find time to learn that skill.

He had seen cables being spliced. He had watched this being done at the camp at Powell River but he had never tried to do it. He thought that was something he could easily learn to do. At his first opportunity he would give it a try on a short section of one of the smaller size cables.

One day Olaf did pick up a piece of small size cable and a marlin spike with the idea of making an eye splice. He soon learned that it was a little trickier than he had realized but he didn't give up. He had learned that there were several kinds of splices with names like Liverpool and Gun Factory splices. He was trying to use the one commonly used in logging operations. It was called the West Coast or Loggers splice.

That splice is done by passing each tucking strand successively under two strands, back over and around one strand and out again under two strands. A second tuck is made with the last four tucking strands in the same manner as the first tuck which completes the splice. He finally got done a useable splice, it was pretty ragged in appearance but useable. He knew that with practice he could do one that was not only useable but neat in appearance.

One of the women working in the cafeteria was a member of the local Indian tribe. Ada was not a full blood, very few of the local tribal members were. Her husband, like she, was an Indian with perhaps also a little white blood in his ancestry. He was descended from a tribe different from that of his wife. When the government began moving Indians to the Siletz Reservation some came not only from the coastal area but from east of the coast range. Ada and Minnie had long conversations where they compared the customs and language of their peoples.

When Minnie went shopping in Toledo, she passed through a little valley called Depot Slough. As she passed by the farms she noticed that they had gardens with vegetables of all kinds. Even driving through Siletz she saw that even the homes in town had vegetable gardens. She talked to her friend Ada about this and mentioned that she wished she had a place where she could have a garden.

When Larry was a year old Minnie went back to her old job working with the cooks and helping in the cafeteria. There were a few other children all a little older than Larry in the camp that pretty much had free rein as they played together. The older ones seemed to look after the younger ones and when they heard a locomotive coming with its string of logs or coming the other way with a string of empty trucks, or perhaps a box car or two they made sure that the smaller ones stayed well away from the railroad track.

The children knew that they had to stay out of the shops and other work places. They could look in the open doors to satisfy their curiosity and often did. The grownups knew all the children and their parents and when they saw any of the children misbehaving someone took care of it. When school was in session, those old enough to be in school were taken by bus to Siletz.

Minnie's friend Ada remembered that Minnie was wishing that she had a place where she could have a garden so one day she told Minnie that there was a place near where she lived that was for rent. Of course Minnie was interested and wanted to know when she and Olaf could see it.

"We could get a look at it right after work today if you would like," Ada answered. It was early December. They knew that they didn't have much time before it got dark. "I'll go over to the shop to let Olaf know. I know he'll want to see it also." Minnie said.

As planned, Minnie, Olaf and Larry followed Ada and she took them directly to the rental. It was a small cottage with a carport on a large piece of ground. Minnie could see that there was a garden space with some carrots and rutabagas still in the ground. She learned that it was a common practice to do that. They kept better that way.

They looked in windows but couldn't see much. They thought it best to go to Ada's home where they could phone the owner to see when they could arrange a meeting. They did that and they would meet the owner the next day as soon after work as they could at the rental. Minnie let Ada know that she liked the look of the place. Ada agreed to be with them at the place to introduce them to the owner.

On the way back to Camp 12 Minnie and Olaf talked about the place. Olaf hadn't said much when they looked at the place. Minnie wondered what he thought about it. He let her know that he wanted to see inside the house and he rather liked the idea of having a garden.

Little Larry now just a little over two years old didn't understand much about what his parents were talking about. Actually he was quite happy because there was one thing he liked to do and that was going some place in the car.

The owner of the rental was Pete Hendricks and he was waiting at the property when Minnie and Olaf with Larry accompanied by Ada arrived. Ada introduced the potential renters and they all went to the cottage. He had unlocked the doors before Minnie and Olaf arrived. Minnie and Olaf did a quick walk through before Pete began to talk about the house and property.

In the quick walk through both Olaf and Minnie liked what they saw. Pete explained that they would be responsible for electricity and propane. There was a fairly large propane tank a small distance from the carport and the propane dealer would come by every so often to fill it. The kitchen range was propane but the clothes dryer was electric. Refrigerator along with washing machine and dryer came with the house.

After some discussion with Pete, Olaf and Minnie agreed with the rental terms and cost. They would always pay ahead for the upcoming month. The approaching weekend would be moving days.

Moving was not difficult. The only furniture was Larry's high chair and his crib and the crib could be taken apart to fit into the car. Pots and pans plus silverware belonged to the Camp 12 cabin. For the rental they would need new pots and pans plus silverware. Minnie had noticed second hand stores in both Toledo and Newport. They would see what was available in those before buying new items.

Saturday forenoon most moving was complete. On Sunday any remaining items would be picked up plus they wanted to leave the cabin cleaned. Saturday afternoon was a time to shop.

Minnie would make their first meal in their new home a simple affair. She had decided on spaghetti along with garlic bread. They had found most of the basic necessities for the kitchen in second hand shops. More could be added later. The refrigerator was well stocked as well as kitchen cabinets.

After dinner Olaf and Minnie sat down to relax, both felt that they had moved into their first real home. Larry too had a happy feeling as he played with his new toy. It was colorful and had things that he had to put in holes where they fit.

Sunday morning came along with not a cloud in the sky. It was an unusually bright sunshiny day, a good omen for a good life in a new home. After a good oatmeal breakfast it was cleaning day at the Camp 12 cabin. It would be left cleaner perhaps than it was when they first came to live there. The little cabin had fit their basic needs but with Larry growing like a weed they knew that the new home would be much better, however there was something that worried her. She could talk to Olaf about that at another time.

Chapter 4

Christmas was just past but the nice little fir tree that Olaf had cut on company property was still up. Minnie had invited Ada and her husband Ivan Johns as well as their friends Jim and Julie to a New Year's Day dinner. Now she was planning the menu. By the way, whenever Ivan's last name Johns was mentioned he always had to explain about that unusual last name and how it had originated when the government moved the various tribes to the Siletz Reservation.

She would do a leg of lamb in the oven, sweet potatoes and string beans would pretty much complete the main menu. There would be a fruit salad on the table. Olaf was going to do some kind of a Scandinavian rice pudding dessert.

Ada had a fairly large collection of baskets, some had been made by her mother but most had been made by her grandmother. There was one that she thought would look nice filled with fruit. It was a rather open weave and Ada thought it was made from spruce roots. She had put apples, oranges and a bunch of grapes in it and given it to Minnie as a house gift just after Minnie and Olaf had moved in. Minnie was happy to display it on the counter between the kitchen and dining area.

New Years Day arrived along with gray skies and a steady drizzle. But with plenty wood for the heating stove the home was warm and cozy. Minnie had found a pair of antique candlesticks which were on the extended dining table with candles ready for lighting and the table was set.

Larry felt important, he knew there would be company and he was helping his dad fill the wood box. This was the kind of day when that wood heater was a treasure. Minnie had explained to Larry that this was a special day. It was a start of a whole new year. He didn't quite understand but he felt that it must be important and he knew the people who were coming to visit.

Dinner was planned for mid afternoon and the leg of lamb was in the oven. Sweet potatoes and string beans were ready for cooking. Olaf's rice pudding was in the refrigerator. First to arrive was Ada and Ivan soon followed by Jim and Julie along with their little girl. Everyone had dressed up for the occasion. Larry wanted every one to notice his new outfit and made a point of letting the company know that his mom and dad had given it to him at Christmas. Of course everyone told him how much they liked it.

Olaf had remembered the punch that his parents had made for special occasions and had managed to find a recipe for Swedish grog. There was a punch bowl on the counter and he was serving.

Everyone except Minnie sat around and discussed the weather. Would it clear or perhaps would it turn colder? This winter had brought frost but no snow. Jim mentioned that the last time he and Olaf had been steelhead fishing their linen lines froze as soon as they put their rods on forked sticks. (They put little warning bells on their rod tips to alert them of a bite as they tried to keep warm by a fire.)

Minnie had the last things cooking and joined the group. As the guys talked about fishing and their work the ladies mentioned the latest gossip at work. Julie had heard someone mentioning that so and so was probably pregnant. Ada spoke up, "I guess I might as well let everyone know it could have been me they were talking about." That caught everyone's attention. "Yes," Ada added, "I recently found that I am pregnant." That brought all sorts of comments, even from the men. Minnie thought to say something but thought better of it. She would save that topic for another time and got up to look after her cooking.

With Olaf carving the lamb Minnie was getting other things to the table with the help of Ada and Julie. Jim and Ivan had brought wine, Olaf already had a white and red open and on the table.

With wine glasses raised there were toasts for the coming year and for the new little ones that would be added to their families later in the year. Minnie was thinking to herself that it was time that she told Olaf the secret she was keeping from him. She vowed to do that tonight when they were alone and Larry was into his night's sleep.

Minnie felt that she had put together a reasonably good dinner and she appreciated it when others commented on how good the roast lamb was and on the dinner in general. Olaf too, felt good as he heard comments like they had never tasted that rice dish before and they liked it.

Different topics of conversation came about. Minnie and Ada spoke a little about their Native American heritage and Ivan mentioned a little of his family's history. Both Jim and Julie mentioned that their ancestors had come to this country before the colonies revolted against British rule. They didn't know much real family history previous to their grandparents. They always suspected that there might have been Native American blood introduced into their family heritage somewhere in the past. They knew that it had been common for instance for a fur trapper to have an Indian wife.

It was only Olaf who was absolutely certain that his ancestors were all Scandinavian. He commented that the more he learned about Native Americans the more respect he had for the culture that existed before it was contaminated by Europeans and he raised his glass in a toast to that. Someone commented that Olaf shouldn't be absolutely certain about pure Scandinavian, those early day Vikings did get around! Olaf smiled.

Larry had been in his high chair and was trying to be heard above all the grown up talk and laughter. He had done a good job cleaning his plate and just wanted to go play with Marie and show her his toys. Minnie told him what a good boy he had been to finish his dinner and drink all his milk. His mom helped him down and he dashed off to join Marie. He was pretty good at figuring out ways to amuse himself but he wasn't perfect, sometimes at just a little over two years old he found things to do that did not meet his parent's approval. He soon learned that his parents had ways to convince him that what he had done was not good.

Minnie brought up the subject of gardens and the one she was planning. She wanted to get started with it as weather permitted. There were some things that could be done in February, Ivan said. In that part of Oregon, often as early as sometime in February it was possible to get ground ready for planting. Ivan continued with "I know a guy who has a tiller machine that he walks behind as it breaks up and makes the ground ready for planting. Not only that but it will work manure fertilizer into the ground at the same time. For a reasonable fee he can do the whole operation for you, including bringing and spreading the manure fertilizer. Ada and I have him prepare our garden and he does a good job."

Doing all that work by hand was something Olaf had pictured himself doing for Minnie. "Tell the guy to contact us. That sounds like a good deal," Olaf responded to Ivan. "Will do," Ivan answered, and then went on to ask, "Have any of you ever enjoyed eating freshly cooked crawfish?" Everyone except Ada answered in the negative.

Ivan went on to explain that there were lots of crawfish in the Siletz River and suggested that as soon as the weather was right and river level was down they should all have a crawfish catching party someplace on the river. He would put together the proper equipment. Everyone thought the idea sounded like fun and told Ivan to let them know when he thought conditions were good.

January had been a month of both rain and frosty weather. February also was not a good month for garden preparation. Minnie and Olaf had made arrangements with the guy Ivan had recommended, his name was Joe Simpson. It was in March when a few days of drying weather gave Joe an opportunity to spread manure all over Minnie and Olaf's marked off garden area. When weather permitted, he would work it into the garden soil.

It was April first and Minnie was eager to get something planted. Ada said that it was too early for some things but lettuce, peas and an early variety of potatoes would be okay. When potatoes were starting to show above ground and hard frost threatened she could just rake a little soil over them and it would protect them. Other potatoes she should plant later. With early spring planting it seemed that one just took their chances and if a late frost killed something, just replant.

When it came to gardening, Minnie was a novice but she was eager to learn. She pretty much followed Ada's advice. When the row of carrots came up, along with the little carrots innumerable little weeds also came up. Along with thinning the carrots there was the somewhat tedious task of separating and pulling out the accompanying weeds.

Larry was watching his mom thinning and pulling weeds. Minnie carefully and patiently explained to Larry that those little plants would grow into carrots that she would take from the ground for him to eat. Perhaps when he was a little older she might mark off a little space for him to have his very own little garden.

Ivan had brought up the subject of crawfish again. He said that it was time to take the group that he had talked to at that New Year's dinner to the river for crawfish. All they had to do was set a date.

Minnie had been unable to keep her secret from Olaf any longer and had informed him that she was pregnant again. She explained to him that since she had such a hard time with Larry's birth she was a little worried. Olaf was quite happy to learn that there would be another baby and tried to reassure her that this time it would be different but they should have a talk with her doctor. Minnie agreed with that and she would announce her secret to the group when they all gathered at the river for crawfish.

Crawfish day had arrived. It was Saturday morning, the agreed on plan was to spend the forenoon at the river then enjoy a potluck picnic lunch. In the evening they would gather at his home for the crawfish feed. He would cook the crawfish; others would provide garlic bread and salad.

Ivan's pickup had a lumber rack and tied on it were three long bamboo poles. In the bed of the pickup were three crawfish rings, similar to crab rings but smaller. Also there were a couple empty cold boxes for the crawfish they expected to catch along with bait for the crawfish rings.

He and Ada led the way to a stretch of river that had a stretch of low open grassy bank beside a slow moving river. The water was flowing over boulders probably about four to six feet or so deep. Through the clear water they could see bottom.

To get to this spot they had to open a gate and drive through a pasture area containing a dozen or so grazing cows that were more interested in their grazing than the three cars driving through their pasture. Ivan knew the owner of this property and had permission to bring his friends to the river.

Ivan told the group to watch what he was doing. He took one of the bamboo poles down and picked up a crawfish ring. It had a long cord attached. He measured off a length of cord from the ring near as long as the pole and attached it to the tip of the pole with a clove hitch. The remaining cord he tied to the pole as near the butt of the pole as it would reach.

Next was the bait, a fair size piece of bacon rind. A section of copper wire in the ring was wired through holes in the rind. Now he had the group watch as he swung the ring out and let it sink to the bottom. It was a bit amazing to see what happened next.

They soon saw first one and then other crawfish appear out of nowhere headed towards the baited ring. When a half dozen or so were attacking the bacon rind Ivan lifted the ring quickly from the water. One managed to escape the ring as he lifted it from the water and swung it around onto the bank. He had to work quickly to get them into one of the cold boxes. "And that is one of a number of ways to catch crawfish," Ivan said. Later he went on to mention a number of other methods.

The others spread out along the river bank. At first Olaf and Jim found that it was a little tricky to raise the ring without the crawfish on it escaping but they got better with each try. They all kept moving to fresh places when action slowed.

Larry wanted to help. One of the crawfish had fallen on the grass but when Larry tried to pick it up he had to cry out to his mom for help. The big crawfish had clamped down on Larry's finger and it hurt. Minnie came to his rescue and then went on to show him how to pick it up without getting pinched.

Minnie never talked baby talk to Larry. In fact Olaf thought that she talked to him as if he were an adult. Minnie defended herself by explaining to Olaf that in her tribe little ones had to be taught at a tender age about the world around them. It was a matter of survival. Little kids had to learn to recognize danger and sometimes they learned the hard way. Larry would be careful when picking up a crawfish or its larger cousin a crab.

It was during their picnic lunch that Minnie informed the group that she was pregnant. She said when she first knew, it made her worry. She was remembering the hard time she had with Larry's birth but after a talk with her doctor she felt better about it. He would see her often and probably plan for a Caesarian birth. Ada and Julie assured her that she had a good doctor. They just knew that this time would be better than before.

Ivan was trying to get a rough count of the crawfish in the cold boxes. He felt that they had plenty for a good feed; he thought most could eat ten or twelve. The plan for the dinner was for Julie and Minnie to each bring a salad of some sort and garlic bread. Ivan and Ada would take care of the rest. It was early afternoon now and he suggested that they all gather at his house later about five or so. Every one agreed to the plan and gathered up the stuff by the river to carry to their cars. Ivan took all the crawfish to his car.

As everyone gathered at Ivan and Ada's home there was an aroma in the air. It was coming from the large pot heating on the stove. Ivan had pickling spices along with some bay leaves in the heating water. There were too many crawfish to cook all at the same time. Ivan had a wire and screen basket that he would lower filled with crawfish into the boiling water just about the same way crabs were cooked for the market over at Newport.

All commented on the beautiful table with two platters piled high with crawfish, a big bowl of garlic bread, a couple salad bowls along with empty bowls at each place setting for crawfish parts not consumed. Ivan had made up a bowl of dipping sauce with his own recipe and there was a little dish for it by each plate. Ivan made his own homebrewed beer and there was that for those who wanted it and fruit juice and tea for others.

Most of the edible part of the crawfish is the tail. There was a little in the larger clawed pinchers. Larry and Marie had their own little table where Julie and Minnie prepared a plate with crawfish meat, salad and bread for each.

As they prepared to eat, Ada gave thanks to the Great Spirit for the fish, the animals, the wild berries and all the things that had sustained her people in this river valley for generations since the beginning of time. Ivan added that in his valley on the other side of the coast range the Great Spirit did the same for his people. Minnie remarked that it was pretty much the same for her people too in a far away part of Canada.

Those who had never tasted crawfish remarked that they liked it. Those who had eaten crab thought it was a little like that but not quite the same. Anyway it was good and Ivan was thanked for the crawfish experience. Marie and Larry asked for more crawfish and juice drink.

Chapter 5

It was birthday party time for Larry. He was a big boy now, FIVE YEARS OLD! Five year old Larry had a little sister named Lisa almost three years old now and she was at his party as well as Ada's little boy Willy. Marie was there with her mother. Three mothers were busy supervising four energetic little youngsters as they shared ice cream and Larry's birthday cake.

These youngsters knew each other quite well and were somewhat organized as they played together. Larry felt protective to his little sister and Marie the oldest was always the organizer. Lisa and Willy being the same age sometimes got together to rebel against Marie's ideas, Marie had developed diplomatic skills enough to enable her to usually convince the others that her ideas were best at the moment.

When Minnie found that she was pregnant she worried that there would be a repeat of the difficulty she suffered with Larry's birth. It didn't happen that way. She and Ada were in the hospital at the same time and on August 31, 1939 each gave birth in a perfectly normal manner for Minnie a baby girl that would be named Lisa and for Ada a baby boy to be named Willy.

Larry had continued to be interested in their garden. A portion of the garden area had been designated as his very own to plant and care for. Minnie had planted short rows of corn about a week apart and Larry's corn row was adjacent to Minnie's latest row. They were harvesting corn from it now. His cucumbers had done well; besides giving some away

Minnie had a crock in which she was making dill pickles. There were carrots that would remain in the ground until they were wanted for eating. One leg of a string bean tripod had been for Larry to plant. His potatoes were ready to be harvested as soon as the tops died down.

The fruit trees at the back edge of the lot had produced cherries for Minnie to can. One tree had prunes that were good to eat fresh as well as being good for canning or drying. One apple tree had an early apple that were now all gone but another tree had fruit that was just getting good and it was a variety called King. They had learned that the earliest apple was a Yellow Transparent, but another kind of apple had been grafted on the same tree and it was a Gravenstein which lasted into the season much longer than the Yellow Transparent.

As much as they liked this place with its garden and it's location in Siletz, Minnie and Olaf where realizing that they needed a larger house. They thought it was time for their two children to have separate rooms. It seemed like Larry and Lisa were growing like weeds! If they couldn't find anything suitable to rent they might consider buying if they found something they could afford. It was something to think about.

It wasn't until February that they saw something of interest advertised. The owner of a large ranch between Toledo and Siletz at the upper end of the valley called Depot Slough was advertising a large home on five acres for sale. It wasn't a realtor advertising, it was for sale by owner. Olaf and Minnie thought it worthwhile enough to drive the few miles for a look.

It turned out that the owner who introduced himself as Fred Johanson had recently lost his wife and his grown up children lived away from the area. He planned to move near his daughter in California. In talking they learned that the five acres with the home was a portion of almost four hundred acres. The five acres was beside the road and mostly level with the logging railroad and a small creek passing through it. The rest of the property had been logged some years previous and now had a good growth of young Douglas fir. He wished to retain that as a tree farm.

They found the house to be well cared for and in reasonably good condition despite its age. Fred said that through the years it had been upgraded by redoing the wiring, modernizing bathroom fixtures and two years ago old roofing had been replaced with thirty year new asphalt shingles. Beside the master bedroom and bath on the ground floor, there were three other bedrooms and bath upstairs. A small laundry room off the kitchen also had its toilet and wash basin.

Kitchen and dining area had some time previously been renovated from separate rooms to a more open plan where the two were separated by only a counter. The living room was fairly large with a large plate glass window facing the road. A large fireplace gave the room a comfortable atmosphere. Separate but connected by a breezeway was a two car garage. Attached to the rear of the garage was a well stocked woodshed.

Fred pointed out the area behind the house has several old apple trees and a cherry tree. A fenced area contained a row of raspberries and boysenberries and cultivated ground for a garden. He mentioned that the fence was important because without it the garden would be eaten up by deer and the chain link fence was high enough that they didn't try to jump over it.

Mr. Johanson told Olaf and Minnie that he had put what he considered a fairly low price on the property because he really wanted to sell as soon as possible so he could live near his daughter and her family. He had a son who was a career Navy Officer with a wife but no children. If they were interested and could pay a quarter of his asking price, he would personally carry a twenty year mortgage at a slightly lower interest rate than banks were charging. Olaf and Minnie said that they were definitely interested but they needed to look over their finances to see if they had sufficient funds for the down payment. They would come by in the morning with their answer.

On the way home they talked about the house. They really liked the feel of the place, and there would be separate rooms for Larry and Lisa. Larry heard his name mentioned with something about his room, he wanted to know what that meant. Minnie explained to him that they wanted a larger house with more bedrooms so he and Lisa could have their own rooms. Larry said he liked having his Lisa where he could look after her but maybe it would be nice to have a room of his very own.

At home they looked over their bank checking and saving accounts. There was also another savings account that they had been paying a little into each month. It was for a new car they planned to buy in a year or so. Perhaps they should just buy new tires for the now four year old Chevy. It still had fairly low miles on it and was running good.

Another thing too, Olaf was now making a higher salary. Logging was to take place in one of the last stands of old growth Douglas fir on company property. He would be part of a team planning the operation. The logging railroad would be ending a short distance above Logsden. Logs would come from the woods by truck for transfer to rail cars at that point. With all the saving they had brought from Canada they did have money enough for a down payment on the property. They felt that mortgage payments wouldn't be a problem.

The next morning Olaf had to go to work. Minnie would go to tell Mr. Johanson that they wished to buy the property. He could start preparing necessary papers and she and Olaf would gather money from savings to checking to enable them to write a check for the down payment.

Fred had coffee made and wanted to share coffee while he told her a little about the property. He had grown up here and as the only child he had inherited the property from his parents. Some of the furniture had been in the family even before his parents owned it. He wanted to keep those items but the remaining furniture items could stay with the house. Also the gas powered garden tiller and various tools he wanted to leave with the property.

The house was on ground a little higher than a meadow area next to the little creek. For the first time Minnie had noticed what appeared to be a barn just where the higher ground met the lower meadow area. She asked about that. Mr. Johanson explained that his parents had kept several beef animals and sometimes hogs mostly for their own meat. Sometimes extra animals were sold locally. Mostly his parent's income was from the timber they sold from time to time.

Fred went on to mention that there was an old Model T Ford truck in the barn that his dad had used mostly on the property especially for bringing fire wood he had cut to the woodshed. It had not been licensed or even run for many years. It would just go with the property. Also in a closet there was an old shotgun, a 22 single shot and his dad's old deer rifle. He didn't want to take them to California, they would go with the property and they could do what they wished with them. He went on to say that after he inherited the property he had never farmed the property. He had managed the timberland and sometimes had a part of it logged. He also inherited a part interest in a hardware store in town where he had worked part time until the partner bought his share.

Minnie and Olaf had let the owner of the home where they lived know that with their larger family they needed a larger house. They were looking for another rental or something that they could afford to buy so he wasn't surprised when informed that they had found a larger home and would be moving as soon as all the paper work was done and the property vacated.

With all paper work completed and Mr. Johanson moved out it was an early Saturday in March when Minnie and Olaf with the help of Jim and Julie plus Ada and Ivan were in the middle of moving day. Larry and Lisa had been told to gather up all their toys and put them in separate cardboard boxes. Minnie had helped Larry gather some carrots that were still in the ground. He was told to walk all around the property to make certain that he had picked up any of his toys left outside.

They were able to get most things loaded in the three vehicles for the move. It was easy to use space in the garage to store things to bring into the house later. What they did do was bring all kitchen things in plus food for the three ladies to prepare a celebrating first meal in the new home. Fred had left the dining room table with its chairs as well as some pots and pans with some assorted kitchen tools in the kitchen.

Their first meal in the new home was a credit to the three ladies who had prepared a fried chicken dinner in an unfamiliar kitchen. They had boiled potatoes and carrots and prepared a green salad as well. There was even chicken gravy for the vegetables. Olaf brought out a bottle of wine from a box in the garage. They could all join in a toast to life in a new home. The youngsters were all at a small separate table and they raised their glasses of fruit juices just like they saw their parents doing.

About the first thing Minnie started doing after all the arrangements with propane, electricity, telephone and new mailing address had been finished, was to start getting pictures on the walls. Creating a homelike atmosphere in wherever she lived was always a priority for Minnie.

Looking at the big garden space Minnie was starting to plan what and where things would be planted. Olaf had checked out the tiller and found it to be in good running condition. He made arrangements with the same person in Siletz that had furnished manure fertilizer for them previously to do it again for their new place. As soon as weather permitted it would be time to take the tiller to the garden area to start working the fertilizer into the soil.

Olaf and Minnie had not forgotten their dream of becoming
U. S. citizens. They had been attending a class in Newport that was designed to familiarize potential citizens with the U.S. constitution and history of the country, in other words the things they would need to know in order to become United States citizens. As soon as a time and place was advertized for them to apply and take tests, they would be ready.

Larry was finding this new place very interesting. He wanted to go exploring. Minnie was quite lenient with him and let him do that but she managed to keep an eye on him as he did. One thing especially was of interest to him, the little creek. He wanted Minnie to come with him so he could show her some things he had seen there.

Bringing his mom and Lisa to the stream he had them get down low and peak over the bank. The water was clear and shallow. There was a deeper spot near the opposite bank just below the shallow part. As they raised their heads several tiny trout spotted the movement and darted for cover in the deeper water near the bank. Then they saw a small crawfish like they had caught in the Siletz River slowly making its way along the bottom. They stood up and the crawfish too spotted what it thought was danger and headed for deeper water. Larry thought it interesting that when the crawfish wanted to move quickly it did so backwards.

Larry was so excited and proud of what he had discovered and was able to show to his mom and Lisa.

At the evening dinner table he was eager to tell his dad about the adventure. Olaf agreed that it was important to see and learn about these things. Also Olaf mentioned that crawfish were often called crawdads. Also it seemed to be that creeks were referred to as "cricks" by most people.

That night after Larry and Lisa were in their beds, Olaf and Minnie sat in the living room listening to news on the radio and discussing the war in Europe.

Chapter 6

It was September 1940 with so many things happening, some good and some not good. Their garden had done well, Larry was proud of the things he had cared for in his little plot. What was exciting for Larry was that he was starting FIRST GRADE in Toledo. He would be riding in a big yellow school bus. He knew slightly several nearby neighbor kids but most riding the bus would be strangers. Minnie had taken him to Toledo to be registered as a new student and there had been a Parents' Day for parents with new students to meet teachers and learn what would be expected of their children.

School had been delayed a week for families to pick evergreen blackberries.

Evergreen blackberries seemed to grow everywhere. They were not native but had been introduced probably from Europe. The plant liked the coastal climate in this part of the state and quickly spread throughout the area. Given a chance they would take over pasture land and were difficult to eradicate once established. Farmers considered them a pest. But at this time of the year the berries were ready for picking and a cannery would send a truck several times a week to buy and pay cash for the berries. A cannery's best customer was the US Military. Anyone in the military from this area would know what kind of blackberry sauce or jam they were being served. They had a distinctive flavor unlike other blackberries.

Important to Minnie and Olaf was that they had now been sworn in as citizens of the United States which would bring new privileges and responsibilities. One responsibility was for Olaf to register for the draft. Congress passed the Selective Service Act September 16, 1940.

When Olaf registered, he was assigned a deferred status III-B, registrant deferred because of dependants and employment in an occupation essential to the war effort.

Because Larry's birthday was late in October he had not been able to start the first grade in Siletz. To make up for that Minnie and Olaf together had taught him a few things. They made learning ABCs and counting a fun game. Larry had a little story book with pictures of animals that he could identify and count. He found out that it was fun to tell Lisa how many toes she had, he could count to ten. He showed her that he had the same number. He didn't say anything about it but he realized that some things about their bodies were not the same.

Larry didn't know what to expect when he got on the school bus for the first time but there were several that would be in his class. One boy in particular living nearby he had met once at a community picnic soon became his friend. Having a friend was good he found when suddenly being among a bunch of strangers.

His first grade teacher was Mrs. Bradbury and she asked the class one by one to tell the class their name and what they thought was the most important thing that had happened to him or her in the past year. Larry thought of several things but ended up telling about moving from Siletz to a new home on the road to

Toledo. That night he felt quite important when telling his little sister all about his first day at school.

Olaf learned that the dairy down the valley occasionally had a bull calf when one of their cows freshened and didn't want to keep it. Olaf bought it and another later. The two calves would be raised for meat. They bought baby chicks shortly after moving and now had chickens that would soon start giving them eggs. Roosters would probably end up in the frying pan.

Opening of deer hunting season every fall was always a big deal in this part of the state. Olaf's friend Jim was a deer hunter and brought up the subject in one of their conversations. Olaf was interested and told Jim that he had a rifle that had come with the house when they bought it. He mentioned that he had no experience with deer hunting rifles and would like to show it to Jim. Jim said that he would like to see what kind of a rifle Olaf was talking about. Olaf commented that the man they bought the house from had said his father had used it for deer hunting.

When Olaf brought the rifle to work to show Jim he was surprised to hear Jim say that he had a fine example of a Winchester 32 Special Model 94 rifle. He explained that most Model 94s he would see were 30-30 caliber. 32 Special was an early model designed to accommodate cartridges loaded with black powder. The ballistics of the two calibers using present day smokeless powder was similar. In other words, Olaf possessed a very fine deer rifle. It wasn't long before Jim and Olaf had venison in the Camp 12 freezer.

Suddenly the distant war in Europe was closer to home. The Japanese had attacked the US Fleet at Pearl

Harbor. Now the US was at war with Japan as well as Germany. Olaf was glad that he had fairly good tires on the old '36 Chevy. New tires were rationed and in short supply. Other things were also being rationed. Fast food coffee drinkers saw signs such as: "Stir like hell, we don't mind the noise." Sugar was in short supply and gasoline was rationed as well.

The first big rain storms of late fall made the little stream on their property become full to the banks. Also salmon could be seen working their way upstream to spawn. Most would be chum salmon, often called dog salmon. Chum salmon normally spawned within fifteen miles from salt water. Chinook and Silver (Coho) salmon entering the Yaquina River from the ocean tended to go farther upstream before spawning.

Native tribes were allowed to take salmon using nets. On the Siletz Ivan was taking advantage of salmon runs to have salmon in his smoke house.

The big mill in Toledo was having trouble with a shortage of workers. So many young people had been drafted or joined the service before being drafted. Two large government projects needed workers. One project was the production of prefabricated housing and the other the mass production of a large number of small tug boats. A station wagon made regular trips to Portland's skid row to hire workers. The trouble with this was that these new employees took their first paycheck to buy wine and no longer showed up for work.

One thing the mill did to help their employees was to lease land for those who didn't have ground for gardens. Employees could have a space for planting a vegetable garden.

Farmers and those such as Olaf and Minnie made good use of their land to raise things for canning as well as fresh use. The bull calves that they continued to get from dairies became either veal or baby beef for selling and personal use.

At long last the war did come to an end. A couple bombs practically destroyed two cities in Japan and Japan surrendered. There were a few local young people who didn't return from their military assignments but most did. Some were able to return to old jobs but many were just looking for whatever jobs they could find.

Olaf received a letter from his mother in Sweden. He had supposed that she and his stepfather had been safe in neutral Sweden even though the Germans had occupied Norway; but that was not the way it was for real.

The Norwegian underground had been smuggling supplies of various sorts that were needed by Norwegians and his mother said that her husband had been helping the Norwegians. The Germans had confiscated food crops and in general made life difficult in Norway. The forested land on the border between Norway and Sweden where Olaf's mother and stepfather lived was in a locality where a great deal of the smuggling was taking place. The Germans knew this and made regular sweeps through the area. A Quisling informer had given the Germans information that caused them to make a surprise sweep through the area and Olaf's stepfather had been caught on the Norwegian side of the border. He and a couple Norwegians had lost their lives in an exchange of gunfire.

After that Olaf's mother was afraid to live in the old home and had decided to live in a city away from the border until the end of the war. Now she had returned to the old home but without her husband she wasn't happy there. Her health was not good and she was planning to sell the old home and move to an assisted living facility in Stockholm. Olaf wrote back to say that he thought she should do that especially since she was alone. He was unhappy about what had happened to his stepfather.

It was about a year and a half later that Olaf received a letter from the assisted care facility that his mother had passed away peacefully in her sleep. With regards to her estate he would be contacted at a later date.

Olaf had known that his stepfather was quite wealthy and that his mother's old home was probably worth something when she sold it to live in the assisted living facility in Stockholm. When Olaf received the check after his mother's estate was settled, he realized that he was now a very wealthy person. He realized that he could retire but elected to remain working until his current assignment was complete. What he did do was take a portion of his new wealth to pay off the mortgage on their property.

Chapter 7

Larry was now in his high school senior year and his sister Lisa was a sophomore. Shortly after the end of WWII the logging railroad that ran through their property on the Siletz road was discontinued. Part of Olaf's job had to do with the removal of all steel rails and ties. When that job was finished Olaf decided this was the right time for him to retire. The right of way was taken over by the state to become a new routing for Highway 229. The old road that ran in front of their home would be called Yasek Way. A short distance from their home Yasek Way met the newly paved highway for a faster way to Siletz or Toledo.

As Larry grew older after moving from Siletz he learned how to catch trout. The best fishing spots were below where a fork in the stream near their home made the stream larger. Neighbors downstream didn't mind his fishing along the stream on their properties and he put a lot of trout on the Peterson table. The old 22 single shot rifle on the property turned out to be a Stevens Favorite in good condition. Larry used it to bring home cottontail rabbits for his mother to cook. Minnie remembered her mother cooking rabbits when she was a little girl. They didn't have 22 rifles but used snares or bow and arrows to get their rabbits. Larry liked to hear his mother tell about her and her brother's life as children in eastern Canada.

Olaf had set up a workshop in part of the double garage, a space shared with their car. He had machine tools such as drill press and metal lathe. He had both arc and acetylene welding equipment. Neighbors all down the valley had learned to bring their broken farm equipment to Olaf for repair. He would take no money for his work, only asked them to share meat when they butchered or other produce that he didn't himself have in their garden. Sometimes he could also use a little tractor work. It was strictly barter and he enjoyed helping his neighbors with their machinery problems.

Larry learned from his dad to use the tools and by the time he was in the eighth grade he was an accomplished welder. In high school he loved his shop and crafts classes. He found biology to his liking also.

As a senior about to graduate he had researched what different colleges had to offer. He found that Oregon State had an Agricultural Program where students learned to become Ag teachers. They learned the various types of Agricultural equipment and about farm crops and much more. Larry had set his goal. He would become a high school Ag teacher.

Some schools in Lincoln County had been consolidated. Siletz High School had been closed and students from Siletz were bussed to Toledo High. Larry was happy about this because his Siletz friends, Marie and Willy were now at Toledo High. Marie was often Larry's date to dances and sometimes a movie. They were not going "steady" but were close friends who had pretty much grown up together. They dated other students as well as each other.

Larry and Willy were good friends and often went fishing together. Larry wasn't interested in basketball or football but he did like track. His specialty was distance running. Willy's only sport was football and he was good enough for Oregon State's football scouts to take notice. The college often offered scholarships to outstanding players. Ada and Ivan were proud of their son and remembered another tribal member from Siletz, Coquille Thompson who had been a star player at Oregon State some years ago.

Marie graduated ahead of Larry and had entered U of O at Eugene. She didn't know for certain what she wanted to do with her life but tentatively considered nursing as a career. Larry planned to enroll at Oregon State come fall, Willy's ambition was to become a football coach. He and Lisa were two years behind Larry in high school. Lisa was a beautiful and talented girl that all the boys wanted to date. She wasn't partial and dated most that asked but refused to go "steady" with any. Like Marie and Larry she and Willy had known each other all their lives and were close friends. They often went to dances or a movie together.

Lisa was a sort of tomboy who liked to go fishing and rabbit hunting with her brother. She was on the girls' basketball team as well as taking parts in school plays.

Larry and Lisa on one of their trips to Newport had discovered that at the Embarcadero Marina they could rent a boat for fishing and crabbing on the bay. The rental boats with motors were known as Livingston's and they were roomy, seaworthy and just great for crabbing and fishing on the bay. They did that often in the summer to bring home crabs, flounders, and sometimes when salmon runs began they brought home a salmon. They found a place in Newport that would cook their crabs in properly spiced boiling water for the correct time.

Speaking of salmon, when steelhead and salmon runs started in the fall on the lower Siletz Jim and Olaf would be on the river.

The '36 Chevy had served them well through the war years but when cars became available again they bought a new '48 Chevy sedan. When Larry became 16 and got his driver's license, Olaf and Minnie upgraded to a '51 Oldsmobile and Larry inherited the '48 Chevy and that was the car that Larry and Lisa used on their trips to the coast. One of these trips took them to Depoe Bay where they went fishing on one of the Tradewinds charter trips. Lisa loved the ocean. This trip would help decide her future.

Larry's family talked a lot around the dinner table about Larry leaving home to start school at Oregon State in the fall. Larry knew that students often joined fraternities and lived at fraternity houses but he was not interested in doing that. Others lived in dormitories usually two to a room. He didn't like the sound of that either. Some married couples lived in apartments off campus. That was more appealing to him, perhaps he could do that but he would have to do it alone. He knew that Willy wanted to join a fraternity when he entered college.

Olaf and Minnie had talked to each other and broached the subject one day at dinner. They had an idea. They knew that they would sometimes like to visit Larry in Corvallis and would have to stay someplace when they did that. Surely they could find a small house or apartment to rent that Larry could live in and they could be in when they came to visit. Larry kind of liked the sound of that idea. Lisa joined in too to voice an opinion. Most likely she would be going to Oregon State too and liked the idea.

As soon as they could Olaf and Minnie drove to Corvallis. They drove around the town to sort of get the lay of the land and then they went to a realtor who introduced herself as Dorothy. They told her that they were looking for a small house or apartment with kitchen facilities to rent or perhaps buy. Dorothy looked through her listings and found several small homes that might match what they were looking for and a couple of house keeping apartments for rent. She would show them if they liked. They looked at two apartments, one with one bedroom and another with two. Then there were three small homes they were shown. All were inside city limits. Only one had three bedrooms, the others had two. They explained why they were looking for a house. Their son would enter Oregon State in the fall as an Ag major and a daughter would also be entering college in two years.

They wanted something where they too could spend a little time. Dorothy said that much of the Ag facilities were on the western part of the campus and that she did have a listing that might fit what they were looking for but it was west of the city limits a ways like out in the country but it was on a bus route that a student could use to get to the campus.

When they saw it they thought it would fit their needs very well. However the owner didn't want to rent it. He wanted to sell it. Dorothy knew the owner and why he wanted to sell. He needed money for some sort of deal in Florida that he and others were trying to invest in. Olaf suggested that perhaps for a quick cash sale he might lower the selling price a bit.

They went back to Dorothy's office to call the owner to say that she had a buyer for his property who was willing to pay cash if he would lower his price a bit. After a couple offers and counter offers a price was set and agreed on. If Dorothy would draw up the papers he would come back tomorrow with a bank draft for full payment. Olaf gave Dorothy a thousand dollar check as earnest money.

As they drove home Olaf and Minnie discussed the purchase of the house. It had three bedrooms which was good. When they came to Corvallis Larry, Lisa and they could all have their own rooms. In general appearance the little light blue bungalow on its three quarter acre lot with attached two car garage had a nice homey comfortable look about it. When Lisa started college in a couple years which they assumed she would, she and Larry could share the home together.

When they arrived home they explained to Larry and Lisa what they had done. Lisa said the whole idea sounded good to her although she wasn't certain yet if she would start college right after graduation. She was thinking of other possibilities but still had plenty of time to make up her mind. Olaf and Minnie agreed that she had time to decide her future but they did hope that she would choose college. Larry liked the whole idea and was eager to see the house.

The next day in Corvallis Olaf and Minnie along with Larry and Lisa were in the realtor's office with the bank draft and were returned the earnest money check. There were papers to sign and property insurance that Dorothy would arrange. She would have electricity turned on and would arrange for telephone service as well as contacting the gas company. Appliances were all natural gas. They all went out to the property for Larry and Lisa to see the property. Dorothy gave them the key to the house and said as soon as final papers, a deed etc. were ready she would call them. She left them all at the house to return to her office.

Both Larry and Lisa were excited about living in this place while they were in college. They both thanked their folks for what they had done. Olaf and Minnie felt that financially what they had done was good for every one.

Going through the rooms they made notes as to what they would need for furniture. There was a sofa as well as a dining room table with leaves and six chairs. The kitchen was separated from the dining area only by a counter. The dining area was open to the living room.

There were several pots and pans in the kitchen. They would need more plus silverware, cups and plates. The bed rooms were empty. They would need beds etc. In other words they could see trips to second hand and thrift stores in their future. Minnie was looking at the bare walls and thinking what she would do about that.

Chapter 8

With graduation past everyone's focus was getting the Corvallis house ready for Larry to live in when he started his classes at Oregon State. After countless shopping tours at second hand and thrift stores the house was becoming more like a home.

There were beds ready for sleeping in the bedrooms. Larry and Lisa had drawn straws to decide who took which bedroom. Larry had a desk and on it was a second hand Underwood typewriter he had found in a thrift shop. He had taken typing in high school and was fairly good with typing.

The kitchen was fully equipped and shelves had an assortment of soups and such. They had rented a locker in town for an assortment of frozen meat and fish. When Olaf and Minnie came to spend a few days in Corvallis they would bring fresh fruit and vegetables.

Minnie had found prints she liked for the walls to make the place homelike and like her mother Lisa had her walls covered with posters and drawings done in Art classes. She had a desk that doubled as a table and on it was a lamp she had made in her craft class. She by now had decided to start college at Oregon State when she finished high school. Other things she had in mind could be taken care of after college.

Larry had applied and been accepted by the college. Now it was just waiting for registration day. In the meantime he was checking out the local fishing streams and lakes. In some of the Willamette River back waters there were crappies but not many places to fish for them without a boat. The upper reaches of the Luckiamute River he was told had good fly fishing for trout. He found a good source for fishing information was a local sport business. The owner was a fisherman who liked to share information.

Larry had a feeling that he was off to a new adventure which of course he was!

Registration day came with its turmoil and confusion but finally he was registered and an entrance exam to take. After that he would be assigned his classes. Because his goal was getting a teaching certificate with an Ag major there would be certain required classes. In high school he had been lucky to have a very demanding English teacher, her students usually scored high on the English parts of the entrance exam.

Larry was happy to learn that he had scored high enough on English that he didn't have to take English 101. He was now free to take some class of his choice. He looked at art and crafts classes but found a class called Recreational Handicraft. The description of the class made him pick that to replace English 101.

As he got into his studies he found some of the courses required for a teaching credential were not of much interest to him but he was serious and did make good grades in them.

The first week of school Minnie stayed at the house with him. She was worried that he would neglect his cooking by eating too much junk food. Actually Larry was a fairly good cook. In his camping along the rivers and at the beach he had learned by trial and error to be a fair camp cook. Sometimes Lisa was with him and they ate well. Larry liked vegetables and fruit plus sometimes in the woods he found extra wild things that were good. And he usually had fish of some kind for his camp cooking.

Getting involved with classes directly related to his major was to his liking. There were so many things related to agriculture he had not previously thought about. Kinds of soils and their management, fertilizers and suitability for different crops would be a part of his studies. He learned that area ranchers brought damaged farm machinery to the college for repair. Students would get hands on experience with welding, etc. There would be biology. The department had green houses and students would learn greenhouse management. Larry hadn't realized that there were so many things about which to learn, but he would have four years to do it.

Larry had learned bait fishing with a bait casting rod. As he fished the upper stretches of the Siletz River he saw other fishermen using fly rods. It was a different kind of fishing that he wished to learn. He made a point of talking to them about their equipments and some gave advice on rods, lines, reels and the flies to purchase. He found a sporting goods store in Newport that had a good assortment of fly fishing tackle and purchased enough equipment to get started on what would become his favorite fishing activity. By observing others along the streams he soon became fairly adept with the sport. One thing he learned was that fly rods alone varied a lot in quality and price. His nine foot split bamboo rod was not the cheapest but it was far from the most expensive.

One part of his Recreational Handicraft class was related to fishing tackle. Fiberglass was becoming popular as a replacement for split bamboo in fishing rods. He learned that he could buy good quality fiberglass blanks for a three piece fly rod along with guides and other parts at a reasonable price and learn how to put it all together as a class project. This he decided to do.

At the end of three quarters Larry had surprised himself. He not only had a beautiful new fly rod but his grades in other subjects had been better than expected. With no distractions he had been able to concentrate on his studies and it had paid off. With summer vacation arriving he needed a job. His parents could well afford to pay for his tuition which they did but he didn't expect them to also furnish his spending money.

With all the locals back from their military service in Toledo and Siletz he doubted that there would be work at the lumber mills in Toledo and logging in the Siletz area. He heard that the Corvallis Post Office sometimes hired extra help. He made a point to talk to the carrier who delivered his mail about that. The carrier said yes extra help was needed at times, carriers took vacations and substitutes were hired to take their place. It would be worth his while to inquire at the post office about a summer job.

Larry did that and was referred to the postmaster for an interview. He learned that whenever possible the post office liked to hire college students for temporary help. He was given application papers to fill out. He would need a recommendation from a responsible person as to character, etc. With these done he was to return for another interview with the postmaster.

To whom he would go to for a recommendation he had to think a bit. He finally thought perhaps the Ag professor with whom he had worked on a project might be a person to help him. It was a good choice. The professor was happy to help and had learned Larry's work habits to the point that he was able to give a good recommendation.

When Larry brought the papers to the post office the postmaster was ready to talk to him. He looked over the questions and answers. He knew that professor and when he read what the professor had written he told Larry that he would be hired as a sub carrier when needed. Also Larry was asked if he had a car. Larry of course said he did. The postmaster explained that sometimes special delivery mail had to be delivered to homes in the area and this he could do when he was available between classes at any time of the year. He would be paid mileage for the use of his car.

A regular carrier explained the mail casing procedure. A case contained a bank of pigeonholes with names and addresses of everyone on a given postal route in the order that a carrier would deliver mail. A carrier stood in front of the case with a handful of letters, etc. to sort them one by one into pigeonholes matching a letter's address.

Larry watched as a carrier demonstrated. Because the carrier was familiar with his route and recognized the letter's address he could almost automatically toss the letter into the correct pigeonhole. Larry found that when he did it he had to search all over the case before locating the correct pigeonhole and was unhappy with his inability to do it quickly. The carrier assured him that it just took practice to do it easily and quickly.

Mail was removed from the case in the order that it would be delivered and into small bundles wrapped with a rubber band. A carrier would walk the route on which he would substitute to familiarize him with it. When Larry finally started to walk a route as a sub carrier he liked that but the beforehand casing he disliked. As he became familiar with various routes his ability to quickly case the mail became much easier and better. Larry would continue his work at the post office the remainder of his time at Oregon State.

Larry was not familiar with the fishing streams in this part of Oregon but he made it his mission to locate and fish at least a few. He had been told about the upper reaches of the Luckiamute River and first chance he had free time that would be his first choice to investigate.

Heading west on Highway 20 through Philomath to a turnoff at Wren, Larry soon reached Kings Valley and the Luckiamute. He found a gravel road heading west that pretty much followed the river. Past a ranch home he continued upstream until he found a good place to park that was a short walk to the stream. Alders and willows lined the river banks but with occasional open areas. At what appeared to be a good fishable stretch of water he stopped to put his rod together along with a new reel and fly line he had purchased to use on the new fiberglass rod he had put together in his Recreational Handicraft class. This would be the first time to use it for fishing. He had however practiced casting with it on a campus lawn and liked the way it handled.

Larry's first cast was over to a shallow riffle that dropped off into deeper water. As his bucktail caddis fly drifted to this deeper water a nice ten inch rainbow was waiting for it and was hooked. Fishermen sometimes have strange superstitions. Some consider a fish caught on a first cast foretells lousy fishing the rest of the day. However with its usual distinctive chatter a kingfisher flew by on its way upstream. Now Larry considered that to be a good omen but which would be the stronger? That was the question.

Size limits here were trout had to be over six inches to keep. Larry remembered that coast streams required they be over eight inches. This was to protect the baby salmon that often remained in the streams until well over six inches.

Larry left the stream when he had enough trout for a couple meals, the five fish all under ten inches he had in his creel would do that. He liked fishing smaller streams like this perhaps because of the challenge involved with landing a fly in the water under overhanging bushes without getting the fly snagged in them. He liked what he could do with his new rod even though a shorter lighter rod might be more suitable for the smaller streams he liked to fish.

Chapter 9
Lucy McCredie

A girl in one of Larry's classes was from the small town of Detroit on the North Santiam River. Her name was Lucy McCredie and she was living with her aunt while going to Oregon State. He learned that her dad was the Ranger at the Detroit Forest Service Office. Larry had asked her to go with him to one of the dances at the college. She did go with him as his date on that occasion and they had a fun evening together. Later they occasionally shared a movie or some school function. Larry was beginning to like this girl very much and Lucy appeared to enjoy their times together.

When Lucy learned that Larry liked to fish for trout she told him that her area had fine fishing streams. The town was at the upper end of Detroit Lake, a reservoir formed by a dam on the North Santiam River. It was a popular lake for trolling for trout. The river both above and below the lake had good fly fishing.

The Breitenbush River joined the North Santiam and the lake at Detroit. It also was a popular fishing stream. Also there were a number of fishable lakes in the mountains above. She had worked in a Detroit general store that sold fishing tackle and supplies and often heard fishermen talk about their fishing success.

Lucy frequently went home on weekends. She told Larry that she sometimes had a late forenoon class on Monday so didn't return to Corvallis until Monday morning. She then had all day free on Sunday and if he would come to Detroit she would pack a picnic lunch and she would show him around the area.

Eventually they did that. She had explained how to find her home which he did. She introduced him to her mom and dad. They expressed their pleasure in meeting the young man their daughter had mentioned as her good friend at Oregon State.

She first had Larry drive east to Idanha so she could show him what the river looked like above the lake. When they reached Idanha Lucy explained that there had been a large lumber mill there and that the railroad also ended there. Its main purpose was to pick up the lumber that the mill produced. After the lake was formed the mill was dismantled and railroad now ended at the lumber mills in Mill City. Leaving Idanha she had him drive back to Detroit and up the road that followed the Breitenbush River. As he drove Larry spotted a stretch of water that he just knew had a trout waiting to be caught. "Lucy" he said, "I just want to stop for a bit to see if there are any fish in that spot." "Ok if you do it quickly because there's a lot more I want to show you." It only took moments for Larry to have his rod together and have a fly landing on the water.

As Larry had thought, there was a nice sized rainbow right where he thought it would be and it liked the look of his fly. As Larry released it he said "go home little fish I'll see you again some time." He quickly took apart his rod and they were ready again to travel on towards Breitenbush Hot Springs. Lucy was amazed at how adept Larry was with his fly casting and told him so. "It just takes practice" Larry said. "I've been fly fishing a lot in the streams along the coast."

At Breitenbush Hot Springs Lucy suggested that they stop here while she explained about the place. There were tables and benches on the grounds where they sat as Lucy talked.

The hot mineral water was supposed to have medicinal qualities. People with rheumatism came to soak in the baths and claimed that it helped to rid them of at least some of their aches and pains. Lucy went on to say that she had worked here several times when they needed extra help. She added that heavy smokers found that it would literally soak the nicotine out of their bodies.

Lucy went on to say that she could remember that before the dam was built, Detroit only had one store and it was a combination post office, grocery and general store all in one. Before the dam stopped them, salmon and steelhead migrated up the rivers to spawn. In springtime Oregon State Fish Commission would create a salmon egg collecting site by putting racks across the river. Salmon eggs would be taken to the main hatchery in Mehama where they were hatched then raised in ponds until large enough for release back to the river. Some steelhead eggs were also collected. They were hatched then raised in a pond at the site. Some were taken in five gallon cans by pack trains for the Forest Service to plant in lakes. The rest were released in fall to the Breitenbush and North Santiam Rivers. "I'm going to take you to one of those lakes where you might catch a descendent of those planted steelhead," Lucy added.

But before they left she went on to say that there were college age boys and girls from other parts of the state, frequently Portland that were hired to work at the place. When things were quiet in mid week they would organize juke box dances. She and others from Detroit would often come to join in the fun.

It seems that so often lakes, streams and valleys were named after bears and elk. They would go to one of these, Elk Lake. Here Lucy elected to spread out the contents of her picnic basket as Larry put the sections of his rod together and started his fly casting. He caught a couple rather small trout that he released before going to join Lucy for lunch. He commented that those fish were essentially rainbows but more silvery in appearance than the rainbow he had caught in the Breitenbush.

Larry complimented Lucy on the lunch she had spread out and as he started to eat, how good were the sandwiches she had made. The cold drinks were still cold as she got them from a cold bag. Larry thought to himself, "this girl certainly knows how to put together a lunch."

These mountain lakes usually had a sizeable mosquito population but Larry was prepared for that, he always had mosquito dope included with his fishing tackle. Lucy too knew about mosquitoes and had mosquito dope in her hand bag. Larry wasn't much surprised about that, he was always a bit amazed at the variety of items women carried in those hand bags.

Back to Detroit as Larry was thanking Lucy for the good day she had set up for him, she said she would be working until school started in the fall at the marina. She would be working with boat rentals. She suggested that if he could find time in what promised to be a busy summer for him he should come up to try trolling for some of the large brown trout that were sometimes caught in the lake. Larry promised to do that.

Larry was a pretty busy guy. This was the time of year that the carriers took their vacations so post office work was a full time job. Things growing in the college green houses didn't take vacations. Normally he would have been expected to care for some of the ongoing projects there but teachers back for refresher courses in the department were taking care of that.

There were things in the garden at home that he was experimenting with that needed attention so that is where he was on some Sundays but he really did want to visit Lucy and troll for the big browns she had told about. One Sunday he did just that.

He called Lucy on a Friday evening to let her know that he planned to come Sunday to see if he could catch one of those big browns she had talked about. He wanted her to reserve a boat and motor for him. She responded to that by saying that she had the use of a boat as one of the perks of the job. She would find a stand-in for the day and take a boat for the both of them to fish together.

Sunday morning early Larry was on the way to Detroit with tackle designed for salmon fishing. On Saturday he had purchased a couple large bass plugs and a salmon lure called a Quickfish. He knew that he would need to fish deep so also bought an Oregon Diver which worked much like the reverse of a kite to take his lure deep.

Lucy was at the Marina when Larry arrived at the lake. She met him with a hug then pointed out the boat they would use so that he could get all his gear from his car to the boat. Lucy planned to fish for trout and had her tackle and some cold drinks and chips already in the boat. Larry had a thermos of coffee and snacks too, they would not go hungry.

Lucy really liked her job at the Marina. She talked about the people who rented boats and their idiosyncrasies. People were so different. Some were so friendly and wanted to talk about the fishing, the weather and other things. When they came back with the boat they commented on how nice it was on the lake even though they had only caught a couple fish. And then there was the guy who didn't like the make of motor they used on their boats. And another who complained about the fishing, he was a expert fisherman who usually caught his limit but had only caught two fish. It was a lousy fishing lake, the fish were small and the motor wouldn't run at the right trolling speed.

As they left the Marina Lucy was running the boat. She explained that she wanted to take him to the part of the lake where the big browns were normally caught. They ran at full speed to where she wanted to go. Lucy has picked a Klamath with 15 hp motor that she knew was one of the most popular rental boats they rented for fishing. It had a Bimini top for shade and amidships control and comfortable seats. Larry liked her choice of boat.

When they reached what was probably the deeper part of the lake Lucy cut the motor back to trolling speed. Larry had his gear ready for fishing and got it in the water. He had decided to start off with a large bass plug called a Brown Bomber. Lucy was using a conventional trout trolling setup called a Ford

Fender with a night crawler on the hook a short distance behind.

As the smooth running Evinrude hummed quietly along Larry and Lucy talked about the coming year at Oregon State. They would be juniors. Larry was looking forward to more Ag training. There would be a required course in Educational Psychology about which he was not much excited. More to his liking would be trouble shooting gas and diesel tractor engines.

When Lucy started her freshman year she hadn't decided on a major. She just wanted a college education. In her sophomore year she realized that she should be thinking about what to do with her life. What were her interests? She talked at length about how hard it was for her to pick a major field to pursue. Living as she did in a home where forestry was always a topic for conversation, she knew a lot about that and she found it interesting also Oregon State offered a major in Forestry. What she did pick as a tentative major was Fish and Game Management; she knew that there were both state and federal jobs in that field. She said she knew it was a field dominated by men but could see no reason why a lady couldn't handle a job there as well as a man. She had hunted deer with her dad. He had taught her how to handle a deer rifle and she had shot a four point buck on one of their hunts and she had helped her dad field dress it.

Lucy always surprised him; he was realizing that he didn't really know her very well. As they talked and munched on potato chips Lucy had hooked two nice rainbows which Larry had netted for her. He had no results on the Brown Bomber so decided to change to his Quickfish.

As Larry was telling Lucy about his sister Lisa starting college this year he saw his rod in its holder suddenly start jerking. When he picked up his rod he knew immediately that he had hooked a heavy fish. Lucy quickly reeled in her line and turned off the motor. She could tell that he was starting to play something big and got the net ready to help him land it. He had been fishing quite deep and that's where that fish wanted to stay. Of course he didn't know how solidly it was hooked so was taking his time to work it up from the depths. When he eventually had it alongside the boat for Lucy to net it looked almost as large as a salmon. Lucy was prepared with a large net she had made a point of having in the boat. She knew the browns in this lake got big. With the fish in the boat they guessed its weight. Larry thought it to be near the size of a 20 lb. salmon he had caught when fishing with his dad and Jim. He guessed it to be 19 lbs. Lucy was a little more generous with 21 lbs. It went in the big cold box. They would weigh it when they returned to the Marina.

Lucy got the motor running again and they agreed that if a fish hit his rod she would handle it and likewise he would pick up the trout rod. Now as they fished it was time for Larry to have coffee and she a cold drink as they munched on their snacks. They wanted to troll awhile longer before they needed a trip to a bathroom. Lucy said some boat owners had portapotties in their boats but this marina didn't offer that service.

About the same time Larry had a trout hit the trout lure Lucy had a heavy fish on. He quickly got the trout into the boat without a net, put it in the cold box and got the big net ready for whatever Lucy had on. She had seen how slowly Larry worked his fish to the boat and she did the same. He netted the brown for her and it appeared to be about the same size as Larry's. Now it really was time for them to wrap up their fishing and head back to the marina and a bathroom. As they headed back Lucy said that was the first big brown for her to catch. Larry commented on the way she handled the fish and she responded by saying that she just did what she had seen him do. Larry said that too was his first big brown although he had caught salmon about the same size and larger.

After a quick trip to the marina rest rooms they carried the cold box ashore. The marina office had a scale and when they weighed his fish it was within an ounce of nineteen and a half lbs. Lucy's brown was very close to nineteen and three quarter lbs. She had beaten him by a quarter lb. They hadn't made any formal bet but Larry said that as soon as school started he would take her for dinner to the finest restaurant in Corvallis. "It's a date," she said and gave him a hug, and this time with a quick kiss. Now they had work to do, there was a fish cleaning station at the marina and plastic bags for their fish. Lucy recorded the weight of their browns and who caught them. There would be a prize for the season's largest brown and Lucy was now in the running with the largest caught so far this season and Larry was so far in second place. He presented her the Quickfish so she could show what lure had been used to catch the fish.

Larry had his fish tightly wrapped in its bag. He got a second bag and was able to surround the brown with ice. He wanted to keep it cool until he could get it in the fridge at home in Corvallis. He added his lone rainbow to Lucy's catch and it was time to thank Lucy for a wonderful day, give her a parting hug and be on the road home.

There was an item in the outdoor news section of a Salem paper about fishing on Detroit Reservoir. Mention was made that the five hundred dollar prize for largest brown caught in the summer season had gone to a young lady from Detroit named Lucy McCredie. Her brown weighed in at nineteen and three quarter pounds. Second prize of three hundred dollars had gone to her fishing partner Larry Peterson. His fish was only about a quarter pound smaller than hers. The article went on to say that the two fishing partners were Oregon State students and the prize money would be going to where it would be much appreciated.

Chapter 10

Larry was happy with sharing the home with Lisa. They took turns with cooking their meals and sometimes working together with something special. They were barely into the new quarter, she as a freshman and he as a junior. They agreed that their parents had surely done a good thing when they bought the cottage in the western outskirts of Corvallis.

Lisa like Larry had scored high enough on the English part of the entrance exam that she could skip English 101. Now she could choose some elective. She would think about this a bit. The problem was that she had so many interests. She had decided on Oceanography as a major. She had seen the ship related to that study that Oregon State kept at Newport. When that ship was at sea someone had to be responsible for navigation, etc. She would see what might be related to that subject. Perhaps enrolling in NROTC might be the answer to that.

Willy too with his football scholarship was enrolled at Oregon State. He was currently living in student housing but expected to join a fraternity in the future. Occasionally Larry and Lisa would invite him for dinner. Larry was looking forward to taking him to new fishing places he had discovered. Larry described at length what it had been like to fish for big browns with Lucy on Detroit Lake.

One evening after a movie Larry and Lucy went to one of the downtown night spots for root beer floats. Instead of taking her home right away he suggested, "Let's go over to the little park by the river to enjoy the balmy evening. There's a nice moon too." Lucy said, "Good idea."

They found a parking spot near the park and walked over to one of the benches where they could sit and see the reflection of the moon on the Willamette. They could see a couple canoes drifting by, obviously from a trip paddling to some attractive spot upriver. "Perhaps they were returning from a large gravel bar up river which with the river so low now exposed an area where very nice petrified wood specimens and sometimes nice agates too could be picked up," Larry commented. Lucy answered that with "Let's do that sometime. We could pack a picnic lunch. I know that there's a place that rents canoes just downriver from here."

As they sat they started discussing the movie they had seen. It was a somewhat sexy movie involving teenagers and their problems. They started talking about their dates. Lucy had something to say about that. "Larry, whenever you've asked me for a date I've always been happy to say yes because I like you and I like you because of the way you act when we're together."

Then Lucy continued with more. "We've never had problems like those kids in the movie. When I was in high school sometimes a date would think because we shared a hug and a couple kisses that was a signal that I would get in the back seat for intercourse with him. That would be the last date for me with that boy. I'm still a virgin and intend to stay that way until I'm certain the time is right to be otherwise."

After that rather long and frank statement from Lucy about all Larry could think to say was, "I just act with you as I think a guy should towards a girl he respects and likes very much. I never had a steady girl friend in high school. Perhaps I dated some more than others but I wanted to be free to ask any girl I wished for a date." Lucy commented, "Since our first date I have not had a date other than with you. That doesn't mean that I want to be your steady girl friend. I want to be free to have dates with others who might ask." Larry responded with, "I feel like if I tell a girl I'm in love with her and want her to go steady with me it's like I want her to spend the rest of our lives together and I'm not yet ready for that. Perhaps I said that in a clumsy way but I think you can understand what I mean." Lucy said, "Seems we're on the same plane and I'd like for two good friends to celebrate that with a big hug and nice kiss."

On the way taking Lucy home Lucy commented on how good it was for them to be able to share their inner feelings with each other. Larry agreed and then went on to mention that his sister Lisa and he took turns cooking but sometimes they worked together on something special. He said, "Lucy I want you to meet Lisa so expect an invitation for dinner with us sometime soon." "I'd like that," Lucy said as they arrived at her aunt's home. At the door they parted with a hug and goodnight kiss.

Willy Johns was performing quite well on the football field. The frosh team coach was happy to have him on the team. However football was not Willy's only interest. His goal was to be a high school football coach but he was aware that in some small isolated schools a coach would be called on to coach a variety of sports. On top of that he might be expected to teach subjects not related to sports. He knew of a coach who taught science classes and another who taught a foreign language.

In high school Willy liked very much his crafts class and the things he learned to do there. Even in elementary school he was using his pocket knife to make wooden chains from alder wood. He was picking crafts as his teaching minor. He would be able to teach ceramics, leather tooling and lacing and perhaps a few other things too. Currently he was in the process of sculpting a fairly large beaver from oak wood. Oregon State students were Beavers just as U of O students in Eugene, their arch rivals in sports, were Ducks. In crafts classes he was always ending up with good grades mainly because he really liked the class and he put a real effort into learning as much as he could about the various crafts as he worked with them.

One of Willy's fellow football team members was also enrolled in this class. He was good with the game of football but was a poor student. His coach had him enroll in the crafts class because he thought this was a class where he could at least make a passing grade. Willy tried to help him but it was hard to help someone who skipped class more days than he was present. Willy kept telling him that if he didn't at least be in class most of the time he would flunk the course. Of course that is what happened.

Representatives of the athletic department came to the instructor to say how important this student was to the football team. Couldn't she at least change his grade to a "D" otherwise he would be dropped from the team. This she refused to do, there was no way she could give a passing grade to a student who was absent from class more than he was there and when he was there he accomplished nothing. They went to the college administration wanting them to pressure the instructor into changing the grade. Willy's crafts instructor was a long time and highly thought of member of the faculty who stood her ground and the football team had no choice but to drop the student. Administration policy was that members of athletic teams had to maintain passing grades in their academic classes.

Larry and Lisa were planning a special dinner; after much thought they decided to do a dinner using only things from the farm on the road to Siletz. Lucy had accepted a dinner invitation with them.

Larry's folks had raised one of the calves to be baby beef. They had a goodly portion of that animal in their freezer locker. They would do a pot roast. There would be potatoes, carrots and peas from their garden. There would be apple pie for dessert using apples also from the farm plus a sweet dessert wine from the abundant Evergreen Blackberries. There would be very little on the table that didn't come from the farm.

It was a typical autumn Sunday afternoon when Lucy arrived to be greeted with a big hug before she and Lisa were introduced. Lucy remembered seeing Lisa before on the campus but of course didn't at the time know who she was. Lisa took Lucy for a tour of the home and the backyard where Larry had put up a small green house beside a small area with several raised beds where he was experimenting with some winter vegetables he had been starting in the greenhouse.

They came in to see what Larry was doing in the kitchen. He had checked the pot roast. Now he could join the girls in the living room. They had been busy getting acquainted with each other by telling a little about themselves. Larry reported that he was about ready to cook the vegetables and the pot roast was almost ready to take from the pot. Lisa suggested, "Larry why don't you open that Pinot Noir that we're having with dinner. We could share a little now." To Lucy she asked, "Do you like red wine? We have some white zinfandel if you'd rather have that." "I like red wine," Lucy responded and Larry left to do as Lisa suggested. He returned with glasses of wine for the girls and returned to the kitchen.

Lisa started telling how their folks had bought this house as an investment and as a place for her and her brother to live while at Oregon State and Lucy said how lucky it was for her to have an aunt living in Corvallis who was ready to give her a room of her own for free in return for helping with housework and meal preparation. So far it had worked well for both.

Needless to say, the dinner was a success. Lucy thought it interesting that the dinner was all homegrown. She and Lisa talked a lot about their majors and plans after college. Lucy talked a bit about her Fish and Game Management major. So far she was happy with the various classes pertaining to it and planned to continue with it. Lisa didn't have too much to say about a major because she hadn't decided for certain what to do. She was considering Oceanography. She loved the ocean and boats. She told Lucy about her first time on the ocean, how they had gone out from Depoe Bay on a charter boat and how she realized that she wanted to do something in later life that involved the ocean.

Lucy had noticed a red Jeep alongside Larry's Chevy in the open garage. She said, "Larry, I didn't know you had a Jeep. When did you get that?" Before Larry could answer Lisa spoke up with "That's not his. It's mine." Then Lisa had to explain that it was a graduation present from her folks when she graduated from high school. She had used it to explore the old logging roads in her area. She said that Jeep was like a tiger so she called it "Tige." She went on to say that she had learned of a number of old roads in this area that she wanted to explore. Lucy was thinking to herself, "Larry's sister is something else again! And I like her."

Larry spoke up to say "I worry sometimes about my intrepid little sister. A Jeep doesn't have much protection for occupants in a rollover. My graduation present for her was a good set of roll bars on that Jeep." "He's right I guess. Some of those back country roads are a bit hairy," Lisa said and then Lucy added "Sometimes I think freeways can be just as bad."

Lisa had been told by a classmate about a rather unusual lake and how to get to it. It was a fairly long lake but narrow with steep hillsides on both sides. The lake had been formed by a slide that dammed up a small stream and it was referred to as Slide Lake. It was beyond the end of a road so one had to walk a half mile more or less to get to the lake. These were the directions she had been given by a classmate. She wanted Willy to go with her to find it. She told Larry that she would like him to go with them too. The Jeep had comfortable front seats but the back seat was rather uncomfortable although it had been upgraded with better upholstery at the same time the front seats had been redone. Larry had sat in the front seats but never in the back.

A Saturday soon after that discussion found Lisa, Willy and Larry with their fishing tackle and lunches in the jeep on the way to search for Slide Lake. Larry and Willy had flipped a coin as to who would be in the back seat first. Whoever sat in the back seat on the way to the lake would get the front seat on the way home. Larry would be first in the back seat. He found that the seat itself was not the problem. The problem was leg room, only by sitting sideways could he stretch out his long legs.

This lake was not nearby. They went west on H20 to a place called Burnt Woods. Here a road turned south which eventually took them over a ridge into another watershed. Then it was downhill to a bridge crossing what they thought to be the Big Elk River. Eventually they passed a logging operation and ridges to where the old logging road appeared to head into another watershed. At last, they found themselves at the end of the road.

There was a trail that appeared to head in the direction of what they could see was a canyon with steep hills on either side. The whole area had the appearance of having been logged some number of years past. They gathered their fishing gear and with lunches in their day packs started hiking the trail. This was fall and the vine maple's foliage on the hill sides were in full red autumn color. As they hiked they could see where on the hillside the slide had originated bringing with it trees, dirt and rock. They had reached a point where the stream had washed away the loose soil to form an outlet through rock. Vegetation gave the appearance that it had been like that forever.

The lakeshore was lined with logs and driftwood. Some logs were large and stable enough to walk out on to fish. There was a bet on for first fish. Larry and Willy were out on logs trying to get their bucktail caddis flies as far out in the lake as they could. Lisa had noticed a fish rise for an insect quite close to the shore. She tied on a small rather insignificant little fly to cast along side a log very near the shore. Larry and Willy quickly had their attention diverted to Lisa when they heard "fish on" from her direction. They watched as she played and landed a nice ten inch rainbow. She beat both boys for first fish.

The best part of the lake to fish they found was among the logs near the shore. That's where trout were feeding on small insects. As they fished they were noticing something else along the shore. Many beer and soft drink cans had been discarded along the shore. They thought this a bit strange because these cans had refund value so as they fished they were also picking up cans and stuffing them into their day packs.

They had almost caught their limits and it was time to relax with lunch. The fly to attract fish the best was the main topic of conversation as they ate. Both Larry and Lisa had learned to tie their own flies. Willy was using flies tied by both. With her more nimble fingers Lisa could tie a neater looking fly than Larry but sometimes the more ragged looking fly looked better to a fish.

In the jeep heading home with limit trout catches and bags of aluminum cans they were passing the active logging operation they had seen previously.

They saw on distant hills rectangular sections of fair size young trees. Next to it was another similar section with trees half the size and near that another with only tiny trees. As they were commenting on this and with the current logging operation behind them they were seeing a beautiful stand of large second growth Douglas fir. Obviously this entire area belonged to a large timber company that was systematically clear cutting and replanting on sections of their timber holdings a little at a time.

This was Saturday. Sunday Larry and Lisa's parents were expected to come for a few days visit. Needless to say there would be a big fish fry Sunday evening.

About those aluminum cans they had collected at the lake, when they were turned in for refund the money they got was enough to pay for a goodly portion of the gas the jeep had used on the trip.

Chapter 11

It was well into spring quarter after a movie, Lucy and Larry were at what had become a favorite place to sit and talk after a date, weather permitting. This was at downtown Corvallis's little park by the Willamette. Lucy wanted to talk about something that had been bothering her.

"Larry" she said and continued with "I have seen Lisa so many times with that Indian football guy, Willy Johns. That worries me, are they having a love affair or something?" "No, I don't think so. They are just good friends and have been for a long time. Why does it worry you?" Larry answered with a question. "Well it's like I don't like to see a black guy with a white girl or the other way around. I don't know why but it bothers me and I guess it's a little like that when I see Lisa with an Indian guy."

Larry responded with "You have to understand that my family and Willy's family have been close friends for as long as I can remember. Willy and Lisa were born on the same day in the same hospital in Toledo. We lived in Siletz at the time and those two grew up together becoming close friends. Willy is my good friend also and a great guy to know."

"I was aware that there was an Indian Reservation at Siletz at one time so I suppose many Indians still live there." Lucy commented. "Yes, there are native tribal members still there as is Willy's mother. His father was from a different tribe here in the Willamette valley and as a child was moved to the reservation by the government. He thinks there is some white blood in his ancestry. Many of the natives and whites have intermarried so there are few full blooded tribal members remaining. What they have done however is put together a tribal association that actively works to preserve their heritage." "I guess you didn't know that Lisa has a little Native American blood in her heritage too."

That statement really caught Lucy by surprise. "That means you do too! How come you never mentioned that to me?" Lucy questioned as she turned to look at Larry. She then added "I always thought you were Swedish. You have what I think of as a Scandinavian look.

Larry answered with "I guess the subject never came up in any of our conversations. I am mostly Swedish. I'll tell you about my dad, when he was about eighteen he came to Canada. He had worked as a logger in Sweden and thought there would be work for him in the Ontario forests. There he met and teamed up with a guy as timber fallers. This person had a sister my dad thought was the most beautiful young lady he had ever seen and yes they did fall in love. After they were married and after many moves they eventually ended up in Siletz, Oregon. That's where I came into this world and by the way, I too think my mom is a beautiful lady."

"But all that doesn't explain how you have Native American blood in your ancestry." "You're right. I'll tell you about my mom's parents. Her dad was Scottish and the manager of a Hudson Bay Company trading post. He married a member of the Chipewyan tribe, native to eastern Canada so you see that my mother is half and half Chipewyan and Scottish. The way I see it, I'm half Swedish, one quarter

Chipewyan and one quarter Scotch. Does that explain every thing for you?"

"Yes, I think so but you just look Scandinavian to me." "May I ask about your ancestry? Larry enquired. "Well, my mother traces her ancestry to the Mayflower landing. My dad's ancestry also goes back to England," Lucy responded. "I read some place that families who trace ancestry back to the time of the Mayflower landing find that along the line some Native American blood got into the mix. As people worked their way west there was constant both friendly and unfriendly contact with the original residents of this large country," Larry commented, and added "I'll bet that if you did a thorough search of your ancestry you would find that those who had been in this country that long very probably picked up Native American blood along the way."

"I guess I've never really given much thought to my ancestry other than what I told you. What you have said does give me food for thought. I'm going to start asking questions as I talk with my folks and some of my relatives," Lucy stated as they left the park.

As they drove towards Lucy's aunt's, Larry said "Lucy you've never met my folks, as soon as we can find a Sunday free of commitments let's drive over to their place for lunch with them." "I'd like that," Lucy responded as they parked at Lucy's aunt's home. Before they parted Lucy said that she was going to ask her aunt a few questions about family history.

Larry had talked a little about Lucy with his folks and now he wanted to bring Lucy with him for a short visit and perhaps lunch. Perhaps Lisa might come with them. "Anytime" his folks said and "just tell us when and we'll put together a lunch for you."

It was less than two weeks later that Larry and Lucy planned to do the visit and Lisa would come with them. Larry called to let his folks know and that Lisa would be with them. When Sunday came even though it would only take a little over an hour for the drive they were on the road before nine o'clock. Larry wanted to drive around Toledo a bit and show Lucy the high School he and Lisa had attended. In Toledo by the waterfront he pointed out where Depot Slough joined Yaquina River and explained that where they were going was on a small tributary of the headwaters of what you see. As they started driving up the road to Siletz Larry pointed out the small stream they were passing. He explained that a tide gate had been installed just upstream from Toledo which stopped the tide from coming a couple miles upstream. The stream at that time was kept clear of brush and other obstructions for small boats to travel with the tides to Toledo.

As they passed a location a short distance further upstream Larry explained that Depot Slough got its name from a depot at this place where supplies came by water to be loaded on wagons for the Government Agency at the Siletz Indian Reservation. Larry further explained, "This is early Oregon History."

"This is home," Larry said as they pulled into his parent's driveway. Larry's folks had seen them drive in and came out of the house to greet them. Larry introduced his folks and Lucy to each other. His folks gave Lucy a warm greeting and said to every one, "Let's go inside."

Inside as they all found a seat Larry's mom said to Lucy, "I'm so glad to meet you in person. Larry has told me a little about you and especially about catching those big fish in Detroit Lake." "Yes, we do have fun doing things like that and he has told me a lot about you and his dad," Lucy responded. Larry's mom looked at Lucy to say, "Lucy, just call me Minnie." His dad also spoke up to say, "Ya, you call me Olaf."

Minnie brought up the subject of lunch and stated that it was almost time for that and wanted the three to go freshen up. That taken care of she asked Lisa to help in the kitchen and told Larry to show Lucy around the place.

He took Lucy upstairs to show her his room. It still had the posters and pictures on the walls from his high school days. They peeked in Lisa's room and Larry said Lisa could show her that later. He wanted to take her outside to see the garden. The weather was nice as he pointed across the meadow to the little stream. "We'll go over there after lunch. I want to show you where Lisa and I caught our first little trout."

There was a call from the house that lunch was ready. On the dining room table there were nice big slices of home baked bread on a plate and another with slices of both white and dark meat chicken. There was a bowl of lettuce leaves fresh from the garden, dill and sweet pickles plus an assortment of other things a person might like in a sandwich. In other words, each would put together a sandwich to suit his or her personal likes. Minnie served coffee, tea or cold fruit juice.

After lunch Larry and Lisa took Lucy across the meadow to the little stream to show Lucy where they had caught their first fish. When they approached the bank they saw a couple small fish dart for shelter down stream. Lisa commented "they could see our movement against the sky. If we had a dark background behind us like trees or brush they wouldn't notice us so easily." Larry pointed out a spot near the bank a little farther downstream to say "that's where Lisa and I found that if we could let the current drift the worm we used for bait into that deeper water near the bank a fish would grab it. The fish here were little but we caught larger fish downstream below where this stream joins a larger stream. By the way we called these streams 'cricks' as did most people around here."

On the way back to the house they showed Lucy the old Model T Ford that Larry's dad had restored to running condition. Back at the house Lisa suggested that they start for home early and go by way of Siletz and Logsden and up the Rock Creek road. She explained to Lucy that they would join H20 at Blodgett. Larry liked that suggestion.

As they prepared to leave Lucy thanked Minnie for the wonderful lunch and told Olaf how happy she was to meet Larry's dad. Minnie and Olaf both let Lucy know how happy they were to meet her and hoped to see her again soon.

As they joined the main highway Larry explained to Lucy that when they had moved from Siletz to the place they had just left, this highway was still a logging railroad. It was shortly after they moved from Siletz that the state took it over and turned it into a new highway. Shortly before crossing the Siletz River and into Siletz, Larry pointed toward where Camp 12 used to be and explained that it was where his folks lived and worked at the time he was born. They drove by the house where they had lived in Siletz before heading towards Logsden. As they passed a bridge crossing the Siletz River Larry told Lisa that if they crossed the river to take that road it would take them over the hills to H20.

As they crossed the river at Logsden, Larry said, "Before we go up the Rock Creek road I want to show you Moonshine Park. It's where a place called Upper Farm used to be. You can find out more about that by getting into the history of the US Government and its Indian Reservation at Siletz. If you were to go up the Siletz River past Moonshine Park you would be going into a part of the Siletz River called the Siletz Gorge. There's very good fly fishing water there. At the park Lucy agreed that it really was as Larry described it and a scenic part of the river too.

Coming to a place called Summit which was where the railroad crossed the summit of the Coast Range Larry mentioned that some years ago there was a major invasion of tent caterpillars. They were so thick on the railroad rails that the Locomotive could only pull one car at a time over the grade even by sanding the rails,

"It was an interesting back road passing alongside the little lake and all" Lucy said as they reached H20 at Blodgett. At Corvallis Lisa said "It's late afternoon. There's spaghetti sauce in the fridge and I can get a spaghetti dinner ready in nothing flat." "Do it." Larry said and then went to look for a bottle of Zinfandel to go with it. He and Lucy got the table all set and shortly they were together at the table with spaghetti on their plates and talking about the days events.

As Larry was taking Lucy home, she was talking. "Larry I've some things I want to say. First when you remarked how you thought your mom was beautiful I sort of thought that it would only be natural for you to say that. I want you to know that your mom really is a beautiful lady and a really nice person." "I know she liked you too." Larry responded.

Lucy continued to talk. "I'm a little confused. I had some sort of a mental picture of what a Native American Indian looked like which most likely was based on cartoon caricatures or some movie I had seen. I've another confession to make. I started asking my aunt a few questions like did you ever hear anything about any of our ancestors marrying or in any way getting Native American blood mixed into our ancestry. My aunt said that there were stories of white colonial girls being kidnapped by Indians and later escaping with their babies and then on both sides of our family some went westward as fur trappers to trade with the Indians way ahead of the general migration and in the process sometimes acquired Indian wives."

"Larry," Lucy said. "According to my aunt there is almost certainly Native American Indian blood somewhere in our family history. It's odd that I never heard anything about this from my parents but I guess the subject just never came up or had no importance. Anyway, knowing this I think changes a bit the way I view interracial relationships." "I rather suspected that you would find something like this if you did thorough search of your genealogy Larry commented as they said their Good Nights with a warm hug and kiss.

Chapter 12

Postal carriers had been taking their vacation time and Larry was kept busy most of the time as an experienced sub carrier. Lisa had signed up for a summer session course that involved short sessions on the college oceanography research vessel at Newport. Lucy had been spending most of her summer as an intern with the Oregon Department of Fish and Wildlife. Now Larry and Lucy were busy with the beginning of their senior year at Oregon State. Lisa was looking forward with anticipation to her sophomore year.

Just to celebrate the end of a good summer, Lisa, Larry and Lucy organized a salmon fishing trip on a charter boat from Depoe Bay. Actually they needed no excuse it was just something they wanted to do. Not only salmon were caught. Larry had a fairly large ling cod to add to his limit of salmon and the girls had each caught a sea bass also called black snappers. Rather than bring their fish back to Corvallis they were left in Depoe Bay to be vacuum packed and fast frozen.

Larry and Lisa had seen polished beach agates in Newport shops. In talking to people about them they learned that Agate Beach just north of Newport was a place where they could be found. The best time to look for them would be at the lowest tide and especially after a storm when sand would be disturbed to expose them.

Another thing that needed to be done was pick up their frozen salmon at Depoe Bay. It so happened that a week after their fishing trip conditions would be good for agate hunting. Early Sunday forenoon Larry, Lisa and Lucy were on Agate Beach carrying plastic bags for the agates they hoped to find. Gravel beds were uncovered and they soon learned that there was a lot more gravel than agates but the agates could be spotted. They soon learned that all agates did not look alike. Some were clear, some had what looked like clouds within them and some were quite red in color. They found some that were opaque and almost red in color. They were aware that different kinds of agates had names but didn't know what they were.

After a lunch in Depoe Bay at a restaurant specializing in clam chowder they picked up their frozen fish and packed it all in the cold box they had brought with them. Larry and Lisa wanted to see their parents on the way home and also to share some salmon and ling cod with them.

Their parents of course were happy for the surprise visit and greeted them warmly, happy too to see Lucy again. When they showed off their agates they were told how lucky they had been to find a newly exposed gravel bed. They had hunted agates in the same area and had found only several after walking over long stretches of beach.

Olaf and Minnie had purchased a freezer for freezing and storing some of their fruit and meat. They knew Larry had rented a locker in a commercial freezer storage facility but they offered to care for some in their freezer if he liked. Larry thought it would be more convenient for him and for Lisa to just use the locker in Corvallis. They would only leave what they were giving to their folks. Minnie put the fish in her freezer and got out a pot roast and a couple packages of ground beef for Larry and Lisa.

As they drove back to Corvallis there was more discussion about agates. Larry knew that agates were found in many parts of the country and wondered why they were on that beach. They all agreed the best way to find the answer to that would be to do a little research at the college library.

In Corvallis they went immediately to get their fish in their freezer locker. Lucy said her aunt had a freezer so elected to take hers there. Before parting they agreed to find a free time for a fish fry at Larry's.

One of Larry's classes involved the repair of farm machinery that farmers had been encouraged to bring to the college for students to get hands on with that part of their education. There was a backlog of projects on hand. Since this was what Larry liked best of his class assignments he often took time on weekends to do a little work of this kind which often required welding or even making a new part for a machine of some sort.

There was some kind of a dredging operation downstream a bit from the little park where Larry and Lucy often spent a little time after a movie. The sand and gravel from the river was being deposited on the river bank. Larry surmised that the purpose of the dredging was not to deepen the river channel but to build up the river bank. Larry noted that a number of knowledgeable local rock hounds had flocked to the freshly dredged material to hunt for agates and pieces of petrified wood. Larry found a little time to join the hunt and did find several nice agates and a fairly large chunk of petrified wood.

Most of these people seemed to know each other. He got into a conversation with one of them and found that they were members of a rock and agate club. He was invited to come to one of their meetings. Larry mentioned that he, his sister and a friend had been lucky to find a freshly exposed gravel bed on Agate Beach north of Newport where they found a goodly number of agates. Again he was reminded of the next meeting date and to bring his friends too. They would be happy to give advice about polishing his agates by tumbling.

When Larry told Lisa about this and showed her the agates he had found she was so interested that she wanted to go down to the river to see if she could find an agate. When he told her about the invitation from the rock club she said "let's go and maybe Lucy might like to go with us too." When Larry called Lucy to explain about finding the agates and the invitation she said "yes, I'd like to go with you." Lisa spoke up to say "I want to talk to Lucy too."

On the phone with Lucy Lisa said that she planned to go to that dredging area to hunt agates and would Lucy like to go with her? Perhaps after a last afternoon class there would be time to do that. Lucy was interested, they agreed on a date.

The two girls did go and each did find a couple agates. The dredged material was getting pretty much picked over. When the time came for the meeting to which they had been invited they went to be seen and welcomed by the man Larry had talked to at the river. They found the program of interest, it was about a recent field trip in eastern Oregon and there was a show and tell about what individuals had collected.

Larry asked how best to find information about rock tumbling and was introduced to a member considered their most knowledgeable on the subject.

For a beginner he recommended a small inexpensive starter kit. He looked through a pile of papers and pamphlets to find a catalog in which there was shown a beginners kit. It included a small tumbler along with the proper grits and an instruction manual. The man was familiar with that particular model and recommended it. He gave Larry the catalog to keep and invited the three to come to the next meeting the following month. He also gave them each a bookmark which had information about the club and their meeting dates.

It was only a few days before Larry had the new tumbler loaded with agates and operating. He and Lisa had decided to just tumble their agates together all at the same time rather than separately. They were determined to follow directions carefully even if tempted to hurry the process with shortcuts because they were so eager to see the results of their first tumbling experience. Lucy would have her turn with the tumbler later.

The agates were looking pretty good. Almost a week had gone by since Larry had started the tumbler charged with coarse grit. Now the agates and tumbler were clean and ready for polishing with tin oxide. He would open the tumbler in a day or so to wash a couple agates in order to judge whether or not they needed more polishing. They were looking good but could stand a bit more, Larry decided.

With classes over for the day Lisa called Lucy to let her know that Larry had finished cleaning all the agates. "Come for dinner" Lisa said and added "I think you'll like the results of Larry's tumbling."

Larry had spread all the agates from the beach separately from river agates out on a cloth and there was a difference between the two. When Lucy arrived she was surprised at the difference between the appearance of the agates before and after tumbling.

"Now it's your turn. The tumbler is all cleaned and ready for you to take home." Larry said. He explained that it was important to clean the agates and tumbler between grits and otherwise just follow directions.

For dinner Larry and Lisa had decided to do the pot roast they had brought from the farm along with carrots, potatoes and onion. Also, Lisa had baked an apple pie using apples from the farm, in other words the whole dinner was from there with the exception of the California zinfandel.

Dinner conversation involved a little about the rock club they had attended before serious talk about this the senior year for Larry and Lucy. They were thinking ahead to graduation and what that would mean for them. Lucy had worked the past summer as an intern in Oregon's Fish and Game Department and was certain that there was a job waiting for her there. With Larry it was different. He knew that he would be going to the college placement secretary to find what schools had openings for an agricultural teacher. Perhaps there might be none but these were things to worry about in the spring quarter. That's when he would be assigned to some high school in the area for student teaching experience.

Sometimes it was amazing how quickly time would pass. Suddenly Christmas break was with them. Lucy was going to be with family in Detroit the entire time. Larry and Lisa would be with their folks at the farm. They knew that there would be time to visit with old friends in Siletz too. They had taken time to socialize occasionally in spite of a busy time with class assignments. The rock club had invited the three to join their club which they learned was a part of a national organization. They had to explain that their classes at the college would be keeping them too busy for taking an active part in the club so they thought it best not to join, at least at the present time.

Chapter 13

It was well into spring quarter with Larry doing his student teaching in nearby Albany. He would be spending the morning half of his day there and then come back to the college for afternoon classes. The ag teacher at Albany High had for a number of years worked with student teachers and pretty much let the student teacher observe and help students with their projects before occasionally turning a class over to Larry to handle by himself. If he noticed a mistake Larry might make with a student or with the class he would later in private call this to Larry's attention and to Larry explained how in his opinion Larry should have handled the particular situation. Larry developed a respect and liking for his master teacher and hoped that he could do as well when he started teaching.

At the present time students were working with repairs to farm equipment that they had brought to class and also learning how to take apart and reassemble small engines that powered lawn mowers and such that had been donated to the school. This was the type of work that Larry liked best to do. It was easy for him to help a student with a problem or to spot mistakes they were making.

His master teacher could see that Larry seemed to know more than he might have learned in his college classes and asked him about this. Larry explained that he had learned from his dad and others how to do these things at an early age. He explained that his dad had worked in the repair shops at a logging camp in Siletz and after retirement had his own shop at their farm.

His favorite thing to do was repair equipment from neighboring farms for free. Some times they gave something in return after butchering a hog or some other farm animal.

It was early April with fishing season open and Larry was on the phone with Lucy saying "Lucy, it's been a long time since we have fished together. My student teaching is going well and I'm pretty well caught up with other class work. How about you? Remember me talking about the little stream west of here where I first fished after coming to Corvallis, the Luckiamute. Would you like to go there with me this coming Sunday?" Lucy answered that with "I'm in good shape with all my class work too. I'd love to do that."

They planned a picnic lunch, Lucy would make sandwiches and Larry would provide drinks and snacking stuff along with some fruit. Lucy had yet to learn fly fishing but would bring her casting rod with some lures and bait. Larry would pick her up at her aunt's about eight thirty Sunday morning.

On the road, Larry just had to talk about his student teaching and the variation in the abilities of students. There was a girl in one class which he had not expected to see. She was sharp and a leader among the students. "She made me think that you were probably much like her when you were in high school," Larry said. Lucy answered that with, "no I never had any desire to be class president or anything like that but I was active in extracurricular activities and did take parts in school plays. I was on the girls' basketball team. Most of the time it was only boys in wood shop but I did take that along with crafts too. I liked to make things and there are still things around my folks' house that I made."

They had left H20 at Wren and were nearing the turn off to the Luckiamute when Larry commented "it won't be long now. I'm going to go to the same general area where I fished before." Lucy commented "I guess spring is here, the alder trees I notice are getting their new leaves."

They passed by the last farm house as they followed the road heading upstream. Larry parked at a spot near the stream saying "we can fish along here for a bit then go farther upstream to some places I remember." They got their fishing gear together and were quickly testing the waters. Water was higher than Larry remembered and commented on that with "it was fall when I was here before and the water was much lower then."

There was an inviting stretch of water in front of them. They moved apart a bit to start fishing. Lucy started fishing with a small lure, a Super Duper it was called. After a couple casts a fish took it. She landed about an eight or nine inch rainbow and held it up as she called Larry to look. He had been so busy changing flies that he had not seen her land that fish. He walked up to get a look at the first fish of the day. She got a high five with "congratulation for first fish but we forgot to name a prize for first fish so what would you like for a prize?" "That's easy" she said. "I'll settle for a hug from my favorite fishing partner?" She got it along with a little bonus kiss.

Larry had an idea. He tied on a bucktail coachman then pinched on a very small lead weight to the tippet next to the fly. He cast that out to a likely spot. Almost immediately he had a ten inch rainbow hooked. "I just needed to get my fly deeper like your Super Duper was the answer to my problem. Let's move upstream now, there's a very nice spot to fish and also have our lunch."

As they moved upstream Larry explained that the road they were on came to an end not far upstream. At the end of the road were old buildings where a railroad coming from the mountains above had ended.

The place where Larry and Lucy came to the stream was beside a sharp bend in the stream. From a long shallow riffle above water flowed into a deep pool at the bend. On the opposite bank were several fairly large alder trees and large willow bushes. It was a good spot to fish which they did. They took turns casting into the riffle and letting the current carry his fly or her Super Duper into the pool. This technique brought Larry and Lucy a couple trout for each and now it was time to forget fishing and have their picnic.

It really was a nice sunny day for a picnic. The only bird activity they had seen was a kingfisher flying by. Nothing unusual about that but now their attention was drawn to some bird activity in one of the larger willows across the stream. A couple robins were coming and going with material for a nest they were building. As they ate and watched how intent those birds were on the job at hand they could see they were paying no attention to the picnickers across the stream.

Lucy came up with a question, "how do you suppose those birds went about picking a mate? To me robins all pretty much look alike. Did they just look at each other and fall in love at first sigh?" Larry looked at Lucy to say "Lucy, you do come up with the darnedest questions. I think that girl bird just looked at that boy bird and thought he might be a good helper with nest building." "You mean that you don't think he fell in love with her and wants her to choose him as a mate?" Lucy questioned and then came up with "Larry, are you in love with me?" I'll have to answer that with a question Larry said. "Lucy, are you in love with me?"

"That's not fair. I asked first." Lucy said. "Yes it is." Larry said and added "Whatever I said would color any comment you might make. Think back to what I once told you in one of our serious discussions and the things you told me about yourself. You are a beautiful girl and any normal guy like me might look at you and think to himself 'I'd like to see her shoes parked under my bed' as I might admit doing." Lucy looked at Larry and thought a bit before saying "I guess you're right with all that and I'll have to admit looking at you and thinking too what it would be like as you say; park my shoes under your bed. Some times girls and boys are alike with their secret thoughts."

They packed up their fishing gear, fished a bit more until each had caught another rainbow. They had all the fish they wanted, probably the limit anyway. Larry wanted to drive to the end of the road to show Lucy the old round house at the railroads end. He understood that there had been a lumber mill at Valsetz which was at the headwaters of the Siletz River. Lumber from that mill had been brought here by rail to be taken away by truck.

Some years back at flood time on the Siletz River the dam at the mill pond at that mill had washed out releasing all the logs in the pond. As flood waters carried these logs down the Siletz River the combination of logs mixed with high water took out the bridge across the river at Siletz leaving the town isolated from Toledo and points south.

They looked at the stream along the railroad and at the hills above. There just had to be some nice fly fishing water upstream, Larry was thinking as he said "Lucy, looking at that stream as it comes down from the hills I think you and I should pick a day to do a little exploring. Wouldn't you like to see what the stream is like further up?" "Why not? It should be easy hiking along the old railroad bed," Lucy answered.

On the way home there was considerable conversation regarding graduation. This was coming soon and it seemed there were so many loose ends needing attention. Even a simple thing like planning for a day of exploring a nearby stream was difficult. Either Lucy or Larry had a conflicting necessary something to interfere.

"I think we should eat some of our trout this evening." Larry commented. "I can take you home after. What do you think about that?" "I'm ready anytime for a fish fry with you, you should know that," Lucy answered.

When they arrived at Larry's Lisa had company. Willy had dropped by for a visit. Lisa had invited him to stay for dinner but she hadn't started cooking anything as yet. Now that Larry and Lucy had arrived with a bunch of trout with plans for a fish fry and saying that there was enough for Willy too, Lisa could stop thinking about what she would cook for dinner. She realized that Lucy and Willy had never met so introduced the two to each other. Lucy mentioned that she of course recognized him. She doubted that any Oregon State student would fail to recognize such an important member of the Beaver's Football Team.

In conversation Lucy found as the evening progressed that Willy was very modest about his football abilities and very serious about his coaching goal. She liked him and realized that he was a far cry from the picture she had in her mind of the character of a so called big shot football star. Willy was interested in where Larry and Lucy had been fishing. Larry explained in detail how Willy could find the stream and recommended that he give it a try.

As Larry was taking Lucy home she was talking about the dinner. "That fish fry was really fun. You are so lucky to have a sister like Lisa. I want you to know that I really liked your friend Willy and you can let Lisa know that. He is a lot different from what I had pictured a big shot football star to be like." They agreed to get together as soon as possible to talk about their graduation and how they might celebrate after. They parted with their usual hug and a kiss. Lucy thought that Larry's hug was a little tighter than usual this time and wondered why.

Immediately after graduation Lucy would be starting work with Oregon's Fish and Wildlife, in what capacity as yet she didn't know.

Larry had checked with the college placement secretary as to what schools had advertised for an Ag teacher. There were a couple in Oregon and one in Madera, California. This was intriguing to Larry because he had read so much that John Muir had written about the Sierra and its beauty. In looking at a map of the area he could see that Madera was within easy driving to Yosemite and surrounding area.

He explained to Lucy why he was considering right after graduation to have the placement secretary send his credentials there and explained in more detail why. If he got the job he would know after a year of teaching whether or not he wanted to stay there. Lucy knew that Larry was serious when he said that the main drawback about going to California was that he would miss her so much. She knew that Larry was in love with her even though he wasn't ready to say so.

It was during the week just before graduation that Larry and Lucy were sitting on their favorite park bench watching the moon's reflection on the Willamette. Larry had his arm around Lucy's shoulder when he turned to look into her eyes and surprised her by saying "Lucy, I love you and I'd like to have you as my wife. In other words would you marry me?" He had caught Lucy a little by surprise but she was ready for him with "I thought you would never ask and I think you knew that I would say YES." That answer came with a big hug and a very warm and sincere kiss.

After a little talk Larry said that he would like to take her to a local jewelry store for her to pick out an engagement ring. Larry wanted to explain an idea he had. He knew that both she and his folks would be in Corvallis for the graduation ceremonies. His idea was that they should plan a dinner at his place in the evening. With her parents and her aunt plus his parents and Lisa that would only be eight people and there was room enough in his house for a nice dinner. That's when he thought would be a good time to announce their engagement to their families. "Lucy what are your thoughts on that idea?" "I like it. If I could have my ring by then I wouldn't be wearing it but some time during the evening I could slip it on. Someone would notice it and that's when we could announce our engagement. I think that would be so much fun and a surprise to our families. I'm so excited. Larry, I just knew that eventually you would tell me you loved me. I was ready to say I was in love with you anytime you would say you were in love with me. I knew you were, we girls can sense things like that. I could hardly wait for you to admit it."

At the jewelers Lucy picked a ring she liked and Larry approved of her choice. The diamond they had picked would be in a modified Tiffany setting with a small ruby on each side. If they came by in late afternoon it would be ready for them.

Lucy wanted to wear and show off the ring but for sure they would meet someone they knew and the secret would be out. The safe thing to do would be to keep it off until bed time. She would sleep with it on her finger and take it off in the morning.

They considered going to a restaurant to celebrate but Larry said that Lisa was expecting him to be there. "I know she's cooking a big stew and there'll be plenty for all of us. I need to plan with her for when our folks will all be at the house and we'll want your ideas too."

At the house as they were all sharing a glass of wine before dinner, Lisa was noticing that there seemed to be something different about the way Larry and Lucy were looking at each other. She couldn't resist speaking out with "are you two hiding something from me? I know you are and you might just as well tell me what it is." "Lucy" Larry said and continued to say "I always have a problem with my little sister. She always reads my mind like an open book and I'm beginning to think that she can read yours too." "I suppose we might as well share with her if she'll promise to keep it a secret," she said to Larry. Larry nodded his head and Lucy showed Lisa her new ring. She gave both Larry and Lucy a big hug as she said "I knew it would happen, I just didn't know when. Lucy, that's a beautiful ring so let me see it on your finger." Lucy put it on then took it off to put back in her handbag saying "I'm going to keep it hidden until the proper time comes to put it on."

The discussion turned to what should be cooked for the graduation party dinner. Several ideas where talked about but it was Lisa's idea that Larry and Lucy liked. Lisa would oven roast two pork loins. She would have everything ready ahead of time then leave for home immediately after graduation ceremonies to turn on the oven and get dinner started. She thought mashed potatoes with gravy would be good and what did they think of carrots mixed with peas. She could pick up a package of frozen peas for that. A little salad and apple pie for dessert would complete the menu.

At graduation ceremonies Larry's and Lucy's parents were proud when honor students were asked to stand and both Larry and Lucy were among those standing. With ceremonies over there was the usual picture taking, high fives, etc. As this was happening Lisa was on her way home to get dinner started.

Lucy and Larry arrived at the cottage some while after their parents had gathered there. That was because Larry and Lucy had taken a little side trip. They wanted a little private time together to sit on their favorite park bench with their arms around each other to share a few words and a celebration kiss in private.

Lisa was in the kitchen and the proud parents were in the living room chatting and getting to know each other better. Lisa had brought out wine and glasses for them to sip as they talked. Lucy and Larry joined Lisa in the kitchen. Now another person was arriving. It was Lucy's aunt Dora, her father's sister. In the kitchen Lucy had heard Dora and came out to see that Dora too had wine to sip. She sat down with the group to say "dinner will soon be on the table." Larry too came from the kitchen to say "Chef Lisa has everything under control. She'll join us in a bit for a little socializing before dinner."

The subject of Larry's plan to apply for a teaching job in Madera, California came up. Larry was trying to explain why he was interested in a job there rather than in Oregon. "I've read so much about the national parks in California, especially Yosemite. John Muir has written a lot about the beauty of the Sierra and I'd like to see some of it for myself. Madera is within easy driving distance from Yosemite and the surrounding mountains." There was a general agreement that Larry's explanation did make sense.

Lisa had joined the group and took the opportunity to say "dinner will be on the table in about twenty minutes. If anyone needs to go to the bathroom now's the time to do it." There were two bathrooms in the cottage and several used her suggestion.

Larry and Lisa had the food on the table. There were wine and filled water glasses at each place and both red and white wine on the table. With this done

Lisa announced "there are place cards on the table. Find your places, it's time to eat."

Lisa had given considerable thought to the seating arrangement. Lisa wanted to be at one of the two corners nearest the kitchen in case there was a need for her to bring an item from there to the table. Her final decision was: looking at the table from the kitchen, to the right would be herself, Dora, her dad and her mom. To the left would be Lucy's mom, her dad, Lucy and Larry.

With everyone seated Lisa said, "Before we eat I propose a toast to our two graduates. After four years of hard work they both graduated with honors and I'm so very proud of them." There were comments from parents of both such as "I'll drink to that, etc." Larry and Lucy both thanked their parents for their four years of encouragement and support.

Every one was finished with toasts and remarks regarding the beauty of the table and how tasty was the food when Lucy's dad sitting beside Lucy noticed something. "Lucy, that looks like a new ring on your finger. Is it what I think it is?" Lucy raised her hand for all to see and said, "Yes, Larry and I decided that this would be a good time for announcing our engagement." Larry leaned over to put his arm around Lucy as they shared a kiss.

Suddenly a dinner party celebrating the graduation of Larry and Lucy had turned into a celebration of their engagement. Among all the congratulations, etc. came the question, "When will there be a wedding?" Larry answered that with, "at the moment we are thinking Christmas vacation break might be a good time for that."

Then there was a discussion about summer plans for Larry, Lucy and Lisa. Larry's papers had been sent to Madera. The placement secretary had thought his chances for getting the Ag teaching job were good and he planned to drive to Madera to talk to the school people there in person. Lucy would start her work with Oregon Fish and Wildlife in the coming week. Lisa planned to continue working with Oceanography studies as in the previous summer.

After all the after dinner conversations were finished it was time for a "Good By" from Lucy's parents who would be driving home to Detroit. Lucy planned to spend a couple days with her folks before starting work but she would drive to Detroit the next day.

Olaf and Minnie planned to spend a few days in Corvallis. As a graduation present for Larry they had set a financial framework within which he could pick a car or pickup of his liking. He had found a two year old GMC pickup with low mileage and in what appeared to be mint condition. That red pickup was in the driveway. Larry's dad wanted to check it out and also drive it before Larry would be driving it to California.

Larry and Lucy wanted to spend a little private time together before her leaving for Detroit. After that big dinner celebration they would not be looking for food, but perhaps a movie if there was anything of interest.

After their evening on the town and leaving their favorite park bench their conversations continued with moments of thought as they drove. "I'll be starting my work with Oregon's Department of Fish and Wildlife in a couple days. In what capacity I don't know but you'll be the first to know as soon as I know," Lucy said to Larry.   Larry came back to that with; "My credentials and job application have been sent to the school people in Madera and I'm going to drive there in a day or two in order to present myself in person.   This'll be a shakedown cruise for the GMC pickup my parents gave me as a graduation present.   I won't know if I have a teaching job there until after meeting with the school principal and perhaps other school officials."

"Sometimes I feel like I'm stepping off a cliff in the dark with my new job and without you to save me I'm falling into darkness, falling and falling----," Lucy said as they were holding each other tight and saying their Good Byes.   Larry responded to that with, "I understand how you feel and I suppose that it's natural for anyone starting an unfamiliar career because I feel a little like that too.   But, I'll be back in a week or so to tell you if I have the Madera job or not."   There were tears in Lucy's eyes as she watched Larry leave.

Chapter 14

After driving through the mountains and checking into a Redding motel Larry was thinking to himself, "I wish Lucy was here with me." Larry was tired and hungry after the day's driving and in what was advertised as the best steak house in Redding Larry savored his steak while reflecting on the day's drive. "I like the way the pickup performed, especially in the mountains but it used a bit more gas than expected." Larry thought to himself.

"I must have been a little more tired than I realized last night." Larry was thinking after sleeping a little later than intended. "Oh well, so what!" Larry thought before his thoughts turned to food and breakfast. The goal for the day would be, "find a motel in Madera by the day's end."

I-5 from Redding to Sacramento and H-99 from Sacramento to Madera, along those two highways Larry had observed orchards, rice fields, hay fields and a variety of vegetable crops. As Larry hungry and tired was sitting in a restaurant waiting for the steak he had ordered to come to his table he couldn't help but wonder what it was going to be like when teaching about all kinds of agriculture to a bunch of high school students.

As he worked on that steak, Larry couldn't help but notice the diverse ethnic groups among patrons of the restaurant, much more diverse than western Oregon. "Oh well, we'll see what happens when I locate the school office tomorrow," Larry was thinking.

At the office of the Assistant Superintendent of the Madera school system to which he had been directed Larry was informed that they had looked over the papers that had been forwarded to them. They liked his qualifications and assigned a member of the staff to take him on a tour of the schools agricultural facilities after which he would have an interview with the Assistant Superintendent Mr. Lewis. Larry realized after seeing the facilities that this was a fairly wealthy school district, the facilities were much better than he had expected to see. Mr. Lewis at the interview informed Larry that if he would accept the offered salary and health insurance provided by the district he would be offered the teaching position. Larry was happy to accept and sign the contract. He would be expected to report in at the school a week before school opened in September.

Larry stopped to talk with the Principals Secretary, he had found that an office secretary was always the best source of information and he wanted to ask a few questions regarding apartments. He introduced himself and found that her name was Patti Roberts. "Welcome to our faculty," Patti said and asked, "Are you married or single?" "Single, but my fiancé and I plan to marry during Christmas break," Larry answered before Patti went on to answer Larry's questions regarding apartments. He learned that several single teachers and a married couple all lived in the same apartment building and appeared to be quite happy with their living facilities. Some couples and especially those with children either owned or rented homes in the area. "Thank you for your help," Larry said and Patti wished him luck as she handed him the address of the apartment she had mentioned.

At the apartment building Larry found that there were several apartments open for rent. One in particular Larry liked because it had full cooking facilities and was completely furnished. It was available for immediate occupancy. As he signed a rental agreement and wrote a check for two months in advance the manager mentioned that they especially liked teachers as tenants because they tended to care for their apartments better than some.

Now Larry was ready to bring belongings from his pickup into what he expected to be his new home for some time and also it was time to go to the nearby super market for food supplies. "I'll not eat in a restaurant nor stay in a motel tonight." Larry was having happy thoughts.

Larry did a lot of thinking, i.e., best described as silently talking to him self. "Why did I want a job in California? It was so that I had a place to be within easy travel distance to Yosemite, Sequoia, and other parts of the Sierra as described by John Muir. My camping gear is in the pickup and now it's time to pack a little camp food. I might want to test a trout stream too so I'll have to get a fishing license for that then I'll drive to Yosemite."

Larry wanted very much to talk to Lucy. He could leave messages for her but because she moved around so much in her job she didn't have a permanent telephone number. It was Lucy who would call him regularly but now it behooved Larry to sit down and write a letter. There was so much to tell Lucy. Most importantly that he had the job he wanted, his new address and his telephone number.

Larry would inform her also that he would be out of touch up in the Sierra for a few days. When his letter was in the envelope there was something else he realized---he didn't know where to send Lucy's letter. He could send it to the Fish and Wildlife Department in Salem but he had no address for them either.

What Larry finally did was write a letter to Lisa to explain everything and then send both letters to her address and asking her to forward Lucy's. Larry was quite certain that Lisa would be in contact with Lucy by telephone.

With all that done it was time now to make certain that he had all the things he might need up in the Sierra. He realized that this was completely new territory for him. Would nights be warm or cold? He had read a few things about sudden thunder and lightning storms along with drenching rain but he had also read stories about John Muir only having a loaf of bread as he headed out into the mountains---how much of this was true?

Studying his California Highway Map Larry realized that Yosemite and the Sierra to the east was a huge area. If he planned to explore even a small part of it he would need more maps. For now he did have a large Yosemite map and his plan for this day would be to go to a campground just outside the H41 entrance to the park. It was just a short bit past a place called Fish Camp. Larry's plan for now was to crowd what exploring he could do in the next three days before returning to Madera.

The next morning early Larry's pickup was loaded and on a back country road that would eventually meet H41 at Coarsegold. He had seen on his map Hensley Lake and was curious about it. By the time he reached Coarsegold he had seen the transition from the flat lands of the San Joaquin Valley to the mountain foothills and now on H41 he had the feeling that he was on the way to some real mountains.

Larry had just passed Fish Camp and pulled into the campground when he noticed a guy coming from downstream with a fly rod and several pan size trout on a stringer. Larry saw the camp spot where the guy was headed and made a mental note to ask him about fishing in the area. But first there were things to care for such as picking out a camp site and paying the camp host the camping fee. The camp host had bundles of camp fire wood for sale too and Larry bought a bundle. This was mid afternoon and warm but Larry was quite certain that at this elevation evenings would be cool and he loved a nice warming fire to sit beside as he sipped a hot chocolate. Shortly before coming to Fish Camp he had noticed an elevation sign and realized that he was in mile high territory.

Another thing Larry had noticed as he crossed over a small stream was a sign on the bridge indicating that this was Big Creek. He had thought it more fitting that the sign say Little Creek.

After Larry had his one man tent set up and his camp stove on a table ready for cooking Larry walked to the camp where the fisherman had gone. He and a lady had a camp fire going and were just talking to each other when Larry walked up to introduce himself as a fellow camper and to say "When I drove into camp I noticed you carrying a fly rod and some trout and thought that you might be able to answer a few questions about fishing in this area. "I'd be happy to help you as best I can. Do I understand that you are new to this area?" was the answer to Larry's question. This was the sort of answer that Larry had hoped for from a fellow fisherman, especially a fly fisherman.

As briefly as he could Larry explained that he had just moved to Madera from Oregon and loved fly fishing. He had read so much about Yosemite that he planned to spend the next day in the park but his hope was to later explore the Sierra outside the park. "I noticed that you caught fish in this stream," Larry commented. "Yes, there are trout here but they are planters and because of the pressure from campers like us they are soon caught out but those planters often are eaten by a few large Browns in the stream. Every once in a while one is hooked but seldom landed. They are big and able to break a light leader. I've heard stories of one weighing almost five pounds being caught in this area and sometimes the store at Fish Camp will have a picture of a big one posted on their bulletin board. If you have a California fishing license and your fly tackle with you I'd say give the stream a try. Come by this evening and I'll tell you a little about the backpacking trips my wife and I have taken together." "Yes I just got a California license and I will give the stream a try and yes I'd like to hear your backpacking stories," Larry answered as he left to break out his fly tackle.

Larry preferred fishing upstream rather than downstream. As he did this while making an occasional cast to ordinary water Larry picked up one pan size trout. "All I want is enough for dinner" Larry was saying to himself as he walked upstream looking for a pool that might hold a slightly larger trout than the one in his creel.

There it was, a perfect pool but with a problem. Most would pass it up because of brush making it all but impossible to cast a fly without it ending up hooked to a willow branch. His fly was a white bucktail Coachman which to a larger trout might appear as a little minnow and a choice morsel. Just above the pool Larry had found a small opening in the willows where he could poke his rod through and just let the current carry his fly to the pool. "This might be worth a try" Larry was saying to himself as he gave the Coachman a couple little twitches as it drifted to the head of the pool.

Just at the head of the pool a fairly large Brown spotted just what he was waiting for, what appeared to be a crippled little minnow. It was a surprised Brown when the little minnow started to fight back as he grabbed it; they just didn't do that. This one grabbed his jaw and wouldn't let go!

Larry had a problem, he had hooked a much larger fish than expected and if he tried to work it upstream it would probably break his leader. "If I really want that fish there's only one thing I can do. I'm going to do what I'm not prepared for. I'm not wearing my waders so I'll just have to get wet. I'll take my billfold out of my pants pocket and put it in my shirt pocket. I don't want the things in it to get wet." All these thoughts ran through Larry's brain before he found himself almost hip deep carefully playing what he thought to be a fifteen or eighteen inch trout in such a way to get it downstream to more open water where he could tire the fish out and land it.

It was a wet and tired Larry that came into the campground with a Brown too large to get in his creel. He was carrying it strung on a willow branch as he had learned to do with the first trout he caught at home on the farm.

When Larry's neighbor camper saw the big Brown that Larry was carrying he walked out to meet Larry and say, "I see you found one of those big Browns I told you about. Before you clean that fish I would like for you to do something special with it. The guy who runs the Fish Camp store is a friend of mine and when anyone catches one of those big Browns which isn't often he likes to measure, weigh it and then take a picture to post on his Bulletin Board and I'd like to go with you." Larry thought that was a reasonable request so answered with "I can do that but before anything else I want to get into some dry clothes. As you can see I'm soaked to the waist." Fortunately Larry had plenty of clothes and a couple pairs of shoes. His wet ones were just tennis shoes.

In dry clothes Larry also had the fish in his cold box in which he wanted to add more ice when he drove by to pick up his neighbor who introduced himself as Joe and they shook hands as Larry shared his name. As Joe had predicted, his friend the store owner was pleased to know that he could have a new fish picture to post. The Brown by the way turned out to be a little over twenty one inches in length and weighing nearly three pounds. The store owner had Larry leave his address so he could send pictures when developed.

Back at camp Larry cleaned his two fish and opened a can of pork and beans to eat with the nine inch rainbow. Finished with his dinner Larry had a cup of hot cocoa in one hand and a folding camp chair in the other as he came to Joe's camp in answer to Joe's earlier invitation.

Joe welcomed Larry and introduced his wife Sarah. Joe and Sarah had been sitting by the fire sipping their hot drinks and as soon as Larry got his chair situated Joe wanted to know more about Larry's catching the big Brown. "You didn't tell me how you got so wet catching that fish. I know there's a story here. Tell me more about where you fished. I notice that you were using a fairly light leader and normally a Brown that size usually just breaks the leader and goes free." "Okay" Larry answered and proceeded to describe the part of the stream where he had fished and why he got so wet in the process of landing the trophy Brown.

Joe had more questions. "What brought you to Madera from Oregon? It couldn't have been for fly fishing. Oregon has lots of fine fly fishing water."

Now Larry had to explain about just graduating from Oregon State as an Ag teacher looking for a job opening and why he chose to apply in Madera. When Joe learned that Larry was a teacher he was quick to volunteer that he and his wife too were teachers. At the high school in Hanford he taught History and Sarah was the Home Ec. Teacher. There was discussion about chances that strangers meeting in a mountain camp ground would turn out to be in the same profession, high school teachers.

Joe commented, "I don't notice a wedding ring on your finger so I take it you're not married." "That's right." Larry answered and went on to explain that he was engaged and that he and his Lucy were planning a wedding during Christmas break.

"You were going to tell me about some of the backpacking trips you and your wife had taken in the Sierra," Larry suggested and added "I'm really interested in learning all I can about California's mountains." This was a subject that Joe liked to talk about. Joe went on to explain that many back country roads had at one time been part of early day logging. They were the road beds left over from old logging railroad road beds. "Some times on these roads you might find an old railroad spike or might see the remains of a trestle crossing a canyon, or stumble onto an old logging camp dump site with rusted cans and sometimes a rare bottle. Most old bottles had been picked up by bottle collectors."

Joe continued with "You may have noticed a road to the right just before descending into Fish Camp. That road leads back to the upper reaches of the stream beside us. At one point a side stream called Rainer Creek enters Big Creek across from the road. That's where most of the water here is from because not far upstream a diversion dam sends most of the Big Creek water into a canal leading off to the west. If you study your maps you'll see that this road can take you into some interesting country bordering Yosemite on the south. In fact at one point the road briefly enters and leaves the park. However, my favorite back country is farther to the south."

"Get on Highway 168 and follow it past Huntington Lake, then follow road signs to Lake Edison. In this area you will find beautiful scenery and fishing both lakes and streams. Edison Lake has Browns that I've seen on display at the Lodge at the lower end of the lake that match the size of a good size Coho salmon. The upper end of the lake is at the border of John Muir Wilderness and Mono Creek enters the lake at this location."

"The lodge operates a pontoon ferry that makes a trip to the head of the lake every morning and again in late afternoon. Mono Creek is one of the best fly fishing streams I've ever fished and if you take the morning ferry you'll have time to hike up the stream, explore and sample the fishing before returning on the late afternoon ferry. You won't need a permit for this but if you plan to back pack you will need a permit easy to get at the ranger station you'll pass on the way to the lake. They'll want to know the vicinity where you'll be and for how long. The first thing though for you to do is get Forest Service maps of the area."

Larry spoke up to say "That was a pretty good sales pitch you gave me and I for sure will plan at least a day trip to Edison Lake and Mono Creek later this summer." "You won't be disappointed," Joe responded,

Sarah who had been sitting silently all this time now spoke up to say "I think the best back packing trip Joe and I ever took was the week we spent along Mono Creek and into the recesses. We even went to the top of 12000 ft. Mono Pass before coming down to camp at a lake a little lower to the west. I've forgotten the name of that lake." Joe voiced his agreement.

Joe also spoke up to say it was time for a refill for the hot cocoa. "I see your cup is empty too. Would you like to join us for a refill?" "I'd be pleased" was Larry's answer to that.

Larry had noticed a blackened old fashioned granite coffee pot on a flat rock beside the fire. It had in it not coffee but hot water. Joe spooned cocoa into the cups before adding hot water from the granite pot. He stirred the mix then picked a brandy bottle from their camp table to add a little to his and Sarah's cups. "Would you like some in yours too? We call these 'cappuccinos' and like them as we sit by our camp fires." "I've never tried that and sure, I'd like to try it," Larry responded and then added "Tomorrow I'm going to spend a little time in the park before heading back to Madera."

"I think the first time most people go to Yosemite they head for the valley where they can see a couple of the famous falls which is good but I think a better place to go where you can get a sense of the vast area the park covers is Glacier Point," 12 Joe volunteered. "I noticed that on my park map and wondered about that. This was a quick trip and some other time I'll take time to spend more time in the park. I'll take your advice with regards to Glacier Point and by the way a little brandy does make the cocoa better, especially while sitting beside a nice campfire as we are."

"I'm going to hit the sack now and I want you to know that I've enjoyed very much visiting with you and I hope that somewhere our paths will cross again. I'm going to get away real early so if I don't see you then I'll say goodbye now," Larry said and Joe responded as the two shook hands, "Do enjoy your trip into the park and good luck with your teaching."

As Larry drove past Oakhurst and turned off on his shortcut back to Madera at Coarsegold Larry just couldn't get his mind off the events of the previous day and what he had seen of Yosemite from Glacier Point. He had only been away from Madera a short time but might there be a letter from Lucy? Then too, the Brown that he had carefully kept covered with ice would need attention.

It was now that Larry realized that among his interests photography had not been one of them. Others had on occasion used their cameras to record events and now he was wishing that he still had the old box camera someone had given him while he was still in grade school.

Larry had an idea as he was taking the brown from the ice chest to the refrigerator. Suppose he had that fish on the grass with the part of his fly rod with the reel alongside for size comparison; wouldn't that make for a good picture? He made a decision, first thing in the morning he would go camera shopping.

Besides the letter he had hoped for from Lucy there was one from Lisa. Lucy told how much she was enjoying her work. She was spending the day at Newport's South Shore Marina. When fishermen or those who had been crabbing came to the boat ramp to haul their boats from the water she would check their catches for size and limit violations. Fishermen knew they would be checked so were careful to follow regulations.

The main problems she mentioned in her letter were those who had for the first time rented crab rings and caught crabs. She soon learned that she could tell if violations were just honest mistakes or deliberate. The common problem was using the gage to measure crab size. Some just didn't use it properly so had an occasional undersized crab. In this case she had to demonstrate the proper way to use the gage then confiscate the undersize crab and return it to the bay. Only in gross violations would she issue a citation which was seldom.

In Lisa's letter she had good things to say about her work on the oceanographic study ship. It was moored near the marina where Lucy worked so they could often spend time with each other. She didn't think most fishermen and crabbers minded being checked by that beautiful young Fish and Wildlife Officer even though she did wear an imposing sidearm.

Both Lucy and Lisa wanted Larry to hurry back to spend a little time with them and this was something he intended to do. One thing Larry had planned for doing in Oregon was in his dad's shop on the farm build in his pickup shell a bunk and storage for camp equipment. Sometimes instead of pitching a tent sleeping in the pickup would be more convenient.

As he had decided to do, right after breakfast Larry was out camera shopping. In one of the chain drug stores he found a well stocked camera department. He had not realized that there was such a range of types and prices in the camera field.

The clerk in that department was very knowledgeable about cameras and when Larry explained that he had no experience with photography the clerk suggested a fairly inexpensive 35mm Eastman camera and film which Larry bought. The clerk loaded the camera and showed how to work the camera settings which were quite simple. The clerk pointed out that some of the expensive cameras had so many adjustments and lens settings that only an experienced photographer would be capable of taking a decent picture with them but they could take good pictures under conditions where his would not. Larry learned that some people liked showing pictures in color using a slide projector and there was film for that that would work in his camera.

Back to his apartment Larry immediately got his fish and fly rod out to the lawn to do the thing he pictured in his mind the evening before. A couple of the other teachers in the apartment who Larry had met saw what Larry was doing and came to admire the big Brown. One offered to use the camera to take a picture of Larry holding the Brown with one hand and holding his fly rod with the other. Responding to requests, before Larry returned to his apartment he had related where and how the Brown had been caught.

With his fish filleted Larry realized that he had enough for four meals. He carefully freezer wrapped three pieces for the freezer. One would be part of this day's dinner. His plan was to have everything packed and ready for an early start for Oregon in the morning.

Approaching Canyonville on I-5 Larry was thinking "I don't want to get to Newport late at night and I like the campground here. I'll spend the night here and get to Newport early enough to find a place to stay. First I'll drive directly to the South Shore Marina to surprise Lucy."

All set up at his campsite and after his dinner Larry was sitting by a nice campfire sipping a hot cocoa laced with a little brandy that he had added to his camp supplies before leaving California. He was aware that in Oregon he would have to go to a state liquor store for that and they weren't open all the time. He had set up his tent for sleeping tonight and now he was mentally planning how he would put together a sleeping arrangement in the pickup. Also he was remembering that Joe had called this hot cocoa with brandy a cappuccino.

Larry considered cutting over to the coast and then on to Newport. That would be the scenic route. He opted for the faster stay on I-5 then west to Newport.

Walking toward the boat ramp he could see Lucy talking to someone who had just pulled a boat from the water. She looked very official he thought with her sidearm and Fish and Wildlife badge prominently displayed. Lucy hadn't noticed Larry approaching until he was quite near. The boat owner she had been talking to was a bit surprised when the Fish and Wildlife officer suddenly excused herself to rush into the arms of a gentleman with whom she proceeded to share hugs and kisses. She noticed that the boat owner was still standing and looking a bit perplexed where she had left him. She thought it best to take Larry with her and to introduce him as her fiancé and explain that they hadn't seen each other for some time.

With no activity at the ramp Larry and Lucy were able to sit on a nearby bench to talk and bring each other at least partially up to date. "Does Lisa know you are here? If she doesn't, her Oceanography ship is in port and I know now's a good time to find her aboard. Why not we have dinner together this evening? I'm going to be pretty busy soon when more people will be coming in from crabbing and fishing. When I know most have their boats out I'll be free for the day." Larry thought Lucy's suggestions were good and said so. "I'll go to the ship now. Then I'll find a place to stay tonight: tomorrow I want to go to the farm," "You can stay with me tonight at my apartment at the Embarcadero. I got one with two bedrooms because quite often my folks like to come for a visit," Lucy said and Larry responded with "I'll take you up on the offer and now I'll go see if I can find Lisa."

Lisa happened to be on deck and spotted Larry parking his pickup. She was on the dock to throw her arms around him as he approached. "I recognized that it was you when I saw you parking your pickup. I'm so happy you're here, come aboard with me. I want to hear about your life in California."

To everyone they met aboard Lisa introduced her big brother. It was hard to say who was most proud, Lisa of her big brother or Larry of his little sister. As they walked around the deck Lisa was explaining how some of the equipment they saw was used. "I saw Lucy at the boat ramp and she wants the three of us to have dinner together this evening. Will you be free to do that?" Larry asked. "My evenings most of the time are free while we're in port. Sure, I'd like that," Lisa answered. Then continued to say "I want to show you where I bunk and work on my studies." Larry was surprised how nice her little stateroom was with its built in bunk and a small desk. It had its own little bathroom with shower and wash basin. Even though small it didn't make her feel too closed in because the bulkhead beside her bunk had a porthole that could be opened or closed. Lisa explained that at sea it would be closed most of the time to keep out the salt spray, sometimes they were out in heavy weather.

Lisa explained that she was studying two things as part of her college studies. One was Oceanography and the other was a part of her Naval Reserve Officer Training program. At sea she was on the bridge studying navigation and ship handling as well as a regular wheel watch and she loved it. She didn't have a rigid ships maintenance schedule while in port. Sometimes she was assigned a deck task such as hosing down the deck or polishing bright work i.e. brass railing, etc. It was the type tasks that would be assigned an ordinary seaman in the merchant marine.

Larry explained that he was staying with Lucy in her apartment this night and planned to go to the farm in the morning. "I want to get started on some ideas I have for making my pickup canopy more useful and now it's getting late enough for Lucy to leave the Marina so should we come by to take you with us?" "No, come by when you leave and I'll see you a little later at her apartment." That settled and Larry was correct, Lucy was ready to leave the Marina.

"I know you know the way to the Embarcadero but there are many apartments so try to follow me but if we get separated in the traffic which can be heavy this time of day, I'll wait for you at the Embarcadero entrance.

As Larry looked out the apartment windows he remarked "What a view. I can see the whole bay and Newport waterfront as well as looking down at the Embarcadero Marina." "Yes, I picked this because I knew my folks would like it. I think when I end up with an assignment somewhere else which I know will happen sometime in the future, my folks will take it over if and when I move." Lucy was responding and showing Larry the bedroom where he could put his travel bag as Lisa walked in.

"Would anyone like something to help us unwind after a busy day?" Lucy asked and added "I can offer coffee, tea or perhaps a glass of wine might be good." Larry answered that with "I could go for a glass of wine." Lisa concurred.

Lucy produced a bottle of Willamette Valley red wine to state "I know you both like red wine which is good because I only have red." She handed the bottle and cork puller to Larry saying "You take care of this while I change to what I call civilian clothes."

With all three settled down relaxing with wine and small talk Larry questioned "Lucy, as I was looking down to the Marina I noticed someone filleting fish and someone else getting crabs from a boat. Couldn't they violate the restrictions on crabbing and get away with it?" "We don't worry much about that here. Most are locals who know the restrictions and abide with them. However, I do sometimes make an appearance at the fish cleaning station. Most know that someone from Fish and Wildlife could appear at any time to check licenses, etc."

The subject turned to dinner. Larry spoke to say "Some years ago I had fried Yaquina Bay oysters at a small restaurant near the waterfront. I don't remember the name of the place or even exactly where it was." Lisa spoke up to say "I think I was with you at the time and I do know the place. Let's all go there." With that settled small talk continued.

"Lucy, a question has been bugging me. I notice that you have about the largest sidearm that I see police carry. In fact most I notice have smaller lighter types. Why weren't you issued the same?" "Larry, in answer to your question, I had a choice. I had read the history of the development of the 1911 Model 45 caliber semi automatic in answer to a need during the Spanish American War. The state had acquired a number of those in a surplus sale after WW II so I had a choice for one of those or the smaller and lighter 9mm models."

"At first the guys at the range where State Police and Fish and Wildlife honed up their shooting skills in a good natured way poked fun at the little girl with the big gun. I was determined to master that 45. My wrists are strong and it wasn't long before my scores were right in there with the best of them. I had earned their respect." Then Lucy went on to say "I hope I never have to shoot someone but if I do it will be for good reason and I want it to be effective." Lucy's experience with the 45 was not new to Lisa but it was new to Larry. He hadn't realized that so much had happened in Lucy's life since he last saw her. "Lucy, why didn't you tell me about all that in your letters?" Lucy answered with "because I thought you'd better understand what I was trying to say if you heard me say it to you in person."

Riding in Lucy's car on the way to the restaurant Lucy took time to explain that rather than drive a state car she kept track of the mileage on her car when she used it for official purposes. "I'm paid so much a mile in that case." She explained and added "It probably costs the state less in the long run."

As they waited for their fried oyster dinner to be served both Lisa and Lucy pressed Larry for a report on his Yosemite trip. Larry answered that with "So much happened on that trip that it'll take more time than we have now to tell it all. However, in my short time within the park I'll say that I got a terrific overview of the park from what I saw at Glacier Point. In the future there'll be time for more exploring in the park. What happened at a campground where I stayed before entering the park, I'll tell about later. I see our dinner coming."

Back at the apartment Lucy and Lisa both said "You were going to tell us more about what happened at that campground." "Oh yes I think that was the best part of the Yosemite trip." Larry answered. "There was a nice little stream alongside the campground. I learned that its name was Big Creek which I thought didn't make much sense. Anyway, when I drove into the camp ground I had noticed a camper with a stringer of pan sized trout. After I got my camp set up I walked over to ask the guy about fishing in the little stream. He said that it was periodically planted with catchable sized trout. They were quickly caught out by campers. However, he said that there were a few large Browns in the stream that grew big on a diet of planted Rainbows. Sometimes one was hooked but seldom landed. Well, I did hook one and I landed it. The little store at Fish Camp took a picture of it and promised to send me one." Larry went on to explain why he was planning another trip to the mountains when he returned to California.

"After all this the neighbor camper invited me to visit by their camp fire later in the evening which I did.

It turned out that he and his wife were teachers at a town south of Fresno and a favorite place where they liked to backpack in summertime was an area south of Yosemite. He described the stream in the area as the best fly fishing stream he had ever fished. When I get back to California I'm gong to check that out. I'll still have time for a quick trip back to Oregon before school starts."

As Lisa was leaving Larry let her know and Lucy too that he would come back to Newport for a day or so before returning to California. It was time now for private talk about future plans. Lucy already knew that Larry planned to come back to Oregon during Christmas break for their marriage and it was up to her to plan the details for that. Now she had some things to say about her work.

There were plans for her to team up with State Police to help with solving a bear poaching problem. It seems that dead bears were being found in forests at widely separated locations but all had things in common. All were missing their paws and their gall bladders had been removed. She didn't know how soon this would happen but when she did she would keep him informed.

Hugs and kisses were shared before going to their separate bedrooms. Secretly Larry was wishing that she would invite him to share her bedroom. Secretly Lucy was wishing that Larry would be sharing her bed but she was determined to keep her virginity until they were married.

After sharing breakfast Larry was getting his travel bag in the pickup as Lucy was getting herself in uniform.   It was time for a hug and a kiss before parting.

As Larry drove to the farm he couldn't help but worry about Lucy.   He knew that Lucy loved her work but he also knew that requiring her to wear a sidearm meant there was always an element of unexpected danger.

Chapter 15

Larry's folks were expecting him but didn't know exactly when but it didn't matter. They were always happy to see him. His dad was interested in what Larry thought of the pickup.

Larry explained that he really liked the pickup but thought a little work in the canopy would make it more useful for camping. He explained to his dad that he knew he could remove the canopy and replace it with an over the cab camper complete with regular living facilities but for now all he wanted to do was build a simple bunk that he could put an air mattress on. There would be space under it for camping equipment, etc. In some camping situations that would be better than setting up his tent.

But before any work like that could begin he would have much conversation about Lucy and Lisa and of course his trip to Yosemite.

Larry went on to explain that he had figured out how he had time yet this summer for going back to California for a quick trip to the mountains south of Yosemite and back to Oregon for a few days before school started in Madera.

Olaf and Minnie were happy to have their son with them. Minnie went all out to cook the kind of food that Larry had always liked. Olaf too was interested in Larry's bunk project and helped go through the available odds and ends of lumber to find what was needed. Between the two it was hardly anytime at all before Larry had his bunk complete with air mattress and sleeping bag. Larry had two sleeping bags. The one he used in the camper canopy and usually when setting up his tent in a campground was a full size bag. For back packing he used a light weight mummy bag along with a cover made with rip stop material on top and damp proof material on bottom.

In good weather that was all he needed for comfort, no tent but if rain threatened he had what was called a tent tarp. It was light weight and had tie loops in various places. It could be set up as a leanto or in a number of other configurations.

It was two days before Larry planned to leave that he had a phone call from Lucy. She was being called to Salem and intended to take the coast and Salmon River route and wished to meet him briefly in the morning at her apartment before she left.

That was why Larry was on his way to Newport wondering, what was the purpose for Lucy's sudden call to the Fish and Wildlife head office in Salem? He was soon to realize what was happening. She met him with open arms and a happy smile along with a warm kiss and big hug then saying "I'm quite certain that what has been considered is now happening."

Lucy went on to say that she would have more to tell after she knew more. She went on to say that it was almost a sure thing that she would be working closely with the Oregon State Police to solve the bear poaching problem. "I've liked the duty here in Newport but it will be somewhat exiting to be doing detective investigations. That bear poaching has to be stopped," Lucy said. "I feel that it's sort of like I'm getting a promotion."

After listening to all this Larry was realizing that Lucy was really happy about this and he didn't want to say anything to put a damper on her enthusiasm. About all he could think to say was "I'm happy that you're happy and I'll be expecting more about the job when you know more." Lucy had her bags almost all packed and as she finished and he was helping load her car Larry was explaining his plans for the rest of summer.

"There's time for me to investigate the area south of Yosemite that the guy in the camp ground told me about. It sounded like an area where you and I could go back packing next summer. He and his wife had done that and loved the area with its good fly fishing. "I'll look forward to that," Lucy commented. Larry continued with "I'll come back to Oregon for a few days visit before my school starts and I meet all the teachers and the students I'll be teaching. Of course I'll have a report on what I find in the mountains. There'll not be time for back packing, just a quick day of learning about the area and a little fishing."

As Larry was saying his goodbyes to Lucy he commented "I planned to see Lisa today and now I can see that her ship is not where it's normally docked. Apparently it's out at sea." "Yes, I saw it leave yesterday afternoon," Lucy answered. Larry and Lucy parted with their usual big hug and a very warm kiss and Larry saying "Have a safe trip sweetheart and remember, I love you so very much." Lucy responded with "The same to you." They both drove from the Embarcadero at the same time, she heading for the coast highway and he back to his folks.

Larry had to explain that he didn't get to say goodbye to Lisa because her ship was out at sea. Also there wasn't much he could say about Lucy except that she was expecting to work with Oregon State Police to solve a bear poaching problem. He wanted his mom to explain to Lisa why he was unable to say goodbye to her as he was seeing Lucy off on her trip to Salem.

That evening at the dinner table there was serious talk about what Larry was expecting to find about his new job once he was actually doing it. Larry knew from his student teaching just about what to expect and was confident about his ability to do well with teaching. About Lucy and her working with the police he confided that he was a bit worried. He mentioned her choice of side arms and with her work with the state police she might be forced to use it. He mentioned that on the practice range with state police she could shoot as well as the best of them. She had earned their respect.

Larry was getting an early start. Minnie had made sandwiches for him plus a stew that he could heat up on his camp stove. He planned to stop one night some place on the way to Madera. After thanking his mom for providing his lunch and dinner plus thanking his dad for his help with the pickup sleeping arrangement and a big hug for both he was on the way back to California.

A couple hours or so later as Larry was crossing the McKenzie River he got to thinking about what he had read and heard about the upper part of that river and its variety of Rainbow trout, the McKenzie Redsides. Question: while he was at Corvallis and so close why hadn't he gone there for a little fly fishing? With no answer to think of, he thought just have to write it off as a missed opportunity.

And later as he was crossing the North Umpqua River Larry got to thinking about all these well known fishing streams like the Rogue that he would cross later in the day. All of which got him to thinking as he drove toward California "Maybe the grass is always greener on the other side of the fence. Oh well! I can always come back." Larry concluded as his thoughts turned to other things such as "Maybe I'll pull off at the next rest stop I come to. I could use their rest room and I have a sandwich to eat and there's coffee in my thermos."

Larry had in his mind to stop shortly after coming into California at a rest stop he had seen where I-5 crossed the Klamath River. He had seen RV's and others stopped for the night there and he would do the same.

At the California Inspection Station he was told that he couldn't bring the Gravenstein apples he had picked at the farm into California. Larry knew his apples were not wormy and tried to convince the inspection officer. "Perhaps not but it's the rule that apples from home orchards can't come in. Those from commercial orchards are inspected at the shipping point.' Larry was determined not to see his apples thrown in the garbage. "If I turn around to come back with them cooked, then could I bring them into California?" Larry asked. "Oh sure, the rule applies only to fresh fruit."

A short distance from the station, passers by could see a pickup parked with a camp stove on the tailgate and a guy cooking something.

Next to a table for his camp stove, Larry was enjoying a dish of still warm applesauce. He had separated enough for a dish without skins and cores and it needed sweetening to make it good. The unwanted remains of cores and skins he would separate when he got to Madera, cooking apples beside a busy highway Larry had thought it best to just cut up whole apples and worry about skins and cores later. He had on the camp stove his moms stew that he would heat up after freshening up at the near by restroom.

As Larry was enjoying his stew, along with soda crackers and hot tea he was noticing the young couple camping near by and on the rear window of their car in big white letters: JUST MARRIED. They had a new looking tent and what appeared to be a brand new camp stove on their table. They appeared to be heating water for hot drinks, he thought cocoa. Other than that they were not cooking anything, they were just eating what appeared to be deli sandwiches.

About the time that Larry started thinking that he might be stopping here for the night with Lucy during Christmas break after their marriage, the couple came by and stopped to admire Larry's camping set up. They had noticed he didn't set up a tent and obviously was sleeping in his pickup canopy.

Larry commented, "I noticed the Just Married sign on your window." "Yes, we were married in Portland and spent last night at a hotel in Salem. What we plan to do is spend our honeymoon in Yosemite. We understand that there are tent cabins to rent there," they explained. Larry answered that with "I was recently in Yosemite and I learned that those tent cabins are usually all reserved ahead of time. I camped at a campground just outside the park near Fish Camp."

"We're new to camping." The couple explained and went on to say that they were going to need pots, etc. "What you'll need depends on what kind of camping you intend to do. Sometimes I'll be in a regular commercial campground and sometimes I'm out in a remote area where I cook over a camp fire or sometimes like this where I can't even have a camp fire but I can cook what ever I have the pots and pans to do it with," Larry answered and continued with, "By the way my name is Larry and if you'd like to join me for breakfast I'll serve eggs and bacon both of which are from my parent's farm. I'm looking at you two newlyweds and thinking how my fiancé and I will be in a similar situation as we travel to my work in Madera next Christmas vacation."

"My name is Tom," the guy responded and his wife spoke up to say that her name was Gerry. "Thank you for your invitation but we planned to have breakfast in Yreka," Tom said. "I'd like to accept Larry's invitation. I want to hear more about Larry's fiancé," Gerry said to her husband. "Good, you'll know breakfast is about ready when you smell it cooking," Larry said and added as they parted "Sleep well."

As Larry was getting ready to start cooking he was thinking about the novice campers he had invited to share his breakfast. There was something intriguing about them. Perhaps it was that they reminded him of his wish that he and Lucy were already married and she was with him now, traveling to Madera.

The smell of fresh coffee and frying bacon brought Tom and Gerry to join Larry as he was stirring up his eggs, he had decided to have his eggs scrambled.

Tom and Gerry brought their own coffee cups and as Larry was serving the eggs and bacon he was noticing the logo of a large Portland department store on the cups.   At the same time Gerry was mentally taking note of Larry's cooking equipment and that he used disposable plates.

"Larry, last evening you made a comment about travelling with your fiancé. I gathered that you are planning a wedding during a Christmas break. All of which stirs up my curiosity, I'd like to hear a little about your fiancé and when you say Christmas break, a break from what?" Gerry asked.

"Okay, in answer to your last question I'll be teaching agriculture at Madera High School and my fiancé and I plan for our marriage during Christmas vacation. About my fiancé, her name is Lucy and we announced our engagement about the same time we both graduated from Oregon State."   "Why did you want to wait so long to get married?"   Gerry questioned.

"Sometimes I wonder a little about that too, but I was just going to be starting a new job at an unfamiliar place, and Lucy was also starting a new job so I guess we thought we should wait to see what would happen with our new jobs." Larry answered.

"Gerry and I both went to a business school in Portland but we didn't meet each other at school. We both went to work for Meier and Frank department store and that's where we met. We dated steady for about six months before we decided to get married. We announced our engagement and ten days later we were married. By the way, what kind of a job does Lucy have?"

"Lucy's ambition was to work with Oregon's Fish and Wildlife and during vacation time had done volunteer work with them. Right after graduation she went to work for that state department and she loves her work but she does intend to resign and come to California with me when we are married. " Larry said.

"I'll bet you wish she were traveling with you now, right?"   "You're right about that." Larry had to answer.

Tom and Gerry helped Larry with cleanup and before parting exchanged addresses for their places of work. All expressed hope that their paths might cross again somewhere sometime as they bid each other good bye.

Driving down I-5 with the latest hit music playing, Larry couldn't help but think about Lucy and the couple he had met at the rest stop. He was thinking about their getting engaged then quickly getting married. If he and Lucy had done that the seat beside him would not be empty. Larry didn't know why but he had a feeling that somewhere sometime he would see that couple again.

After a good night sleep and a hearty breakfast Larry was busy making a list of what he would need for his trip to the mountains. He was remembering what he had been told about a part of the Sierra south of Yosemite. He was determined to see for himself if that part of the Sierra was as great as he was told.

If three or perhaps four days were used for this there would still be time for a quick trip back to Oregon before school opening. His plan was to have everything ready for an early start in the morning.

Chapter 16

Larry's plan involved taking a day to get to Lake Edison. Studying his map it appeared that in miles the distance from Madera was not great but Larry knew that many of those miles would be on slow mountain roads and he wanted to take his time

He had done that, had passed Shaver Lake which he later learned was a good fishing lake. While enjoying his lunch beside beautiful Huntington Lake he realized that he had reached a fairly high elevation and looking at his map he could see that in a very short climb the road would take him to Kaiser Pass at elevation 9200 ft. There were sail boats on the lake to watch but now it was time to move on,

After Kaiser Pass he found the road in places not wide enough for two cars to pass when meeting but there were turnouts. When coming to sharp turns it seemed a good idea to sound his horn and drive slowly.

Coming to a Ranger Station he learned that for passing the wilderness boundary at the head of Lake Edison if he were only going on Mono Creek for a day he would not need any paper work, but if he were planning to back pack he would need papers indicating planned destinations and length of stay. After listening to the ranger's description of the general area, Larry purchased a detailed map of the Edison Lake Mono Creek area and a map of the entire John Muir Wilderness area.

At a fork in the road were signs indicating go right to Florence Lake and left for Mono Hot Springs. There was now a drop in elevation to crossing the upper reaches of the San Joaquin River before climbing again to his destination, Edison Lake.

The first thing he saw was the large earthen dam that formed the lake. And the lake itself was larger than he had expected, in fact it was about seven miles long he later learned. He found that there was a regular campground a little past the turn in to the lodge but he thought that for his purposes using the lodge parking area would be best.

With tickets for next days ferry ride and return he got out his camp stove to heat up his dinner which in this case came mostly from cans. His plan was to have cold cereal with milk and instant coffee for breakfast. In the morning he would make sandwiches for his lunch.

After his dinner he thought it a bit early to crawl into his sleeping bag and when he was at the lodge he had noticed a large Brown on ice in a display case. He wanted to ask a few questions about that.

In talking to the lodge clerk Larry learned that in Vermilion Valley before the lake was built there was a large population of Browns in Mono Creek as it flowed through the valley. The Browns in the lake were usually caught by trolling deep with bass plugs or similar lures. The clerk said that there was a good population of smaller Browns in Mono Creek above the lake. Some probably migrated into the lake and with its plentiful food they grew big. Larry thought the one on display looked more like a fair sized salmon than a trout. Larry chose not to mention that he and his girl friend had caught similar sized Browns in Oregon's Detroit Lake.

On the ferry in the morning there was a rather mixed group of people. At the end of the lake Larry had along with his day pack his creel slung over his shoulder and his fly rod sections ready to put together. He was noticing his fellow passengers. Several had picnic baskets and looked like they just planned to spend the day in the vicinity. There were two young ladies together with a yellow Lab. One had a professional looking camera and he could see her immediately taking pictures of bushes along the stream.

With his fly rod assembled Larry started hiking on the trail that most of the time was near the stream. Sometimes Larry couldn't resist casting his fly to a fishable stretch of water. The fish he caught were released because his plan was to explore up stream as far as he could before returning downstream. He would catch trout on the way back downstream. Normally he preferred to fish travelling upstream but his purpose now was to see as much as he could of Mono Creek.

Not far up the trail a small stream from the left joined Mono Creek. Looking at his map he saw that it was Mono Creek's North Fork. Also he could see that the trail forked with one fork following the North Fork and the other climbing a high rise and away from Mono Creek for a distance before dropping back along the stream.

There was a bridge crossing the stream and he could see that by crossing to the south side of Mono Creek he could follow the stream rather than climbing up and dropping back to the stream. The reason for the bridge was that there was a trail called John Muir Trail continuing on to the south. However Larry could see what looked like an old unused trail that followed the stream. Hiking up that trail he soon realized that at some time in the past trail maintenance had ended. It was passable by climbing over or around fallen trees and it was a little brushy; however, it did pass by some fishable water before coming to a beautiful little waterfall. Looking down in the pool below could be seen in the crystal clear water a sizable trout.

On the bank and back a bit was a large rock outcropping. A large slab had broken off to form a low table and near it was an opening between two rocks with ashes from what he could see had been a perfect cooking fire. More in the open and off to the side were ashes from a campfire. It appeared that the site had not been used for some time. Looking across the stream where the trail came closer to the stream was a large campsite with several rock campfire rings, the sort of camp that a packer with horses would use.

Studying this spot and looking over to a well used campsite Larry made a promise to himself "Next year when I backpack to Mono Creek, if no one is using it this is where I'll spend my first night." Larry made use of a big logjam just upstream for crossing the stream to continue his hike upstream.

When Larry figured that he had come upstream somewhere between three or four miles and looking at his map it appeared that the first recess was yet a ways upstream. He wanted to take his time going back downstream and do a little fishing and he would follow the well used trail all the way. Where it joined the North Fork trail it was a ways up from where he had crossed Mono Creek. Going upstream the way he did he had avoided an uphill climb.

By the time he was back at the ferry landing his creel had a limit of nine to ten inch trout cleaned and packed in wet grass and leaves from alongside the stream. This would keep his fish cool until he put them on ice in his pickup. His plan was to start home as soon as the ferry landed.

On the ferry the young lady with the camera spoke to him. She said she had noticed his empty creel and now she could see that it was no longer empty. He did open the creel to show the trout and did remark that fly fishing was good on Mono Creek.

At his pickup Larry found that he still had ice in his cold box for his fish and left immediately. He felt that he could drive home in a lot less time than it had taken him to come to the lake and be home not too late for a trout dinner. He knew how the next day would be spent; he would be getting everything ready for his return to Oregon.

As Larry enjoyed a trout dinner his mind was busy planning the next several days. There would be phone calls to let people know his plans. He even considered trying to drive all the way with no overnight stop on the way but gave up that idea. It would be better to arrive at his destination sometime in the afternoon rather than at night. Perhaps the campground by the Rogue River near Grants Pass would be a good place to stop for the night and then he was thinking "Why do I make such a big deal out of a simple drive to Oregon?" It was then that Larry realized that it wasn't the drive that was a big deal. "It was that this visit would be the last chance to spend a little time with the most important people in his life before Christmas break."

Larry was finding that trying to contact some people was frustrating. Lisa was out at sea. Lucy was out in the field somewhere but he was able to leave a message for her to call him that evening. He did talk to his folks to let them know that he expected to arrive sometime in the afternoon the next day.

Trout had been on Larry's dinner menu the previous night and now it was again when Lucy called. About the first thing Larry had to say after he let Lucy know when he expected to arrive at the farm was "Lucy, you are going to love where I'm going to take you back packing next summer. It's a beautiful area and fly fishing is great." Larry went on to describe his trip to the Sierra in detail. Lucy let him know that she would be looking forward to that. Now that she knew when he would be there she said "I'll be working on getting some free time for us to get together and I'll call you at the farm."

Larry had his last trout for dinner parked beside the Rogue River the night before and now as he drove into his parent's driveway in mid afternoon he was wondering what his mom would be planning for dinner.

Those thoughts were put aside as he saw his mom and dad coming to greet him even before he was out of his pickup. After all the hugs and greetings and in the house Olaf, Minnie and Larry were all trying to talk at once. Having fresh brewed coffee as they sat and talked Minnie let Larry know that Lisa would come the next day to spend the night at the farm.

After saying that his trip to the mountains had been worthwhile Larry said "When Lisa is here I can tell all of you at the same time about what I found on my trip to the Sierra."

They were all enjoying a roast pork dinner when Lucy called to say that she would be coming to the farm the next day and intended to spend at least a couple days at Newport before returning to Salem.

Olaf talked about his neighbors. The word had gotten around that he could repair just about any kind of farm equipment and would accept in payment no money, only some product from their farm that he could use such as the pork roast they were enjoying. Larry commented "Dad, maybe you should go into business like opening up a fixit shop. In the morning I want to see what kind of a machine you are working on now."

In the morning what he saw was an old time drag saw or rather the parts thereof. Olaf explained that mechanically the saw was in good shape but the wood frame had so much decay that it was falling apart. He was building a new hardwood frame. He had told the owner what he would need and the owner had provided the materials. Larry had good reason to be impressed by his dad's woodworking skills.

Lisa arrived at the farm in time to have lunch with the family. She had brought with her three cooked crabs. She explained that when the oceanographic ship was at sea they frequently had a commercial sized crab pot at some location. The buoy marking its location had markings that identified it as part of a marine study. It was placed at varying locations and records kept of the catch. A good share of the catch was usually released but sometimes a few were kept for their own use and these were brought to a commercial cooker in Newport for cooking.

Lisa, Larry and their mom were busy cracking crab when Lucy arrived. There were hugs all around. Olaf too had come in from his shop to get his hug. He and Lucy joined in the cracking operation and it was soon done with. Lisa and her mom were planning a large Crab Louie as main dish for dinner. They would come up with something to go with it.

Lucy explained that she had been given time for two days stay in Newport and planned to go back to the apartment at the Embarcadero tonight. She wanted Larry to come to her apartment in the morning. Larry said "I'll do that." Lisa commented "I have to go back to the ship in the morning too. I think we're planning to head out to sea for a few days."

While everyone was at the dinner table Larry went into detail about his short trip to Edison Lake and Mono Creek. He told about his plans for back packing next summer in the area. Lucy commented "I'm looking forward to that."

The next two days at the coast were filled with so many shared experiences. They hunted agates at Agate beach and climbed the spiral stairs to the light at Yaquina Head lighthouse. There was a fried oyster dinner at Larry's favorite restaurant in Newport and they went out on a whale watching trip out of Depoe Bay and Larry was happy that Lucy didn't get seasick. The restaurant overlooking the harbor with its commercial fishing fleet and pleasure craft was famous for its sea food dinners and after the two hour time on the ocean they were ready for their baked salmon dinner.

Lucy explained a little about her work with the state police on the bear poaching problem. They were learning a few things about such things as bear paw soup and bear gall bladders. Through connections with San Francisco police they had learned that San Francisco's Chinatown was where gall bladders and bear paws removed from poached bears were being marketed.

They were getting a few leads as to the identity of the poachers but even if they knew their identities that was not enough. They had to be caught with the bear parts or caught in the act of poaching. She and the State Police were determined to put an end to this poaching. Bringing these poachers to justice had become a personal thing.

Larry told Lucy about the couple he had met at the Klamath River rest stop and how they had met each other not at the school from which they graduated but at the Portland department store where they started working. They fell in love, got engaged and shortly after got married. Larry said he was beginning to think that waiting for Christmas break to get married was a mistake. Lucy said "I'll admit to sometimes thinking the same thing. I'm reading your mind; I know that you would like for us to get married right now." Larry answered that with "That's correct." Lucy then had to say "I would like to do what you want but now I'm stuck. I'm so deep in this poaching investigation that I just can't resign until it's over. We're learning enough about suspects that I think in a month or so the poachers will be in jail. Note that I used the plural, we are quite certain that three people are involved.

Larry understood Lucy's determination. She was a person who didn't give up when faced with a problem. About all he could say was "I understand."

The next morning as Lucy was preparing to return to Salem they agreed that the past two days together had been wonderful. Both were thinking to themselves they didn't like knowing that events were going to keep them apart even longer.

Parting was difficult. As they hugged and kissed along with their goodbyes Lucy had tears in her eyes. With a last "I love you" they both got in their cars and left the Embarcadero at the same time.

At the farm Larry in talking to his mom confided how hard it had been to say goodbye to Lucy and that he didn't let her know how worried he was that her job would get her into some dangerous situation. She was so confident in her ability to take care of herself and loved her work so much that he couldn't bring himself to let her know how worried he really was. She answered to that with "That's the way it is with those we love."

Larry had noticed some stock grazing in the meadow. Asking about that he learned that the pasture was rented to a neighbor who needed more pasture for his stock. He spent most of the afternoon helping his dad with the drag saw frame project. Larry was thinking "Between the two of us if we had a fixit business we could fix just about anything."

The next morning after a hot cake with maple syrup breakfast Larry was ready to hit the road. As usual his mom had loaded him up with food for the road and more.

As Larry had done on his last trip south he stopped at the Klamath River Rest Stop. This time he brought no fresh fruit to declare at the border check station and he didn't meet up with interesting people as he had done before. He walked over to the river and found that was quite low which was probably normal for this time of year. After heating the dinner his mom had prepared for him and sipping a cup of hot tea he just turned in for a good nights sleep.

Breakfast time he thought about the couple that shared breakfast with him the last time he was at this rest stop, Tom and Gerry. They were headed for Yosemite. Would he ever get to talk to them about that?

Larry found that on the rest of the way to Madera just listening to music and news turned up loud was the best way to drive worries about Lucy out of his mind.

What he had to think about now was that he would be reporting to his first teaching job in just a few days. Driving to his apartment building Larry was thinking "I've been gone for a while and there will probably be spoiled things in the fridge for me to throw out. I'll have to make a grocery list and go shopping before dinner."

Chapter 17

At the welcome to a new school year meeting of Madera High School Teachers there were greetings and pep talks by the district superintendent and the high school principal. Larry had met the teachers who lived in his apartment building but it would be a while before he got to know others.

School would start the coming Monday but now there would be time for him to look over his facilities and make appropriate plans for opening day. At this school things were comparable to where he had done his student teaching so he saw no problem. He was ready.

As Larry was enjoying his Monday evening dinner he was thinking about his first day of classes. Meeting his students for the first time he had seen that they were of diverse ethnicity which was reflected in the names of students in his classes. Most of the time meeting his students for the first time was spent checking his lists of student names to see who was present and who was missing. Names of missing students he had turned in at the days end.

This was a three year high school. In Junior High ninth grade boys and girls had completed a semester each of any two wood shop, metal shop or home economics classes. Now in tenth grade their counselors had to make class assignments which were often subject to change.

Since Agriculture as a subject hadn't been offered in Junior High his two tenth grade Ag classes were beginning classes. His eleventh and twelve grade classes were both advanced classes. Out of a five period day he had one period with no class called a preparation period.

One thing Larry had planned to do was visit the farms and ranches from which his students came. In talking to counselors he learned that parents of many of his beginning students were migrant workers who followed certain crop harvest times. He could expect many of these to be dropped and new names added to class lists through out the school year. The parents of some boys and girls were permanent workers on the larger ranches and those students often elected to continue in advanced classes. Larry was beginning to get the big picture as to how he should organize his teaching.

Larry soon learned that in his beginning classes there were those who were there only because there had been no other place to put them. Many of these could care less about learning and sometimes became a class problem. Those whose parents were really interested in their sons and daughters education were his best students and he really enjoyed working with them.

Several weeks after school opening there was Parents Night. A chance for parents to meet the teachers and Larry realized afterwards that it had been the parents of those he considered his better students who had come to visit with him in his classroom.

Things had pretty well settled in to routine with Larry's teaching. He had visited several farms, the homes of students in his classes. One was a fairly large cattle ranch in the lower foothills and another completely different, with a peach, fig and cherry orchard.

In talking with ranch owners Larry was getting an education as to the problems that a diverse group of farmers had in common. There were the fluctuations in market demands, sometimes unpredictable weather and always the insect pests.

Lucy called almost every night. Because she was constantly at different locations about the only way he could contact her was to leave a message with her department in Salem. She let him know that there was a lot that she was not at liberty to talk about regarding the poaching problem but she was confident that it would soon be wrapped up. Larry liked these calls not only for what news she passed on to him but she was someone he could talk to about personal matters. They always ended their conversations with a "love you" to each other.

What Lucy wanted to tell Larry but couldn't for security reasons was that they could now follow the movements of the leader of the poaching trio. As his car was being serviced, oil changed etc. a bug had been planted in the car. At least they knew where his car was and it would be a good guess that the three poachers were with it. The team followed but always kept their distance. They wore civilian clothing with their badges out of sight and the three usually separated at restaurants and in public with Lucy and one of the police together and with the other apart from the two. They also drove an older model unmarked car.

Lisa and Larry frequently talked to each other. She was back at school now and living in the Corvallis home so he was able to call her there. Their folks were often with her, bringing produce from the farm. Lucy frequently called her too and she said the usual topic in their conversation was Larry and what they were hearing from him.

The poacher car was driving some side roads in the vicinity of Noti, a small community west of Eugene. This was interesting to the two police and Lucy because they knew that there was a bear in the vicinity. Oregon Fish and Wildlife was aware of this bear because it was a problem bear. Because it had caused trouble in the Noti community Fish and Wildlife had trapped the bear and released it in a remote area. At the same time a radio tracking device had been attached. Now that bear was slowly working its way back to where it had previously caused trouble especially with its habit of getting into garbage cans and scattering the contents. Bee keepers too had their hives destroyed by the bear as it tried to get at the honey inside.

The next morning the poacher's car was parked on the back road where it had been driven the day before. Apparently the poachers were now entering the forest to find and kill the bear. They didn't know its exact location as did the officers.

The plan now was for the officers to wait at the edge of the forest. They would know that the poachers had located the bear when they heard gunshots. A police backup unit and ambulance was at the scene. The officers had decided that just the three would quietly approach and surprise the poachers in the act of removing the bears paws and gall bladder. They were prepared for gun fire and wearing armored vests but were hoping that the poachers would just surrender when surprised by the officers. They would be in radio contact with the back up officers.

There is an old Scotch saying about the best laid plans of mice and men not going as planned. As the officers were approaching the bear kill the poachers bear hound started barking. The poachers stopped what they were doing to pick up their rifles so when the officers stepped into the open they had rifles pointed at them. The officers were in plain clothes but with their badges in conspicuous view. One officer ordered "Drop your guns, you're under arrest."

Lucy happened to be facing the big guy, the poacher leader and she was watching closely his eyes as they flicked quickly over the situation. At the moment it was a standoff. Thoughts were racing through the big guys mind as he assessed the situation. He was facing a slight young female with what he recognized as an old style military 45 and she probably couldn't hit the broad side of a barn with it. The other two young officers appeared to him as rookies.

The leader had been in jails and done prison time as had his partners. None wanted to go back to prison and were ready to shoot their way out of this situation to prevent it and their rifles were still pointed at the officers. As Lucy watched the leader's eyes and facial expressions she saw him give a slight nod which she took as a signal to his partners to shoot. She pulled the trigger on her 45 and had the satisfaction of seeing him fall to the ground. Actually, her 45 bullet had hit his heart and to all intents and purposes he was dead before he hit the ground. When the partners saw their leader down they dropped their rifles and raised their hands. One was severely wounded and the other slightly so.

One officer had not been hit and the other had a 30-06 bullet graze his vest without penetrating. Lucy's vest had been no match for a bullet from an H&H 300 Magnum cartridge. A direct hit had penetrated her vest and in so doing had fully mushroomed to create a very serious wound. She had dropped to her knees and struggling to keep from falling to the ground.

As soon as the Police backup unit and medics had heard the volley of gunshots they had not waited for a radio call but had immediately entered the forest. The bear kill was about a mile from the road and it was only minutes before they were at the scene. The medics recognized Lucy as the most seriously wounded and with her vest removed were applying a compress to her wound to stop the bleeding. The seriously wounded poacher had a compress taped on his wound.

The backup officers with the two handcuffed poachers and the medics with Lucy on a stretcher were leaving the scene with only Lucy's two police partners and a police photographer remaining at the site. They would remain until a crew arrived to remove the dead body, the dead bear and the bear hound that was still tied to a sapling.

It was late forenoon when another teacher entered Larry's classroom to say "I'll take over your class. You are wanted in the office immediately." Larry had a sinking feeling and was picturing something serious happening to Lucy as he hurried to the school office. He was met by Patti the secretary saying "Your fiancé is in a hospital at Eugene. Go home to pick up what you will need for a few days in Oregon then go to the airfield. An Oregon State Police plane is on its way to meet you there and take you to Eugene." Patti was trying to understand what Larry was thinking as he stood speechless with a shocked expression on his face. She said "If you're worried about your classes, they will be covered by a substitute until you return." About all that Larry could think to say was "Thank you, I'll do as you say" as he left.

At his apartment Larry quickly had essentials and a couple changes of clothing in his suitcase and left for the nearby Madera Airport. He left his pickup in the long term parking area and was walking to the landing area as the Oregon Police plane was coming in for landing. As soon as the plane taxied to a stop Larry was at the plane to meet the pilot and establish his identity. After a quick refueling they were in the air.

Larry was curious as to what had happened to Lucy. Why was she in the hospital? Larry just knew in his mind that there had been shooting and Lucy had been wounded but he wanted to hear the facts. About all the pilot could say was that he really didn't know the particulars. He thought she had been wounded in some sort of police activity.

An Oregon State Police car was waiting at the airport and Larry was immediately on his way to the hospital.

Chapter 18

Lisa was waiting for Larry at the hospital entrance. She had arrived earlier to find that Lucy was still in surgery and that's when she learned that Larry was in the air on his way to the hospital and would soon arrive to be brought to the hospital by police. She wanted to meet Larry before he went to see Lucy so they could go there together. Lucy would soon be out of surgery she thought.

Lisa met her brother with a hug and as they walked into the hospital she said "Larry I know you've been worried about Lucy. In the radio news this afternoon I've been hearing that Lucy personally shot dead the leader of a bear poaching group. However, in the gun battle she was wounded. That's all I know about what happened. I'm sure there's a lot more we'll find out later on."

In the hospital room they found only Lucy's parents. The lead surgeon had discussed Lucy's condition with them. She was out of surgery and would be in Intensive Care for a short time. Internal bleeding from a serious wound had been stopped but there was much damage. He had stated that only the quick response by medics had saved her life. She was currently receiving blood transfusions and had not as yet recovered consciousness after anesthesia.

Larry, Lisa and Lucy's parents could only wait for Lucy to come to the room. They discussed what little they knew about the confrontation with the bear poachers. Their leader had died after being shot by Lucy. One other was wounded and in the hospital and the third was in jail. Radio news reports were sometimes confusing.

As they waited Lucy's parents were asking questions about Larry's teaching job. He was describing his school's agricultural program when interrupted by the arrival of Lucy on her bed with a needle in her arm with a tube connected to a bottle with liquid hanging at the foot of the bed. She had sensor wires leading to a monitor on its table attended by a nurse.

Lucy's eyes were closed and the nurse commented that she was still pretty sleepy as well as sedated. Larry leaned over the bed to kiss her on the forehead, her eyes opened and she spoke "Larry! I knew you'd come. I was waiting for you." Larry thought about that statement as she closed her eyes for a few minutes before speaking again to say "Larry, you once wondered why I had chosen that heavy 45. It did what it was supposed to do. My one shot put the lead poacher on the ground and I'm proud of that." "I'm proud of you too." Larry answered.

The sedative was making her so sleepy she was struggling to stay awake. Lucy's eyes closed and as she slept Larry noticed that her breathing was a little difficult. Each breath was short and shallow. He saw too that Lucy's nurse was watching closely the monitor.

It was almost a half hour before Lucy opened her eyes again to say "Larry, please hold my hand." He took her hand and gave it a little squeeze and she squeezed back. She looked at him and he saw her mouth "I love you." He looked at her and before she closed her eyes again, he whispered "I love you too."

As he continued to hold her hand she kept a firm grip on his.

Suddenly, her grip relaxed and her breathing stopped. What Larry feared had happened. All he could do was lean over to kiss her on the forehead and say "Goodbye, Lucy," and then bury his head in his arms on the edge of the bed to let go the single sob he could not hold back. There was a straight line on the monitor and Lucy's mom was sobbing in the arms of Lucy's dad. The nurse had called the doctor on duty and he arrived to verify her death.

They were all leaving the room except Lucy's dad. He had to answer questions as to body disposition, etc. A nurse took them to a waiting room where they would wait for him. They had paid no attention to time and now it was after ten o'clock. They had not eaten since breakfast it turned out except for some snacks. There was food in the hospital and they agreed that as soon as Lucy's dad returned they should at least have a sandwich and something to drink.

It was now that the two State Police Officers who had been Lucy's partners in the poacher affair arrived at the hospital to see Lucy. When informed that she had only minutes ago died they were taken to the room where parents and friends were. Lucy's dad arrived as they were expressing their condolences.

They spoke about Lucy's bravery and how when they first met her at the Police Shooting Range they had kidded her as being the little girl with the big gun. She was so determined to master that 1911 Model 45 that it wasn't long before she could hold her own with the best of them in target practice. They answered a few questions about how the bear poachers were traced and finally taken down.

As the group moved to the cafeteria the Police Officers took their leave and the talk turned to their next move; Lucy's parents mentioned that they planned to find a hotel to stay the night. They planned to pick up Lucy's car the next day. It was in the police parking lot at Salem. Lisa mentioned that she and Larry were going to their place in Corvallis and suggested that Lucy's parents come with them. They agreed to that and after finishing their sandwiches and coffee were in Lisa's jeep heading for Corvallis.

Riding in the jeep was comfortable for Lisa and Lucy's mom but in the back seat the problem was leg room. Larry and Lucy's dad had to sit a bit sideways to make room for their long legs. Fortunately the trip from Eugene to Corvallis only took a little over an hour.

About the first thing that Lisa did was go to her room for a letter from Lucy to give to Larry. Lisa had been told to give it to Larry only if anything happened to cause her death.

Larry opened it and started reading. What he read was: "Dearest Larry: The only reason you are reading this is that I am no longer alive. Even if you didn't talk much about it I knew all the time that you were worried about my safety. I was aware that when I was assigned to work side by side with the State Police there might be situations where I would be in danger and I accepted that.

I loved you very much and often looked forward to our marriage during Christmas break with anticipation. Now that is past and I want you to think about the future. I want you to have the ring you gave me. I know that you will meet and fall in love with someone in the future and since I am no longer here to wear it I can only think it proper for you to place it on the finger of that person you wish to become your wife.

As I write this I'm thinking of the good times we have spent together and how much I love you. Think of me as someone you have loved and then let me fade into the past as you face your future. Lucy."

There were tears in Larry's eyes as without a word he handed the letter over for the rest of the group to read. As each read it there were tears in their eyes too as they read without comment. Everyone kept their thoughts to themselves. Lisa and Larry would discus it later in private.

When Lucy was prepared for surgery it was routine for all her jewelry to be removed. Later it along with the rest of Lucy's belongings had been given to Lucy's dad. He had already given to Larry Lucy's engagement ring.

In the morning Aunt Dora was contacted by Lucy's dad. She agreed to take them to Salem where Lucy's car was. Of course she had heard and read all about the bear poachers and Lucy's death.

After Lucy's parents left with Aunt Dora Larry started thinking about his return to Madera. It was now Sunday and if he took a bus today he might be ready to return to his school some time Monday. Lisa suggested that instead of the long bus ride wouldn't it be better to fly out of Portland to Fresno on Monday. He could get the short distance to Madera using local transportation and be ready to return to his school Tuesday morning. Larry agreed with Lisa. He liked that idea.

It turned out that there was a flight originating in Portland that made a stop in Salem, and several other towns along the way to Fresno. Lisa would take Larry to Salem early Monday morning and they would have the rest of Sunday together. Since there was plenty of time left in the day for a trip to see their folks and return to Corvallis by evening they decided to do that.

They called the farm and Minnie was happy to hear from them. She would have lunch waiting for them.

Lisa with Larry pulled into the farms driveway soon enough that Minnie didn't have to wait lunch; she hadn't started making it as yet. After the hugs and greetings both Minnie and Olaf were expressing how sad they were when learning of Lucy's death. They knew that even if Larry didn't outwardly show his grief, he had lost a very important person in his life.

Gathered around the table enjoying Minnie's ham sandwiches on homemade bread it was a time to talk about more pleasant things. Olaf was interested in Larry's Ag teaching. He was quite interested in the part of the Ag program where students brought in farm equipment for repair.

Students were learning acetylene and arc welding as well as blacksmithing. The schools Ag facilities were first class. They had a couple greenhouses too but the part where students were taught ways to repair the various pieces of farm equipment was the part Larry liked best.

After lunch Olaf took Larry out to his garage work shop to show off his latest project. He had cut willows along the creek and peeled parts for a couple easy chairs that he planned to give to his friends Jim and Julia.

Later in the afternoon Lisa said they should soon be leaving. Minnie wanted them to stay for an early dinner but Lisa declined the invitation explaining that she was taking Larry to Salem early the next morning to catch a flight to Fresno. After hugs and good-byes Larry and Lisa were on the road back to Corvallis.

Most of their conversation was about Lisa's school work except for comments about the road work they saw. They knew that future plans involved building whole new stretches of highway designed to eliminate narrow stretches and sharp curves.

In Corvallis Lisa put together a quick dinner mostly consisting of leftovers. Lisa brought up the subject of Lucy's letter to Larry. She knew that it was on Larry's mind also and she wanted to be sure that Larry really understood what Lucy was telling him.

She started by saying "Larry I know you are blaming yourself for not insisting on not waiting until Christmas time to get married." It seemed to Larry a bit uncanny how his sister was able to know what was on his mind. Larry answered Lisa with "Yes I can't help but think about the couple I met at an overnight stop on a drive to Madera. They told about meeting at their workplace, falling in love and with no time wasted getting married. They had never regretted doing that."

Lisa answered that with "Larry, that was different. That couple worked at the same business but you and Lucy had two completely different work goals. Remember that Lucy had been volunteering with Fish and Wildlife during summer vacations and had her mind set on becoming a member of Oregon's Fish and

Wildlife Department after graduation. She may have loved you enough to go along with your wishes and go with you to California but in the back of her mind there would be a question. Had she made the right decision?"

Larry had to admit that Lisa had made a valid point. Lisa went on to say "It's possible that Lucy may have thought that although giving up her job to get married at Christmas time, after a year of teaching in California you might be ready to start teaching in Oregon and she could get her Fish and Wildlife job back. We don't know that to be a fact but it's something to think about."

Lisa didn't wish to see her brother withdraw into a shell as she knew some did after losing a loved one. She thought he might be receptive to some sisterly advice as "Larry you can't let yourself in your grieving withdraw into a shell. Try to become even more creative in your job and do socialize with your fellow teachers as much as possible. Promise me you'll do your best to follow my suggestions." "I promise," Larry said.

After an early breakfast Larry and Lisa were on the way to Salem when the topic of conversation turned to Christmas planning. Larry, of course, planned to return to Oregon during Christmas break. Larry suggested "Let's plan to celebrate Christmas at the farm with our folks. We could visit with our old friends in Siletz too." "I like that idea." Lisa said and added "I'll bring up the subject with our folks. I'm sure they'll be happy for us all to be together for a time."

Larry bought his ticket to Fresno. The plane's arrival was delayed for some reason so there was a little wait before Larry would give Lisa a hug and thank her for all she had done for him as he said his goodbye and left to board the plane.

During the flight to Fresno Larry was lucky enough to get a window seat. He could try to not think of recent events; just concentrate on trying to identify the places he was seeing. There was a quick stop at Eugene to drop off a passenger and pickup another.

In Fresno there was only a short wait to board the bus that would take him back to Madera where he had to get a taxi to take him from the bus stop to the airport for his pickup.

Back to his apartment he called the school to let them know he would return for work the next morning. Now it was time to think about food for dinner. He might need to take a trip to the grocery.

Later other teachers in the same apartment building had learned that Larry was back from Oregon. They came to welcome him back and to express their condolences. At school the next morning everyone seemed to know what had happened in Oregon and that it was his fiancé who had been shot; they came to express in various ways their sympathy.

Chapter 19

Larry threw himself into his teaching. He was making an effort to meet the parents of all his students at their ranches. There were some students especially in the beginning classes who were not from farms. For various reasons they had enrolled in the Ag class, a few just thought it might be an easy class but some were truly interested. These planned to get jobs on ranches or perhaps have a farm of their own someday. Students in this category usually became good students whereas those who thought it would be an easy class soon dropped out or later just flunked the course.

As Larry visited the different kinds of small farms and large ranches he was especially interested in the many different kinds of equipment it took to handle the various crops. It was often a full time job in some cases for someone to just keep the equipment in working condition.

Greenhouse management was an important part of the Ag program. There was the starting of new plants from seed and then preventing their being lost to bugs or disease.

There were large orchards in the area. Larry had noticed that older trees were continually being removed and young trees often of a different kind were replacing them. Sometimes a different rootstock from the desired variety of a particular fruit was grown that would have a twig from the desired variety grafted to it. These were some of the things that were included in the Ag program. Larry's favorite part of his teaching was repair of tools and farm equipment. Students usually brought simple repair equipment but sometimes complicated machines that required the making of new parts. Madera High School had shop equipment that in some cases was shared between the Industrial Arts Department and the Agriculture Department.

It was almost a month after Larry had returned from Oregon that Lisa called to let him know that there would be a memorial service at the State Capital Building in Salem for Lucy. It would be on the coming Saturday and she thought that he should be there for that. If he could have Friday off to fly to Salem she would meet him at the airport. He could fly back on Sunday and be back teaching on Monday. This was early in the week, Larry said he would see about taking Friday off and get back to her.

When Larry explained to the principal's secretary what he needed to do, she conferred with the principal and came back with an answer. It was a valid reason for an absence. A substitute would be provided for the coming Friday and if for any reason he couldn't be back on Monday, call to let them know and his classes would be covered then also.

Larry called Lisa to let her know that he would catch a flight to Salem on Friday and she said she would be there to meet him. After he called the airport in Fresno for flight time he would call to let her know what time he would arrive in Salem.

Friday all went as planned. Lisa and Larry were sharing lunch in Salem before driving the thirty five miles back to Corvallis. They read in the Salem newspaper that the Memorial for Lucy was scheduled for one o'clock Saturday.

Back in Corvallis Lisa and Larry were discussing what they should do about Friday night's dinner when Larry thought to ask about their friend Willy. Lisa hadn't talked to him for some time but she had learned that he had a girl friend. Larry suggested "Why don't we get in touch with him and invite him and his girl friend to have dinner with us?" "I'll see what I can do." Lisa answered.

Willy had joined a fraternity and was now living at the fraternity house. Lisa called there and was lucky enough to find him there. Lisa broached the subject of dinner with her and Larry. "I have a date with my girl friend. We were planning for a dinner together and later a movie. I haven't talked with Larry for a long time and I'd really like to see him. Of course I've heard on the news about Lucy. I'm sure my friend Wilma won't mind a change of plans. I'll be happy for us to have dinner with you." "I'll be looking forward to meeting Wilma. I'll plan for dinner around six but come anytime after five," Lisa replied.

Now Lisa and Larry really had to hurry a plan for dinner. "I have some salmon fillets in the freezer locker downtown that I brought from Newport. If I go for those could you do them on the barbecue?" Barbecuing salmon was the kind of cooking that Larry liked. Of course he agreed to that.

Back with the salmon Lisa unwrapped and put the fillets in plastic bags. The bags were placed in water to hasten a thaw. Lisa had fruit on hand for a fruit salad. Mashed potatoes and frozen peas with baby onions would pretty much complete the menu except for dessert. There wasn't time enough for pie baking;

they would settle for ice cream and cookies which Lisa had on hand.

Willy and his lady friend arrived a little after five. Willy was met with a handshake from Larry and a hug from Lisa. Then introductions began. "Larry and Lisa I want you to meet my friend Wilma Morrison and Wilma these are my long time friends I've told you about."

About the first thing that Willy had to say as they all prepared to sit down for talk was "Larry I'm so sorry about what happened to Lucy." Larry put his arm around Willy to just say "Thank you."

Willy mentioned that he had read about Saturday's Memorial for Lucy and planned to be there. He looked towards Wilma to say "I might be able to talk Wilma into coming with me." Wilma smiled.

Larry spoke up to ask "Willy where did you find this pretty young lady?" "It was in a class we shared. I needed a date to take to a dance so I just asked her if she would go to that dance with me and she said 'why not' and that was our first date." Wilma spoke up with "A lot of the girls had their eyes on that good looking football guy and I got lucky." That remark brought a good laugh from Larry and Lisa.

Of course Larry and Lisa wanted to know a little more about Wilma. During the course of the conversation before dinner Willy stated that Wilma was from Tillamook and one of her grandparents had been a member of the tribe native to that vicinity. Willy explained to Wilma that Larry and Lisa's mother was half Chipewyan, native to eastern Canada.

In the course of the conversation the subject of Tillamook cheese came up and Wilma commented "All the milk from my parents' dairy is sold to the Tillamook Cheese Factory. If you ever get a chance for a tour of the factory you would find it very interesting." Both Larry and Lisa said that they had been with their folks some years ago and had done that. They remembered snacking on cheese curds and liking it.

As Willy and Wilma were leaving they were both commenting on how much they enjoyed the dinner and Larry and Lisa both commented how happy they were to meet Wilma.

After they were gone Larry and Lisa agreed that Willy had found just the right person for a girl friend. Lisa added "I'll bet that Willy's folks will like her too."

Early Saturday morning Minnie and Olaf called to say they wanted to go with Larry and Lisa to Lucy's Memorial Service. Lisa had answered the phone and said "Do come we can all drive together in your car. Larry and I were going to take my Jeep but your car will be better for the four of us. The Memorial is at one o'clock. I hope you'll stay Saturday night to visit a little with Larry. I'm taking him to Salem Sunday morning to catch his flight back to California." Minnie said "We'll be on the road in a bit and be there around ten o'clock."

They did just that and when the Peterson family arrived at the State Capital Building in Salem shortly before one o'clock they were surprised by the gathering crowd's size. One of the police officers who had worked with Lucy and had met Larry at the hospital in Eugene recognized Larry. A special reserved area had been set aside for Lucy's family and close friends and the Peterson family was taken to that seating area by the police officer. They were greeted by Lucy's parents and Lucy's Aunt Dora already there.

The Director of Oregon's Fish and Wildlife Department stepped up to the podium and the audience quieted. After a few words of welcome to the audience he was silent for a moment before continuing with "We are here today to remember and honor a special member of our organization, Lucy McCredie who gave her life as a serious poaching problem came to a violent end. We wish also to officially offer our condolences to Lucy's family and to Lucy's fiancé who are with us here today."

The director read a letter from the Governor. He was commissioning the making of a bronze plaque to be placed on the wall in the main office of the Fish and Wildlife Department. It would be honoring the bravery and dedication to duty exhibited by Lucy McCredie who gave her life during the violent ending of a serious poaching problem.

Next the two State Police officers who had formed the team with Lucy were called to the podium to give a brief account of the bear poaching problem that existed in the state and how they eventually learned the identity of the poachers. They told of Lucy's determination to end the poaching problem. Knowing the danger but with no hesitation Lucy was eager to have a part in the final push to end the bear poaching. She was credited with personally putting down the poachers' leader while at the same time receiving a wound that later became fatal.

The Director thanked all for coming and said any questions should be directed to the offices of State Police or Fish and Wildlife. As the crowd started to leave he came to have a few private words with the families of Lucy and Larry.

As Larry's group were leaving Willy and Wilma came to say hello. After a few parting words they left and Larry was approached by a couple. "Remember us?" They both spoke at the same time. "Of course I do. How could I ever forget Tom and Gerry?" Larry responded. He called Lisa to come meet the couple he had told her of meeting at the rest stop by the Klamath River.

They wanted to offer their condolences and to thank him for the advice he had given them about Yosemite.   Their visit to the park had been an experience to treasure. If he ever had occasion to be in Portland please come to see them at Meier and Frank Department store. Larry promised to do that as they parted.

On the short trip back to Corvallis nothing much was said about the Memorial service but it was on their minds. Olaf and Minnie were going to spend the night in Corvallis. Minnie planned to do a little shopping before returning to the farm. Now the question about dinner came up. Larry said "Let's keep it simple. Lisa, do you have all we need for a spaghetti dinner?" "Yes, except let's stop at a market for some ground beef to mix with the spaghetti sauce I have. Or I think there's still some in our downtown locker. We could go for that." "Oh, let's just pick up some fresh at a market so we won't have to thaw it out," Larry said. Olaf was driving and asked for directions. "I'll guide you," Lisa spoke up to say.

Later at the table enjoying their spaghetti along with their favorite red wine, zinfandel, they did have a few words to say about the memorial and the governor's plaque. Minnie thought proper recognition had been given to Lucy's part in the breaking up of the bear poaching group. Lisa said that she knew all the time how obsessed Lucy was with breaking up the bear poaching. She thought that if the bear poaching had still been happening at Christmas time when she was to marry Larry, she would have wanted to postpone the marriage. After thinking about that a bit, Larry spoke up to agree that probably Lucy's obsession was so strong that she would not have been ready to resign from Fish and Wildlife to marry and return with him to Madera.

The next morning after saying goodbye to his folks, Larry and Lisa were on the way to Salem. Larry was not talkative, he seemed to be deep in thought and Lisa was quite certain as to what was on her brother's mind. As they neared the Salem Airport Lisa said "Larry, remember the things Lucy said in her letter to you. Please try to forget these recent bad happenings. They belong to the past. There will be good things in the future like the Christmas get-together at the farm. We'll be meeting with our friends from Siletz. You might even get to meet a guy I like a lot." This last statement really got Larry's attention. "You have a boyfriend?" Larry asked. "Well not really but there is a guy who likes me and I like who I've dated a few times."

There was no time to discus that subject, there was only time for Larry to give his sister a hug, say good bye and leave for boarding his flight.

Back on the job, Larry did his best to follow his sister's advice and surprisingly the time did seem to pass by rather quickly.

So quickly in fact that it was Christmas break and Larry was on the way to Oregon. He knew that Lisa was already at the farm so decided to cut over to the coast at Sutherlin, a route that brought him to the coast highway at Reedsport. A short distance up the coast just south of Florence was a Forest Service campground beside beautiful Takenitch Lake and that's where Larry would camp.

He was tired and here was a great place to relax but looking at the lake he did wish he had an inflatable raft of some sort. He knew that there were several kinds of fish in this lake. Even though it was winter time he knew that even now there were catchable fish in that lake.

In the morning he walked to the nearby boat launch where he observed a person fishing from the boat tie up float which extended aways out into the lake. That's when he decided to spend an extra day at Takenitch Lake.

On the road again early the next morning Larry was thinking he had been lucky. He had Eastern Perch for dinner last night caught from the boat float. Perch are not very large, only a little over six inches in length but quite meaty for their length.

On the farm about the first topic in Larry's conversation was his description of the part of his trip from Madera on the coast highway. It was slow and curvy in places but followed a beautiful stretch of Oregon's Coast.

Christmas dinner promised to be quite an event. Lisa and her mom were full of menu ideas but at the same time wanted to keep it simple. The main meat dish would be ham, but Willy's dad, Ivan, was also bringing roast Chinook salmon, fresh caught in the Siletz River.

Willy's girl friend was driving down from Tillamook to join the group and Olaf's fishing and hunting buddy, Jim and his wife Julie would also be with them. They were bringing a venison roast. Their daughter Marie was spending Christmas with her boy friend's parents in Seattle. Lisa would drive to Newport to pick up her friend since he had no car. Charlie was a crew member on a Coast Guard cutter stationed in Newport. Lisa was not quite ready to call him her boyfriend.

Counting, it looked to Larry that there would be eleven people all told at Christmas dinner, a time of getting together for old and new friends. Luckily the big old dining table had extra leaves to seat twelve.

Needless to say but that dinner was a success. Even though these people were all hearty eaters there were goodly portions for all to take home afterwards. This had been a repeat of past Christmases except for Wilma and Charlie. Lisa hadn't talked much about her friend so when she returned from Newport with him even before she introduced him, they could see that the young man in dress uniform was a Petty Officer first class in the Coast Guard. Larry knew that Lisa was very particular when choosing close friends and after listening to Charlie's conversation a bit he thought Lisa had used good judgment; he liked Charlie.

Before ending his visit at the farm, Larry and Lisa went steelhead fishing on the Siletz River with their dad. Three steelhead were laid out to cut and wrap for the freezer. Larry and Olaf each had a steelhead when they were about to leave the river. It looked like Lisa was about to be skunked until she made one more cast and caught the best fish of the day, a nice eight pounder. Of course all didn't go in the freezer; Larry barbecued enough for a dinner the Peterson family enjoyed with a little left over.

Lisa would take several steelhead packages to put in the freezer compartment of the fridge rather than the one in downtown Corvallis. Larry would be leaving first and his would be in his cold box with dry ice to keep them frozen until he got back to Madera.

In her conversations with Larry, Lisa could see that Larry even though he still thought about Lucy he was not letting losing her dominate his thoughts. She was happy when Larry said "I like your judgment when picking boyfriends. I really liked Charlie. I think he's a keeper!"

Lisa said "We first met at a dance at the 'Nat' and I liked dancing with him. We've gone to several movies together. That was last summer when I was on the research ship. I'd only seen him a couple times when I came from Corvallis to go to dances at the 'Nat' with him."

(Note: For those not familiar with the "Nat" it is a heated sea water natatorium at the edge of Newport's Nye Beach. Up stairs in one end of the building is a very popular dance hall with dances every Saturday night.)

Chapter 20

Back from Christmas break Larry was soon immersed in his teaching routine. By this time in the school year Larry's students were intent on completing their projects; some of which were somewhat complex involving major repairs to farm equipment.

One major summer plan always on Larry's mind was planning a five day back packing trip to explore Mono Creek and the recesses or as much as he could.

When the last day of school arrived parents came to pick up the projects on which students had made repairs. Seniors would not be back next school year and he knew that some of those would be missed; they were his best students and a pleasure to work with.

Summer didn't come to the high country as early as it did in the San Joaquin Valley. His plan was to spend the early part of summer in Oregon and then come back for his back packing in August.

Larry decided to spend a little time in Corvallis before going to the farm. Even though he knew Lisa was already there preparing to return to her summer job on the ship.

One thing Larry wanted to do was drive to Detroit. The main thing was to touch bases with Lucy's parents and perhaps do a little fishing in Detroit Lake. In talking to Lucy's dad he learned that he had taken half of Lucy's ashes with him on a routine helicopter flight around the Detroit area. Her ashes were scattered over areas where they had hunted together and shot her first deer. Some fell in the upper Santiam River and would end up in the lake she loved. The other half of her ashes would be buried in their family plot.

Larry rented a boat for a bit of fishing in the lake. He didn't try for a trophy Brown only trolling for trout. He did catch several nice rainbows before returning the boat but he wasn't happy on the lake; it just wasn't the same as when he was on the lake with Lucy.

In Corvallis, Larry went to the Ag Department to see if there might be someone there he knew. He did talk a bit about his teaching in Madera with former instructors.

Before going to the farm there was one bit of nostalgia that he wanted to relive. The first stream he had fished after coming to Corvallis was the Luckiamute and he just wanted to fish it once more. The first time he fished there he was alone and that was the part he wanted to remember even though later he had fished there with both Lucy and Lisa.

On the banks of the Luckiamute at the spot where he had first cast a fly it seemed like the same Kingfisher was flying by with its familiar chatter. A trout made a pass at his fly on his first cast. The trout came back to take the fly on Larry's second cast. Larry carefully unhooked and released it. He had his nostalgia moment and now he was ready to return to Corvallis and leave for the coast and the farm the next day.

At the farm he caught small trout in the stream where he and Lisa had caught their first trout. He released what he caught; they were small and there were larger trout waiting for him in the Siletz Gorge.

Olaf as usual was repairing some equipment for a neighbor. Larry joined his dad to help and commented that he thought a repair and fixit kind of business would be something he would like.

In general he liked teaching but at times it was frustrating especially with some beginning students. While most were receptive to learning there were some that just seemed determined to not learn anything. Even though those were in the minority his failure to interest them in learning really bothered and bugged him. Sometimes it made him feel that he was a failure and his fault that those few kids didn't want to learn anything.

Larry's dad agreed that a fixit business would be interesting but personally at his age he wouldn't like being tied down to a regular job routine again. He was in good health and enjoyed doing what he wanted to do when he wanted to do it.

Time at the farm went by so quickly it seemed. There was a big garden that he was able to help with a bit. Once Lisa came for an overnight visit and a couple times Larry drove to spend a day in Newport with Lisa and once with Charlie on his ship.

With goodbyes said to all Larry was again on the road back to Madera. This time was different; he was planning to take the Coast Highway all the way to south of Eureka where he would cut over to meet I-5 at Red Bluff.

This really was a scenic drive with many stops along the way just to admire the many beauty spots along the coast. He made it to a campground near Brookings before stopping for the night. By rights he should have been pooped but wasn't that tired because he had taken his time and was under no pressure to hurry.

Two days later Larry was gathering together all his back packing gear and fly fishing tackle as well as making a list of the special dehydrated food that he would need for five days. He knew that he could just about live on the fish he could catch. He had tied up a few experimental flies and had extra leaders and tippet material.

Larry didn't use a tent; instead he had what was called a tent tarp. It would shed rain and with its ties and grommets could be set up in a number of configurations. He had a lightweight mummy bag which he placed inside a special sack he had made. It was made of a breathable rip stop material above and a damp proof material for next to the ground. Depending on the weather sometimes that was all he needed and didn't use the tent tarp.

Even in August the weather was sometimes unpredictable. Sudden thunderstorms with hail or rain showers could happen. A light weight raincoat or poncho was a needed item. Dressing with layer combinations he had learned was a good idea. Hiking up hill with a fifty pound pack could warm up a person. A heavy wool shirt and a windbreaker were two clothing items he liked.

Larry found a store in Madera that had all the dehydrated food supplies he needed. He had Lipton's tea bags, instant coffee, and cocoa. He also had a pint of brandy that he had taken from its heavy glass bottle to a plastic container. Larry had found that a cup of hot cocoa with a little brandy added was a good drink to sip as he watched the flickering flames in his campfire before slipping into his sleeping bag for the night.

With everything checked and double checked and in his pickup Larry felt that he was ready to head to Edison Lake in the morning.

He did that and was all set to sleep in his pickup in the lodge parking area. He had his ferry tickets and would be ready to board the ferry in the morning. He noticed in a farther away part of the parking area a lady and a large dog beside a station wagon; it looked like she was preparing to sleep in her vehicle just as he was doing.

In the morning after a breakfast in the lodge, Larry gathered up his pack and fishing tackle, locked his pickup and joined the group already on the ferry. On the ferry he realized that the lady with the large dog was the same lady he had talked with the previous summer. She recognized him at the same time and they started to introduce themselves to each other.

"I'm Larry Peterson and I'm an Ag teacher in Madera and that's a nice Lab you have." Larry volunteered. "My name is Georgia Brown and I start teaching in Oakhurst this fall and my dog's name is Girlie. You can see that she is carrying her own food," Georgia answered.

Larry and Georgia were the only passengers with back packs. After getting off the ferry as they started walking up the trail together Georgia explained that she was taking pictures of streamside plants on Mono Creek and hoped to eventually write a book on the subject. Larry was thinking as they walked "I wonder if we'll be making camp together tonight and I wonder what sort of a person is Georgia Brown?"

Chapter 21
Georgia Louisa Brown

At a hospital in Fresno, Betty Brown and her husband George were loading their '31 Ford sedan with belongings including a bassinette for their two day old baby girl. Betty got herself situated in the passenger seat ready for a nurse to hand her little Georgia.

As George drove toward Firebaugh he remarked, "BB, I was just thinking about us leaving home in a rush to get to the hospital with little time to spare because your time came several days sooner than expected. Now the drive is almost leisurely."

George always called his wife BB because that was her nickname in school. They were classmates and she was his sweetheart. At that time her name was Betty Boone and now it was Betty Brown, the nickname still fit.

BB and George had talked about getting married after they graduated but after graduation George wanted to fulfill a dream, he had always wanted to be a Navy Sailor. They talked it over, should they get married now or wait until he completed his four year enlistment? They decided to wait the four years. George enlisted right after graduation in 1932. While George was in the Navy, BB found an office job in Firebaugh and as soon as she had earned enough for a down payment she bought a used '31 Ford which they were now driving.

The farm near Firebaugh had been in the family for a long time. George's grandfather had acquired the property in 1906 after returning from Alaska. He had been lucky in a card game during the gold rush. Like many others luck with finding gold had not been with him. It was George's father who started raising Black Angus cattle both for beef and for breeding stock shortly after George was born.

After George completed his enlistment and left the Navy as a Machinist Mate 2nd Class in 1936, George said "BB, now it's time to do what we talked about." After they were married his parents turned the management of the farm over to him and moved up to Bass Lake. The family had owned for a long time a cabin on a choice bit of property there. Now after two years of marriage little Georgia had come into their lives on July 1, 1938.

In 1940 congress passed the Selective Service Act and George had to register for the draft. Because of his occupation in an essential industry and his prior military service he was given a deferment, III-C. This was because of dependents and employment in an agricultural occupation. He could also have been deferred because of previously completing military service, IV-A.

The little cabin at Bass Lake had been enlarged and a roomy deck added. This was the scene where George was just finishing a speech pretty much covering the forgoing information. It was Georgia's 18th birthday and family with close friends had gathered to celebrate the occasion.

High school had been fun. She had been on the girl's basketball team. She liked reading and learning, especially biological sciences. For a senior project she had identified and photographed the plant life along the irrigation canal banks in the surrounding area. It was only natural that she would be active in the schools

4H program. She had raised several Black Angus for the market.

She was ready now to enter Fresno State. Her wish was to become a science teacher. Botany would be a special interest. She wished also to sharpen her photography skills regarding her interest in plant life photography. A combination graduation and birthday present from her parents was the most suitable camera for that purpose that they could find.

At home in Firebaugh she had her own well equipped darkroom where she developed her film and did her enlargements. She had done well with her old camera. Now with professional equipment she could do even better.

Georgia's foreign language in high school had been Spanish, mainly because for many farm workers in the surrounding area Spanish was the usual language used. Now in college she realized that she needed Latin because Latin was used for the botanical names for plants.

Sharon had been Georgia's best friend since elementary school and was with Georgia now at Fresno State. The two girls shared an apartment near the college. Sharon wanted a degree in business technology. They shared several classes but most were different.

Both girls had been very popular in high school and if either had given any of their boyfriends any encouragement they would now be married. Now they were happy that they had not done that.

Sharon and Georgia remembered the fun they had with basketball in high school and discussed the pros and cons as to trying out for the Fresno State Girls basketball team. Their final decision was no. Better that they should put all their efforts into studies relating to their major fields. They were well aware that high marks at graduation would affect chances for finding the jobs they would look for in the future.

Georgia was finding that to qualify for a teaching certificate there were certain required courses such as psychology and school law that had nothing to do with her major interests such as plant life. As a general science teacher she understood that she had to know at least a little about many things. Science survey courses covered everything from astronomy to basic chemistry.

Georgia's work in 4H plus farm life in general had been an education by itself. She already had a basic understanding of the chemistry involved with sprays, fertilizers, and the medicines prescribed for farm animals.

Her mind had been focused on high school teaching and she was finding that among her fellow students, some wanted to work with primary age children while other's goal was college teaching. Some were looking at school administration as a goal.

Sharon too was finding that her major could take her in many directions. She could find secretarial work in large corporations or small businesses of many kinds. A starting job could be a stepping stone to other and various positions within a large business enterprise.

Studying the structure of a large corporation she realized that some operated on a worldwide basis. One such corporation that had been selected for study was Bechtel. Within that company were engineers specializing in everything from building oil refineries in foreign nations to dams in the United States. Then there was management. She was surprised to learn that the Superintendant in charge when the dam was built in Vermillion Valley that formed Edison Lake just three hours driving time east from Fresno had graduated from Dos Palos High School. Dos Palos was a neighboring town to her home town, Firebaugh.

Sharon was a bit curious about how this so called local boy had risen to a position such as being in charge of the building of the Vermillion Valley Dam. She found that his personal ambition and drive was a factor, but there were other things too. He understood the work and problems of those he supervised because he had started working for Bechtel as a cat skinner in the building of Shasta Dam in northern California. He was successful with getting things done because he had the loyalty of those he supervised.

Both Georgia and Sharon were now in their senior year and had been given assignments which required them to turn in a paper relating to a study of something relating to their major field. The two girls talked about this at length. Just about what should they write?

Sharon thought that she might get an idea from seeing the dam that Bechtel had built. Georgia too was interested in seeing Edison Lake. They decided to get an early start one Saturday morning for the drive to Edison Lake. They had read a little about the lake and knew that there was a lodge and campground at the lake. They would gather up enough camping equipment for an overnight stay.

They found that to be a very interesting drive. Past beautiful Huntington Lake there was a steep climb to over 9,000 ft. elevation high Kaiser Pass and then down to a crossing of an upper reach of the San Joaquin River and then up again to over 7,000 ft. elevation Edison Lake.

It was a surprise that the lake appeared much larger than they had imagined it would be. They found out that the lake was about seven miles long and that there was a trail where they could hike to the upper end of the lake. If they didn't wish to hike they could take a ferry which made a run to the upper end of the lake every morning and again in late afternoon.

There would be a change in plans. There was no good reason why they couldn't stay over Sunday night and return to Fresno Monday morning. They would miss a couple forenoon classes but be there for afternoon classes.

The plan would be to spend Saturday around the dam and lake, then on Sunday take the morning ferry to the upper end to spend the day along Mono Creek then catch the afternoon ferry back to camp.

They were at the resort to buy their round trip ferry tickets with time to spare. Their lunches with drinks along were in day packs. Georgia had her camera on a strap over her shoulder, and with notebook in her pocket she was ready to take notes as she took pictures. She didn't know what sort of streamside plants she would find along Mono Creek.

As passengers picked up their belongings they noticed that several had large back packs and it was obvious that they planned to be in the wilderness area for some time. She also learned that those who planned to do that had to have a Wilderness Pass. It would state how long the person planned to be in the wilderness and the general area where the person planned to be.

For what Georgia and Sharon were doing passes were not necessary.

About the first thing Georgia noticed was that some stretches along the stream had willows so thick that it was almost impossible to get to the waters edge. However, she noticed that in some areas the willows were a little different, they were larger and their leaves were a little different too.

Suddenly Georgia had the answer to something that had been bothering her. "Sharon, now I know the subject I'll write about. I'll research willows, pick out a specific variety and find out all I can about it. It'll be one of the kinds we see here," Georgia excitedly turned to Sharon to say. Sharon answered to that with, "great idea." Georgia took pictures of leaves and bark on the different kinds and in her notebook she noted where each grew. Georgia noted that some were only at the stream bank while others were often well away from the stream.

On the return ferry among the passengers were several with large packs. It was obvious that they were returning from time having been spent in the wilderness. They were talking about places called "recesses." Curious, Georgia asked one of them, "I hear you talking about something called a recess, what's that?" The man explained, "There are four side streams along Mono Creek. They are to the south and have their sources at small lakes." "I see that I'll have to pick up some Muir Wilderness Maps," Georgia responded. "If you plan to spend time in this area, they are a necessity," the man answered.

On the morning trip they had noticed one person with only a day pack. He had a creel and a fly rod taken apart. Now on the return trip they could see that the creel was not empty like it was in the morning. Georgia commented on that. He opened the creel to show a limit of nice trout to say, "Mono Creek is always good fishing, especially with flies." Back at the resort Georgia and Sharon noted that the guy got in his pickup and left. He wasn't camping.

Sharon and Georgia were up early to break camp and get on the road home. They would miss morning classes but they intended to be home for afternoon classes. Sharon talked about ideas for the paper she was going to write. She understood that the dam and Edison Lake had destroyed a beautiful area. To Georgia she said, "I think that my paper will explain how commercial interests had destroyed a thing of value while creating another of perhaps greater value. What do you think of that idea?" "I think that lake will probably attract more people that the valley ever did. Your idea can make for just the kind of paper your professor is looking for.

Georgia spent some time in the college library digging up as much information as she could on willow varieties. She learned that the willow family was large. Some varieties were quite large while some grew hardly taller than a person. She had noticed a small variety and photographed it on Mono Creek. It was the one she was considering as the main subject for her paper.

Georgia found that researching willows was not as easy as she had thought it would be, it was difficult. With 350 willow varieties narrowing down to a specific photograph and memory of the plants appearance, about the time she found one that seemed to match her plants appearance she would discover that it was not found above 3,000 ft. elevation She realized that what she should do was collect twig and leaf specimens of the ones she wanted to write about. She was certain that some streamside plant specialist could identify what she had. She must make another trip to Edison Lake.

Chapter 22

Georgia and Sharon had graduated with honors. Their papers had received high marks. Now their challenge was finding where they would make use of what they had learned from four years of study at Fresno State. Sharon had done all that research on Bechtel as part of a study of international business organizations. Her plan now was to investigate the possibility of an entry level job in that company

Georgia had done her student teaching in Clovis. The Teacher Placement Secretary at Fresno State had given her a list of school districts around the state with job openings for teachers in her field. One that immediately caught her eye was at the high school in Oakhurst. That would be an easy drive from Bass Lake where she could live. She asked the Placement Secretary to send her qualification papers there and arrange for an interview date.

The date and time had come and Georgia was at the School District office for her interview. She found that they were looking for a teacher for ninth grade general science and at the same time be qualified to teach twelfth grade physical science and a class in plant biology. Georgia felt that she was well qualified to do this and let the assistant principal know that. He and the principal had of course already read her college record and they wondered about her high school life and her other than school personal interests. Georgia told about her high school experiences and growing up on a farm in Firebaugh. With regard to plant biology she mentioned the senior study of vegetation along the irrigation canals that she had done and also the paper she had done on a particular willow on Mono Creek.

She was told that she would receive in the mail their decision regarding her job application. The letter came, she was offered the job. There was a contract to sign showing what her starting salary would be, etc. She was happy to sign and return it.

She explained to Sharon what had happened and was ready to move all her belongings to the cabin at Bass Lake. Sharon too had some news for Georgia. She had found someone to talk to at Bechtel and had been directed to a person in charge of hiring. In her interview she was asked, "What foreign languages do you speak?" Looking at her college record and learning that she was fluent with Spanish, she was asked if she would be willing to consider working in Spain. It was explained that Bechtel was working on a possible contract concerning the building of an electrical power generating plant. This was a thing that Bechtel had done previously in other countries.

Sharon didn't have an objection to working in Spain, however she had never had occasion to travel out of the United States and didn't have a passport. She was told that if she would acquire a passport and be willing to work in Spain, Bechtel would definitely use her in some capacity there. She said that she would apply for a passport immediately and let him know when she had it.

Georgia and Sharon just had to drive over to Firebaugh right away to tell their parents the good news about jobs. Naturally, the parents of both were very happy to learn their daughters' success with job hunting. Sharon's parents were not too happy about her not being closer to home with her job, but realized that it would probably work out to be a good thing.

Georgia's parents were happy that Georgia would be living in the cabin at Bass Lake. Especially now since George's parents were planning to move to a care facility in Fresno. Their health was such that it was becoming more and more difficult to maintain a normal day to day life at Bass Lake.

George was a duck hunter and always had a couple Labradors at the farm. He had a friend who owned a male yellow Lab that was not only a very good duck retriever but was also a great pheasant pointer and retriever of wounded birds that were sometimes quite difficult to find. George had used that Lab to breed his female. In the resultant litter there was a yellow female pup that he had in mind to keep and train as a gift for Georgia. Now he thought was the time to give it to her. It was almost a year old and was trained to heel off leash as well as being house broken That pup was smart and learned quickly that there were things it was not supposed to do in the house.

George was aware that there would need to be an all weather kennel arrangement for the dog when Georgia was not at home and couldn't have the dog with her. He would come to Bass Lake to take care of that after explaining to Georgia what he had in mind.

Georgia immediately fell in love with her gift and her parents were happy to see that the young Lab seemed quite attracted to Georgia as well. As George was training the pup he had just called her Girlie. If Georgia didn't like that she could easily train the young dog to answer to another name. Georgia thought the name was quite fitting, at least for now.

Georgia had all her belongings at Bass Lake and she had tentative lesson plans ready for school opening. She knew that they might need changes after she met her students. She had visited the classrooms and seen the equipment available for her teaching.

Another thing that Georgia had done was go to a store in Fresno that specialized in backpacking equipment and supplies. Georgia had a vague idea; she would like to do a book with pictures and descriptions of the streamside plants along Mono Creek. She knew that she couldn't accomplish what she wanted to do with just day trips. She picked out a backpack that fit her needs along with nesting pots for cooking. Georgia knew that sometimes there could be sudden thunder and lightning storms with rain or hail. She learned that generally the weather was best for back packing in August. She found a lightweight one person tent, plus a lightweight mummy bag and pad. The store had a good assortment of freeze dried food and Georgia bought a good supply of what she thought she would like. In the store she also found saddle bags for Girlie. With dry dog food plus doggie snacks, Girlie she thought should carry at least most of her own food.

With all that new equipment Georgia had a plan. She would go to Mono Creek to hike upstream as far as she comfortably could just to see what the stream was like above the part she had seen. If she found a comfortable camp site, she might just use it as a base camp as she studied the streamside vegetation in the area. Georgia would plan for four nights camping and have her Wilderness Pass for that period of time. She not only had her Wilderness Pass but also two maps of the Mono Creek area. One was a topo map.

On the ferry one of the passengers seemed familiar to her. He too had noticed her and stepped over to speak to her. "Didn't I speak with you and another young lady here on the ferry last year?" "Yes, and you showed me a creel with a limit of trout," Georgia answered. "I see that you are equipped for more than a day hike this time," he commented. Georgia explained that she planned to hike upstream a comfortable distance to camp. She explained that she planned to do a study of streamside plants for a book she wanted to do. She only planned to camp for four nights.

The guy seemed quite interested. He said that he just liked to fly fish Mono Creek and planned to camp five nights. "By the way my name is Larry Peterson. I teach Agriculture at Madera High School." Georgia responded to that with, "My name is Georgia Brown and I'm going to start my first year teaching as a Science teacher at the High School in Oakhurst." "Welcome to the world of teaching," Larry said as they shook hands. Then added, "That's a nice Lab you have." Georgia said, "Yes, she's a great companion. Her name is Girlie and she's carrying most of her own food."

The only ferry passengers to get off with backpacks were Larry and Georgia. As they started walking up the trail together Georgia wondered, would she be making camp tonight with a man she hardly knew? Really, who is this guy who calls himself Larry Peterson?

Chapter 23
Larry and Georgia

As Larry and Georgia walked up the trail together they talked. At one point he was explaining the advantages for crossing the river on a bridge. The reason for the bridge was a trail going south and not a trail they would follow but there was an old trail no longer maintained that followed Mono creek to the camp spot he wanted to camp tonight.

He suggested that if Georgia looked at her trail map she would see that the maintained trail went up a fairly steep climb to where it forked with the one to the north following the north fork of Mono Creek. The fork to the east would eventually come back to following the main stream. He thought from his experience the summer before that it would be the best route to follow when returning to Edison Lake.

Larry went on to describe the campsite he had seen the summer before and liked. "There was space between two flat rocks for a cooking fire and with a large flat rock to use as a table for cooking pots and meal preparation etc. Also there is a previously used spot for a social fire. He had seen a spot under a spruce tree where branches touched the ground. There was just enough room on top of a bed of spruce needles for rolling out a sleeping bag and near by was a flat area good for her little tent that I can see rolled up at the bottom of your pack. You're welcome to join me there. It's a good campsite for two or three people."

Georgia indicated that she thought camping this night with him would be a good idea. Larry went on to say that he was sure that he could catch trout enough for both by dinner time.

As they worked their way following the overgrown old trail Larry sometimes stopped to cast a fly to a likely spot. Georgia watched as Larry landed another trout for their dinner. There were several times that they had to climb over aspens that had fallen across what had been a path.

Larry was surprised when Georgia suddenly started laughing. He hadn't said anything he thought to be funny. He just had to ask "Georgia, what made you start laughing?"

Georgia answered "Well, I just got to thinking about a guy and a gal, school teachers who hardly know each other picking their way along a creek where the guy is catching fish for dinner at a campsite where they plan to camp together!" Larry did have to admit that yes there was a little humor in an unusual situation.

Larry was thinking to himself "I like the way Georgia looks at things in life with its sometimes strange happenings. She seems to be serious about life in a light hearted way."

When they reached the camp spot Larry had described Georgia had to say "I see why you wanted to camp here and I like the sound that nearby little water fall makes. It's a musical sound." "I think so too," Larry responded.

Georgia looked around for the best spot for her tent and parked her pack against a tree. Larry set his pack down and immediately started laying out cooking utensils on the flat rock beside where the cooking fire would be. He had a lightweight little grate to place across the opening where the cooking fire would be. Nature had arranged the flat rocks perfectly. Behind those was the massive rock from which they had broken away.

Georgia had been watching Larry's work and commented that she too had nesting utensils and a nine inch fry pan like his and was ready to share if needed. Larry had caught and released trout but kept four between eight and nine inches. There was discussion about cooking trout. "Some cut off the heads but I like to fry them with heads on. Besides, the little trout cheeks are a delicacy," Larry commented. "Cooking trout is something where I have no experience. My dad was a hunter, not a fisherman so I learned a lot about cooking ducks and pheasants that my dad brought home," was Georgia's answer.

"Why not if we are to camp and cook together that we share food supplies and work? I have dehydrated potatoes and string beans that I think would go well with your fish," Georgia offered. "Sounds good to me" was an answer Georgia liked.

Larry had bacon grease he always saved just for frying trout and he had a container of a mix he had worked out for coating his trout before frying. The upshot of all this was that their meal together was a good one and now they were sitting on a log in front of their social fire as they talked and sipped hot tea.

Georgia and Larry were slowly getting a little more acquainted with each other. Larry was describing his Ag teaching and Georgia was describing what she hoped to do in her science classes. They talked about the areas where they grew up and a little about their families. Georgia had noticed the ring that Larry wore on a chain around his neck and could no longer contain her curiosity. "Larry, I'm curious about the ring you wear on the chain around your neck? Is there some special significance attached to it?"

Larry said "yes" and went on to explain that it was the ring he had given to his fiancé. They planned to marry during Christmas break the year before last Christmas but she had lost her life to gun fire during an Oregon Fish and Wildlife breaking up of a bear poaching operation before that could happen.

Larry did go on to tell a little about meeting Lucy at Oregon State and her goal which was becoming a member of Oregon's Department of Fish and Wildlife which she did.

The conversation eventually turned to plans for the next day. Georgia would study the plant life along nearby sections of the stream and camp another night at this same place. Larry spoke up to say that he planned to fish up stream to First Recess. "If that looks interesting I may explore it a bit. I'll plan to come back here and if you can stand another trout dinner I'll bring back enough for that." Georgia came back with "Those trout were so good. Sure, I'm ready for more."

Getting ready for sleep time involved getting their food sacks out of reach of a wandering bear. Larry had long nylon line. He put a rock in a little sack on the end and tossed it over a long limb on the nearest tree. The rock weight was lowered and food sacks were hoisted out of a bear's reach. A point was made to secure the tie down well to the side.

Well aware that nature would call they had established the directions into the trees for each. Larry was happy to see that Georgia carried a garden trowel when she answered natures call. He had a little light weigh hardened aluminum shovel with a short wood handle. He had made the thing in a school shop class.

During breakfast after commenting on how well they slept the discussion turned to the comparison of powdered eggs to fresh. "Not bad when mixed with a few bacon bits," was Larry's comment." "Go's good too with that bread you call bannock bread that you did in your fry pan," Georgia added.

Larry was talking as he was stuffing some things in his day pack and saying "Georgia, I know you get out in the stream to take pictures of things. Be careful, those rocks are slippery." "I try to be careful. What I really need is a pair of those felt sole shoes made to wear on fisherman's waders. I don't see you using them," Georgia said and Larry commented, "that's because I fish mainly from the banks of the stream rather than wading."

Larry picked up his fly rod and headed up stream saying "I'll be back in late afternoon with enough trout for dinner." To that Georgia said "YOU be careful and have a good day." Georgia picked up her notebook and camera and headed back downstream to check out some plants she had seen as they hiked to their campsite the previous day. Girlie trotted on ahead, with her saddle bags left in camp. Given a chance she could have a swim; she loved getting in the water.

Georgia instead of just thinking to herself frequently shared her thoughts with Girlie. "Girlie, I didn't know how sharing a campsite with a guy I didn't know would be. I rather like this Larry guy and I think you do too." Girlie wagged her tail; she liked it when Georgia talked to her.

As Larry hiked up the trail there were frequent stops to fish an inviting stretch of water. He was discovering that in certain stretches of water he caught rainbow and brown trout, in others only rainbow and in another only eastern brooks. He was releasing all he caught at this time; his intentions were in the afternoon to save enough for dinner.

Thinking about dinner made him think a bit about the attractive young lady with whom he was sharing a camp. It wasn't her good looks as much as her personality that Larry was thinking about. At the same time as she was quite serious about the book she planned to write and her teaching plans, she seemed to take her life in a light hearted manner. There was always something to smile or laugh about.

Larry cast his fly to deep holes and shallow riffles and trout rose to have a look at it. Those he caught and released, he thought were more curious than hungry when they took his fly. Mono Creek had plenty natural food for trout.

It was lunch time when Larry came to Second Recess with its sizeable stream entering Mono Creek from the south. Nearby was a well used camp spot. As he ate his lunch he made plans; this is where he would make camp the next day. He could camp here for two nights giving him time to explore the Second Recess as well as a nearby stream coming from the north.

Larry realized that he had climbed quite a bit in elevation; some places on the trail that had been quite steep. His goal now as he headed back toward camp was to catch and keep enough trout for dinner for two and they had to be between eight and nine inch fish to fit their fry pans and it would be nice to have a camping companion.

It was well into the afternoon when Larry walked into camp. He had released quite a number of smaller and larger trout before reaching his size goal. Girlie had seen him coming and rushed to greet him. Georgia smiled and said "I think Girlie has found a new friend." And she thought to herself that perhaps she had too.

Georgia had gathered wood for both the cooking fire and the social fire and she had both of them started. Before starting to cook they sat down by the social fire while Larry described his trip upstream and the campsite near Second Recess. He explained his plan for camping two nights there while exploring both Second Recess and the stream coming from the north.

As they started preparing dinner sharing trail food from both their packs and the trout, Georgia explained that she had studied the streamside vegetation both upstream and down. She had made notes and taken pictures and she too was ready to head upstream the next day. "The campsite you described sounds good to me and I'd like to share it with you if you wouldn't mind," Georgia said. Larry answered that with "I'd like that."

The next morning as they hiked on the trail heading upstream Larry couldn't resist even with a heavy pack on his back flipping his fly into an inviting pool. And of course a rainbow trout couldn't resist that strange bug just a little different from her usual diet. And Georgia couldn't resist a comment on the tableau as it unfolded---Larry at the edge of a pool casually flipping his fly and as it settled near the opposite bank a trout leaping to grab it. "That was like an artist with one stroke of a brush creating a picture, you really are an artist with that fly rod."

Larry had to think a moment as he released the trout; he didn't have a ready answer to Georgia's comment. He finally answered with "I never thought of my fly fishing that way. I like the challenge just getting my fly to a particular spot without getting it caught in bush or something and by the way would you like trout for dinner again tonight? The answer to that was "I think fresh trout beats our freeze dried food by a mile. Sure, I'm always ready for a trout dinner or perhaps lunch too."

"I'll wait until this afternoon before I save fish for dinner," Larry commented and the two hikers with their heavy packs didn't do much talking as they hiked. They had to save their breath; there were some rough and steep spots along the trail.

It was about midday and time for rest and lunch when they came to a particularly scenic spot. A narrow channel in bedrock shot a fast flow of water into a deep pool. Streamside plants draped over the bank along the far side. Georgia looked at that and got out her camera and notebook to make a record of the scene and specifically the streamside plants of which there were several.

As they hiked Larry made frequent stops at choice fly water places. By the time they reached their new campsite Larry had a trout dinner wrapped in damp weeds in the special canvas fish creel he had designed and made. As soon as they had their packs off Larry pointed to the clouds building up over the mountains above and said the first thing we'd better do is get our rain shelters up. With a thunder storm we'll be getting rain or hail and maybe both.

It didn't take long for Georgia to set up and stake down her tent and Larry set up his tarp with three corners staked down and the fourth tied to a convenient tree branch. And then the sky cut loose with not rain but hail big as marbles. Girlie was a bit surprised and didn't like it a bit to be hit on the head with heavy hailstones and immediately took advantage of Georgia's tent.

This campsite was well used. The stone ringed fire pit had on one side flat rocks arranged in such a matter that Larry's grate could be laid across for cooking.

As they shared their food supplies Larry commented on the big difference between his experiences in the Oregon forests and here. "Always in the Oregon forest and along the streams there's always something good to eat like blackberries, huckleberries and sometimes wild hazelnuts if you could get them before the chipmunks did. Other berries I liked were the salalberries, the thimbleberries and the salmonberries. Blue elderberries were edible even though I didn't like their taste. Red elderberries were good for wild pigeons but not people. There were other things too that I've probably neglected to mention. I'll have to admit that the altitude has a lot to do with it. I think you've probably noticed that even the plants at streamside change as we gain altitude."

Georgia answered to all that with "Yes, I've noticed a change and I'll have to remember to comment on that when I organize my notes and pictures for my book. And you make the Oregon forests sound so inviting that you should be a member of the Oregon Chamber of Commerce if there is such a thing." Larry responded to that with, "Getting lost in an Oregon forest is not that bad except in winter when one might have to subsist on the little fern roots found in the thick moss on maples and alders. Not too bad though; it tastes a little like licorice. In fact that's what the little fern is called."

How good a meal of trout and freeze dried food can be seemed to be the usual gist of after dinner comments before Larry and Georgia built up the fire a bit and found seats beside it to sip what had become usual, a cup of hot cocoa. Larry had taken a pint of brandy and transferred it from the heavy glass bottle to a lighter plastic bottle. He had explained to Georgia how much better he found hot cocoa to be with a little added brandy. After a taste Georgia was happy to share a little of Larry's brandy in her hot cocoa as they enjoyed their social fire.

The thunder storm had passed for which Girlie was thankful. She also let everyone know how much she liked the trout heads and bones she was given and then it was pure bliss to find a comfy spot where she could curl up and feel the warmth from the fire.

Day four arrived with a clear sky. Georgia's plan was to spend the day checking out the vegetation upstream as far as she could then spend another night at this campground and the next morning hike down to catch the late afternoon ferry.

Larry's plan was to explore the Second Recess and perhaps a little of the small stream that came in from the north. Larry had a suggestion. "Tonight will be the last night we camp together. I know we both have freeze dried beef stew. I've noticed wild onions growing along the stream. I think those added to the stew would make it better. We can fry the fish I bring back and wrap them up to eat cold for lunch the next day. What do you think of that idea?" "Sounds good to me," Georgia answered and added "I have some pudding to cool in the stream and that'll be good for dessert. I have some dried fruit that I can put to soak; I don't think we eat enough fruit when we're back packing."

They both left camp with day packs with bannock bread and cheese for lunch. Larry with his fly rod would explore Second Recess; Georgia with her camera and notebook would do her thing upstream.

Last night for Larry and Georgia to share a campground; this would be the fourth night for that. This had been a productive day for both Larry and Georgia. Larry had much to say about his day of fishing and the beauty of where he had been.

Georgia had found plants along the stream that she had not noticed before; she didn't know what they were but took pictures and would find out what they were later. She was happy with what she had seen and photographed.

This evening as they sat by their campfire sipping hot cocoa and making small talk each had their private thoughts about how chance had brought them to sharing camp grounds together.

After a shared breakfast Georgia stated "today I'm not going to do anything with streamside studies; I'm just going to take my time hiking down hill with

Girlie to catch the afternoon ferry and enjoy our beautiful surroundings."

Larry announced his plan for the day. "I'm going to fish and hike upstream until I come to a good campsite. I'll make camp then explore and fish upstream a bit before evening. The next morning I'll do the same as you; just head down the trail to catch the afternoon ferry."

Before parting Larry and Georgia did exchange telephone numbers and both tried to express how much they had enjoyed each others company as they camped together.

Chapter 24

As Larry rode the ferry he reflected on his last several days experiences. Sharing camp with a lady and her dog had been an interesting and pleasant experience; in fact making camp alone last night he really missed the company he had the previous four nights.

At his pickup, Larry was preparing to head for Madera when he noticed Georgia's station wagon still parked where it had been before leaving on the ferry. He knew Georgia planned to leave a day earlier. He had a feeling that something not good had happened to Georgia. At the lodge he inquired if she had been on yesterdays afternoon ferry and the answer to that was no.

Larry changed his mind about leaving. He got out his camp stove to prepare a tailgate meal. He had picked up ice for his cold box and his trout were already on ice. This time he had kept larger fish but there were a couple that would fit his fry pan. That and a can of pork and beans would be his dinner.

Going over in his mind the hike down the trail to the ferry from his last camp Larry visualized what he had seen along the way and there had been no sign of Georgia. Then he remembered something; when he was in the vicinity of the juncture of the North Fork trail he had noticed the smell of camp fire smoke. This might be a clue as to Georgia's whereabouts.

As Larry ate his dinner a mental picture began to appear. Georgia had come to the North Fork trail early enough in the day to hike up it a small distance. Along the stream she had spotted some plants that she would like in her picture collection. He had seen her habit of removing her hiking shoes and getting tennis shoes on for getting out in the stream to a good position for taking the picture she wanted. Picking her way over wet slippery rocks she had slipped and sprained her ankle and it hurt so much that she couldn't put her weight on it.

In Larry's mind there was a picture of Georgia hobbling around with a makeshift crutch. She had put up her tent and with Girlie's help had gathered wood for a fire. She had spelled out the word HELP with toilet tissue in case a search plane might be looking for her.

Larry knew what he had to do. At the lodge when he tried to rent a boat and motor for the morning the lodge gave him the use of the boat and motor with no charge. Also the lodge had a pair of crutches for him to borrow. Larry added an ace bandage and tape to his first aid kit in the day pack; in his mind he was certain it was a sprain or broken bone in Georgia's ankle that was keeping her from walking. Early in the morning he would go to the head of the lake on a rescue mission.

It was still fairly early in the morning when Larry secured the boat at the head of the lake and started hiking up the trail. When he reached the North Fork trail he detected a faint odor of camp fire smoke and knew that Georgia was up and about in her camp.

Hiking up the trail alongside the stream it wasn't long before he could see Georgia's camp just as he had pictured it complete with the toilet paper HELP sign. Girlie spotted Larry before Georgia and with a little bark came to greet him. Georgia had a surprised look on her face as she stood with her makeshift crutch.

As he approached Georgia spoke up with LARRY! She dropped her crutch stick to throw both arms about his neck and gave him a solid kiss. Then next came the question "Larry, what made you come looking for me and how did you know where to find me?" "I knew you were in trouble when I saw your station wagon still parked at the lodge. Then I saw your toilet paper call for help." Now Georgia was puzzled. "How could you see that?" she wanted to know. "I'll explain later" and added "let's have a look at that swollen ankle and take these crutches. Can you tell if your ankle is sprained or has a broken bone? "All I know is that when I put any weight on it the pain is too much for me doing that."

Larry thought wrapping with the ace bandage would relieve the pain a bit. Getting to a doctor for an x-ray was the important thing to do as soon as possible. Together they worked to pack up for leaving. Larry picked up the toilet paper call for help to burn before watering down the little campfire. Larry shouldered her pack and his day pack and Girlie carried what remained of her food. With the crutches Georgia was able to keep weight off her foot as they slowly worked their way down the trail.

When they reached the lake the ferry had come and gone. Several people had come to spend the day around Mono Creek and the head of Edison Lake. Out on the lake as they did the seven mile or so trip down the lake they discussed what they should do next. Since it was Georgia's left ankle that was damaged she felt that she could drive. Larry would follow behind.

But where should they go? "You'll need an x-ray of that ankle. Do we go to Fresno?" Larry asked. "No, I want to go to Oakhurst. That's where my doctor is and they can take an x-ray there too," Georgia answered. At the lodge Larry wanted to buy the crutches he had borrowed but the answer he got was no. They liked to have a pair on hand for emergencies so all they wished him to do was mail them back when Georgia could buy new ones.

They had agreed to stop at Shaver Lake for a quick lunch which they did and at the same time Georgia called her doctor to explain her problem and about when she expected to get to Oakhurst. As they passed along the west side of Bass Lake Georgia stopped to point across the lake to where she lived.

When Georgia's doctor examined her ankle it was his opinion that it was a bad sprain with no broken bones but he did want an x-ray. By the time the doctor studied the x-ray picture and determined that there were no broken bones and explained what she should do with hot and cold packs it was getting fairly late in the afternoon.

Georgia commented that if there were no pressing reasons for Larry to hurry on to Madera she would like him to come with her to her house. She had what she needed to whip up a spaghetti dinner and there was a spare bedroom for him to spend the night.

Larry expressed some reservations that Georgia should have about inviting a stranger to her home to spend the night. Georgia's answer to that was "Larry we camped together for four nights. You may have been a stranger when we got off that ferry but after camping with you for four days you are no stranger.

And then you came to rescue me when I got into trouble; Larry I owe you big time! Please let me cook a dinner for you. I'll have a fire in the fireplace; we can talk and enjoy an evening together. The first thing I want is a hot shower and I'll bet you'd like one too."

After listening to the way Georgia expressed her invitation there was only one thing for Larry to do and it was accept her invitation. At her home in Bass Lake after Georgia had her shower and she was starting her work in the kitchen Larry got fresh clothes from the camper and took his turn in the shower. Joining Georgia in the kitchen Larry commented "A hot shower is a lot better than a washcloth bath in the cold waters of Mono Creek." Georgia agreed with that.

Georgia explained that all she had to do for spaghetti sauce was take a container of it from the freezer. She made it from scratch and always kept some in the freezer ready for use. Larry found this to be interesting and commented "that's what my mom does too."

After dinner as they sat and talked in front of a cozy fire in the fireplace Georgia mentioned that when they had camped together and talked a little about Larry's parents and his sister it was just enough for her to want to hear more about them. "How did your dad and your mom meet each other?" Georgia asked.

Larry explained that his dad came to Canada from Sweden and had teamed up with a guy as timber fallers. The partner was half Scotch and Chipewyan native. It was his timber falling partners sister that he had fallen in love with and married. "That would mean that you are half Swedish and one quarter Scotch and one quarter Chipewyan," Georgia questioned. "That's correct," Larry answered. "That's really quite interesting. There was always a little talk in my family that my dad might have a little American native blood in his ancestry." Georgia responded and then wanted to know more about the sister he had mentioned.

Larry was proud of his sister Lisa and liked telling Georgia about her ambitions and summer work on the Oceanography ship in Newport Oregon. Georgia said she had always wished that she had a sister or brother. She told a little about her best friend Sharon who was always so much like a sister.

The next morning the combination of hot and cold packs the night before had reduced swelling in the ankle a bit but it hurt too much when she tried to put any weight on it to do that. After breakfast they rode together in Georgia's car with Girlie along to shop for a pair of crutches so Larry could mail the borrowed pair back to Edison Lodge.

That accomplished, Georgia wanted to drive Larry not only around the business district but around the residential areas. Larry was learning that Oakhurst was a much larger community than he had first thought.

Back at Bass Lake Georgia prepared a nice lunch. She was getting quite proficient with getting around on crutches. Larry commented on that and hoped for her ankle to recover sooner than later. Before leaving for Madera they agreed to keep in touch. Actually it wouldn't be long before school opening for them both and Georgia expressed a hope that she would be off crutches by that time. They parted with a warm hug and Georgia couldn't resist from giving Larry a little kiss on his check.

Watching Larry drive away Georgia hated to see him leave. As Larry was driving away he was thinking that it would have been nice to spend more time with Georgia.

Back to his apartment in Madera it was time for Larry to call Lisa. As he waited for Lisa to answer his call he wondered how in the world he could begin to describe the events of the last few days.

Lisa answered with "Larry I've been waiting to hear from you; I thought that you'd be back from your back packing trip a day or two ago." "Well, things happened that held me up a couple days. You probably might not believe it when I tell you that I have camped in the mountains for four days with a beautiful lady and then had to return to rescue her when she couldn't walk because she had slipped on some rocks and sprained her ankle. And yes, the fishing was good."

Now Lisa knew Larry well enough to know that there was more to this story than what he had just said and told him so. "Yes I suppose there is. You might be interested to know that she makes spaghetti sauce from scratch and keeps a supply in her freezer just like our mom does," Larry answered. The more Larry said the more Lisa sensed that there was something that Larry wasn't saying. She would learn more in the future so she changed the subject to talk about herself.

The coming year would be her last year at Oregon State. Her Coast Guard boyfriend wanted them to be engaged. She admitted being in love with him but didn't want to commit herself until after graduation. Larry let her know that he thought that was good thinking on her part. Before they terminated their conversation Larry told Lisa that the lady with whom he had camped was named Georgia Brown and that she would be starting her first year as a science teacher at the High School in Oakhurst.

Chapter 25

With school starting for both, Larry and Georgia were busy people but they did manage to talk on the phone at least once a week. It was a month or so after school started that on a Sunday Larry enquired if her ankle was well enough for her to go to a dance with him. He explained that the music of the big bands was coming to Fresno the next Saturday. They could meet some place for dinner before the dance which will be at the Civic Auditorium from eight to midnight.

Georgia answered with "Of course I'd like to go dancing with you and yes I'm no longer using the crutches. My ankle is pretty much back to normal." Larry suggested "You know Fresno better than I do so you pick the restaurant where we would meet." "I can do that. I'll think a bit about restaurants and get back to you in a couple days with directions," Georgia answered.

Three days later Georgia called to say "An easy place for you to find would be the Fresno County Courthouse parking lot. If we meet around five thirty the lot should be about empty and we'd have plenty time to visit before I guide you to a little Armenian restaurant I like. Is that okay?' Larry said that was fine with him and that's what they agreed to do.

At the Court House parking lot they met with a hug and Georgia suggested walking to the grounds where there were benches. As they discussed the events of the past several days they were admiring the statue of the unfortunate kid holding up his leaking boot.

Larry didn't think it a good idea to leave his pickup in the Court House lot; he would rather follow Georgia to the restaurant which Georgia said was nearby. They did get separated at a traffic stop but Larry was able to get behind her again to park next to each other at the restaurant.

Lamb and rice are both items popular in Armenian cuisine and Larry found the featured dinner that Georgia suggested much to his liking and made a point of thanking her for her guidance.

Georgia didn't plan to return to Bass Lake after the dance. Instead she would drive to nearby Firebaugh to spend the night at the ranch with her parents. She had an invitation for Larry.

"Larry, tomorrow around ten in the forenoon I want you to come to Firebaugh to meet my parents. We'll have lunch and then in late afternoon I'll go home to Bass Lake and you can go back to Madera. This will give us time for a good visit and I think you'll find the little Black Angus cattle ranch of interest too." "I'd like that but you'll have to explain to me how to find the ranch," Larry commented.

Georgia sketched out a little map on a napkin for Larry. It would be an easy place for him to find, she thought.

At the Civic Auditorium they found parking near each other and as Larry was getting their tickets they could hear music in the style of Glenn Miller playing. Dancing together was a new experience for Larry and Georgia but they were soon finding that they were in the rhythm of the music together as good dance partners. Georgia just had to say "I like dancing with you and the way you move so smoothly." Larry responded to that with "thank you and I'll say the same to you."

Parting at their cars at eleven because of the distance they would drive and commenting on the good time they had dancing to good music added to their usual parting hugs was a warm kiss and it was much different from their sometimes peck on the check! Somehow it was just the natural thing for them to do.

Driving the short distance to Firebaugh Sunday forenoon and finding the ranch was no problem. He knew he was there when he saw the Black Angus cattle in the pasture and Georgia's station wagon parked in the driveway.

Before Larry had a chance to touch the doorbell button the door opened and Georgia came out to greet him with a hug and a quick kiss. She had seen him coming in the driveway.

Georgia's dad George was in the living room when Georgia entered with Larry. George and Larry were properly introduced to each other which they acknowledged with a handshake. Georgia's mom in the kitchen heard the talk in the living room. When she entered the living room Georgia started to introduce the two but her mom didn't wait for that. She spoke to Larry with "So you are the Larry that my daughter has told me so much about!" As she greeted him with a hug she said "I'm very happy to meet you in person, Georgia has talked so much about you."

Georgia was blushing; she didn't like having Larry know that she had talked so much about him to her mom. Larry was smiling as he said "I can say the same to you; Georgia has told me so much about you. I'm very happy to meet you too."

"I want you to tell my dad a little about your Ag teaching at Madera High. I've tried to explain a little about it but I know he'd like to know more," Georgia said as she left to help her mom with lunch preparations in the kitchen.

"Yes, I'm interested. I happen to be on the local School Board and I like to keep in touch with what is being taught about agriculture in other schools since agriculture in some form or another is so important here," Georgia's dad said.

Larry had been handed a big order. He did his best to describe what he taught in his beginning and advanced classes without getting too much into detail. "I think our high school Ag program is somewhat similar although I don't think our Ag teacher gets much into equipment repair. I guess around here if something needs repair we just take it to whatever kind of repair shop is needed."

"That's the point of why I include equipment repair in my teaching. Some of my students will find jobs in some of those repair shops you mentioned," Larry commented. "Good point," Georgia's dad said as Georgia came to announce "lunch is on the table."

Georgia and her mom had gone all out to put a very special Sunday lunch on the table. There was a large platter with open face sandwiches with assorted toppings. For drink there was a choice for tea, coffee or just iced water. When Larry commented on the wonderful lunch, Georgia commented "We always eat well at this house; when duck season arrives I want you here for one of my mom's duck dinners." "And that's an invitation," Georgia's mom added.

After lunch George took Larry out to see the cattle and the rest of the farm. George explained that raising choice Black Angus breeding stock was the specialty of the farm. There was a garden area where they grew various vegetables in season. All kinds of melons did well in this area; in fact it was important commercially here but in their garden what they grew was only for their own use. Larry asked "do you have any equipment that needs repair? I could take it with me if I could get it in my pickup for my students to work on." "No, I don't have anything at the moment but thanks for the offer," George responded.

Back in the house and time to leave, Larry thanked Georgia's folks for their hospitality and especially BB. She had told Larry to call her that just as did everyone else. Georgia came out to his pickup with Larry to say goodbye with a hug and a kiss. She would be leaving too for her drive back to Bass Lake.

Driving back to Madera Larry was thinking about the phone call he would make to Lisa. There would be so much to say about dancing with Georgia and the visit with her parents at their farm.

In fact when he did talk to Lisa later that evening, he did describe how much fun it was dancing with Georgia and then went into detail about Georgia's parents and the luncheon.

After that conversation Lisa was quite certain that her brother was in love with Georgia even though he probably wouldn't admit it.

Chapter 26

Occasionally, Larry and Georgia had met for dinner and a movie in Fresno. They had much to share about their teaching experiences. Suddenly it seemed, time had come for Christmas break.

Larry, of course, was planning to join the family and friends in Oregon.

Georgia would be relaxing at Bass Lake but the several days around Christmas day she would be with her folks.

Shortly before Larry planned to leave, Georgia called to invite him to her home in Bass Lake to visit for a day or two. Larry thought there might be some special reason for this but he couldn't imagine what it might be. Perhaps she just wanted to visit a bit.

At Bass Lake, of course, Georgia wanted to visit a bit but that wasn't all. After dinner as they sat in front of Georgia's fireplace staring into the glowing embers and sharing hot coco laced with a little brandy Georgia said, "One reason I wanted you here is because of something you said to me some time ago as you were talking about your Ag teaching. In general you liked what you taught but your favorite part was teaching the repair of farm equipment and fixing things. You thought perhaps having a fixit sort of business might be more to your liking than teaching."

"Yes, I remember that and sometimes I do think I'd like that," Larry answered. "Well, you might be interested in what I have to say. A long time family friend in Oakhurst, Oliver Johnson, has a sort of what you might call a fixit shop. He repairs electrical appliances and small engines like lawn mowers and chain saws. A large part of his business is that he is a chain saw dealer and sharpens the chains as well as other kinds of saws. A few days ago as I was talking to him he indicated that he was getting up in years and before he was too old to travel he was thinking of selling his business so he'd have time to do that. He hasn't advertised the business for sale but was thinking about it. I told him that I had a friend who might be interested in having a business like his and he indicated that he would like to meet that person who is of course you," Georgia explained.

Larry thought what Georgia said was quite interesting and told her so. "I'd like to meet your friend and see his business but I imagine that his selling price would be a lot more than I could afford," Larry added. "I'm quite sure that he would carry a mortgage after a reasonable down payment," Georgia answered to that and added that she would take Larry to see the business in the morning.

The fire in the fireplace had burned itself out and it was time for sharing a hug and kiss as Georgia and Larry parted with "good night and sleep tight."

Georgia got to thinking before she went to sleep; she would propose that she become a partner in a potential purchase. They could pool their resources.

At the same time Larry was doing some serious thinking; not about buying the business that Georgia had described which did interest him, but something more serious than that. He had come to realize that he not only liked Georgia very much but had fallen in love with her. There was only one way to find out if she would say yes if he proposed and that was to propose.

He would show Georgia the letter that Lucy had written and then propose at breakfast time.

Larry awoke in the morning to the sound of noises from the kitchen and to the smell of fresh coffee. Freshly shaved and showered he was met in the kitchen with a "Good Morning" and a warm kiss. "I'm getting ready to cook bacon and eggs for breakfast and I hope you like your eggs scrambled because as you can see I've already whisked them up," Georgia said and Larry responded with "I think I'd like your eggs cooked any way you did it and yes, I like scrambled eggs." Georgia smiled and gave Larry another kiss before pouring a cup of coffee for him.

At the table Georgia brought up the subject of Oliver Johnson's shop. "I know that shop would be a good investment and I have a proposal for you. After you see the business and find out what a down payment would be and if you become seriously interested I would like to join you as a partner in the purchase. I have some savings and know that I could borrow more from my parents."

"Thank you but before I answer that I want you to read this letter," Larry said as he got Lucy's letter from his pocket and handed it to her. As Georgia finished reading the letter Larry could see tears in her eyes as she tried to talk and couldn't. "Now I have a proposal for you," Larry said and added "I would like you to be my partner for life. Would you accept this ring I wear around my neck as he removed it and took it from the chain?"

This turn of events had caught Georgia only a little surprised; she had known in her mind that eventually he would realize that he loved her and would say so. She wished that he would not wait forever to do it. She looked across the table at Larry with tears in her eyes, got up from her chair to come around to his side of the table. When Larry saw her rise from her chair he did the same to meet and take her in his arms as she said "YES" and sealed it with a kiss. She was happy to have Larry put the ring on her finger and yes, it fit!

Oliver Johnson's shop was on the north side of H-81 where the highway left Oakhurst toward Yosemite. It was on an acre sized lot that he had purchased many years before when his shop building stood alone. Through the years other businesses had moved in nearby and on both sides of the highway.

Above the shop was an apartment where he lived. At the time he bought the lot and put up the building he was newly married but shortly after moving in his wife lost her life in an auto accident and he had never remarried and had no close relatives.

The first thing Larry noticed as Georgia parked was the prominent Husqvarna chain saw sign on the store front in addition to Oliver's Fixit Shop.

Inside Georgia introduced Larry to Oliver Johnson mentioning that she had told Larry that this business might come up for sale in the future. She explained that Larry was an Ag teacher in Madera and that a part of his teaching was the repair of various kinds of farm equipment.

Oliver commented, "Georgia, I see a very nice ring on your finger that was not there the last time I saw you. Is this the guy who put it there?" "That's right," Georgia answered and Oliver said "Congratulations and Larry, I've known Georgia since she was a wee tot and you are a very lucky guy." Larry smiled and said "I know that!"

As Oliver explained a little about the business Larry could see chainsaw chain sharpening equipment. Oliver explained that this and other saw sharpening was the larger part of his business. Small engine repair, especially chain saw engines was important too. There were various sizes of new Husqvarna saws on display for sale as well as saws that had been taken in trade and reconditioned.

Georgia asked a few questions as to when he might be selling the business. Oliver hadn't decided as yet but it would probably be in spring or early summer. Georgia explained that if Larry decided to leave his teaching job to have a business such as this they would as partners pool their resources to make a purchase. "That is if pooling resources would be enough for a down payment on the asking price, whatever that would be," Georgia added. She was aware that it wasn't only the business Oliver planned to sell; it was building and land too.

Larry let Oliver know that he liked the business but would have to know if they could raise enough funds for a down payment before making a definite commitment. Oliver hadn't decided on an asking price as yet but would probably like a third down and carry a mortgage himself on the remainder. He also promised before publicly advertising the property for sale he would contact Georgia and Larry.

Back at Bass Lake over lunch Larry said he could see room for expansion the way the building was situated on the lot. He thought work space was a bit cramped at present. Georgia and Larry agreed to explain the situation to their parents to find out if and how much they could help.

Larry had learned a lesson and wanted Georgia to know that he would like a marriage to happen as soon as possible. "I agree but when and where that should happen is a question," Georgia commented.

Georgia and Larry agreed that they would want their parents and close friends to be present for the occasion. Georgia said she would like it to be at her parent's farm and Larry thought it would be nice for it to be at his in Oregon. They must think up a compromise of some sort.

One thing was apparent. The current Christmas break would not give them enough time to get families organized and as a practical matter they would need to put it off until the end of school in the spring. Larry said there was one thing that there was time for during their Christmas break. "I want to bring you to Oregon to meet my family and at the same time work on wedding plans." "That's what I would like too since you've already met mine," Georgia agreed.

At dinner they planned. Larry's first thought was that they would drive in his pickup and camp once or twice along the way; but on second thought realized that this was winter time and some mountain roads could have heavy snow. Better that they fly from Fresno to Salem where they could rent a car.

Georgia agreed with all that and said, "In the morning I'll pack clothing and stuff I'll need and drive to Firebaugh. My folks can care for Girlie. You go to Madera to gather what you'll need then meet me at my folks where we'll spend the night then in the morning we can drive to Fresno to catch the flight to Salem."

Larry thought all that sounded quite logical and said so. They each spent the rest of the evening with note pads in hand as they talked of many things and made lists of things to not forget.

In the morning Georgia was still packing her car as Larry left for Madera. As he drove he was thinking of things to add to his notes. One thing he would do in Madera would be to call his folks from his own phone to alert them to his and Georgia's plans which included spending Christmas with them and New Years day with Georgia's folks.

In Madera Larry was talking to his mom and after letting her know that he was bringing Georgia for Christmas his mom said she would like very much to meet Georgia. She also commented "Lisa has told me that from your conversations with her she knew sooner than later that something like this would happen. She seems always able to know you better than you know yourself." Larry had to admit "Yes, some times it seems that way."

When Larry got to Georgia's folks in Firebaugh Georgia was already there. She had explained to her folks the plans about flying to Oregon for Christmas but that they would be back to spend New Years with them. She had also shown them the new ring she was now wearing. Georgia's mom welcomed Larry with a big hug and her dad had a warm handshake for his future son-in-law. Georgia's parents had always been happy with the people Georgia chose as friends and now they were especially happy with her pick as a person to marry.

At lunch and after there was naturally much discussion as to when and where the marriage would be. On that subject about the only sure thing was that it would be after both their schools closed for summer vacation.

During dinner Georgia brought up the subject of their interest in the business Oliver Johnson planned to sell in the future. George knew Oliver and the business so was quite interested in what Georgia was saying about she and Larry forming a partnership to make some sort of a deal with Oliver to take over the business. At this time they had no idea as to what he would want as a down payment. Whether Georgia and Larry's combined savings would be enough for that was a question with no answer at this time

In the morning they loaded everything they would take to Oregon into Georgia's car and after hugs and goodbyes they were on the way to the Fresno Airport.

Later in the air Larry was happy that they were not driving to Oregon when he could see all the white as they passed over Mt. Shasta. Even when they arrived in Salem there was white in the nearby foothills.

Larry didn't know if Lisa was in Corvallis or at the farm so called his folks at the farm to let them know he was now in Salem. He learned that Lisa was at the farm so would not waste time going to the Corvallis place. He and Georgia would be coming straight to the ranch.

It was late afternoon when Larry and Georgia arrived to greet his parents and introduce Georgia. Larry's mom welcomed Georgia with a hug as she let Georgia know how happy she was to meet her. Larry's dad came out of his garage workshop to say to Larry as he shook Georgia's hand "Ja, it's about time you brought your girl friend to meet us!" and to Georgia he said "Velkommen, Georgia." Lisa had heard Larry arrive. She came out drying her hands; she had been out in the garden getting carrots for dinner. "I knew my brother for sure would bring you here as a Christmas present for us," as she welcomed Georgia with a hug. She was the first to notice the ring on Georgia's finger and called everyone's attention to it. Now Larry's mom and dad as well as Lisa had to let Georgia know how happy they were to welcome her as a new member of the Peterson family. It was Lisa who finally said "Why are we standing here in the driveway? Let's go inside."

Larry's mom went to the kitchen to continue with her cooking. Lisa took Georgia to show her the guest bedroom and bathroom She well knew that after much time on the road Georgia would like to freshen up a bit. She went with Georgia to the rental car to help bring Georgia's things to her room.

Georgia was feeling a bit overwhelmed but at the same time comforted by the warm reception she was receiving. The Peterson family was so much like her family. Tomorrow would be the day before Christmas and the Christmas tree was up and decorated. Larry and Georgia could see already several presents under the tree; they had done their Christmas shopping early and would put their presents to each other under the tree later in the evening.

At the moment in the living room everyone except Minnie was relaxing and sipping their wine as they engaged in conversation which of course was mainly about Larry's engagement to Georgia. Minnie was in the kitchen putting last touches to dinner.

Judging from the mouth watering smells in the air everyone knew it would be especially good.

Lisa left the living room group to help her mom put the dinner on the table as she warned everyone "If there's anything you need to do before dinner, do it now." Minnie had decided to do a pork roast with carrots and rutabagas, root vegetables fresh from the garden, plus boiled potatoes and gravy. It was a simple dinner and a family favorite.

Conversation at the dinner table turned to Larry and Georgia's engagement. Lisa said, "Larry, I knew that eventually you were going to put that ring on Georgia's finger but how did you make it happen at this particular time? Did you get down on the traditional bended knee to ask for her hand in marriage?" "No, it wasn't like that at all." Larry answered.

"Georgia and I were discussing a business that I was some what interested in and what it would cost when she said if I liked the business she'd like to be my partner in its purchase. I answered to that by letting her know I'd accept her offer but only under one condition." Larry explained.

"What was that condition?" Lisa wanted to know. "I took the ring off the chain that I had been wearing around my neck, then had Georgia read the letter that Lucy had written before her death. When she was finished I said I'd accept her business partner offer if she would wear that ring and be my real life partner. Georgia said YES and slipped the ring on her finger and that's how it happened," Larry finished explaining.

Now everyone wanted to know about this business Larry and Georgia were considering. "I'd like to see that business," Larry's dad said after Georgia and Larry together described the business.

The next morning at breakfast the subject of marriage came up. When and where would this happen was the question. Georgia and Larry explained that it would happen after the school year ended in the spring. The big question for them was "where?"

After breakfast Larry was taking Georgia on a tour of the farm. He showed her the old Model T Ford truck that his dad had restored. What he most wanted to show was where he had caught his first trout. He explained that small streams like this in these parts were usually called "cricks" as opposed to larger streams such as Mono Creek where they had first met.

Later when they came back to the house Lisa asked "Larry, did you tell Georgia about the calf that fell in the crick?" Larry just shook his head and said "Nope." That caught Georgia's attention so she looked at Lisa to ask "Lisa, what's this about Larry and a calf in the crick?"

Lisa answered with "one morning when we gathered for breakfast Larry said we've got to go get that calf out of the crick." Of course every one wanted to know "What about a calf in the crick?" Lisa went on to explain that Larry insisted that one of the calves in the meadow has fallen in the creek and couldn't get out; when they all went to look, sure enough, there it was. A calf was in the creek trying to get out but couldn't. "Dad had to lift that calf back out of the crick back to the meadow and Larry never really explained how he knew the calf was in the crick."

Georgia turned to Lisa to say, "When Larry came to rescue me after I injured my ankle so badly on Mono

Creek's north fork I asked how he knew where to find me. All he said was that he had seen the help signal I had printed out with toilet paper. That didn't make sense because there had been no aircraft flying over." Larry was about to say something but was interrupted by his dad coming in from his shop to say, "Larry, I want to show you a project I'm working on." "Some time in the future Larry will probably explain," Lisa looked at Georgia to say.

Lisa and her brother shared a secret. After the calf incident Larry confided to Lisa that things happened for which he had no explanation. He went on to say, "Lisa, sometimes when I'm sleeping I kind of but not really wake up to find that I can look at my body in the bed asleep as I float around looking down at the cows in the meadow and other things around the farm. It's like that guy that had a magic carpet to ride on but I don't have a magic carpet. I don't say anything about this to anyone because they would probably just say I'm having nightmares or hallucinations; but to me it's real.

To himself and later to Lisa, Larry had explained the calf incident probably being caused by his subconscious mind remembering his seeing that calf on the edge of the crick bank and thinking if a bit of the bank broke off the calf would fall in the crick.

It seemed that every time the family was together, the subject of Larry and Georgia's wedding was the topic of conversation. Where would it be was the question. The final approval as to where would belong to Larry and Georgia.

It was Olaf who came up with an idea that he explained, "Larry and Georgia have talked about a fixit business that they are interested in buying. If I might loan money to help with a down payment; I'd like to see the business. If the wedding were in that vicinity I could do two things at once."

"We could do it at my house in Bass Lake except that for the number of people who would come to the wedding it would be too crowded," Georgia volunteered but added, "there are parks on the west side of the lake where group picnics and weddings often occur. I know my folks would love that as would my friends."

Georgia gave Olaf a big hug as she thanked him for coming up with his idea. Everyone agreed and a date would be set depending on Larry's and Georgia's schools closing for summer vacation.

There was another important date to consider, Lisa's graduation from Oregon State in the spring. The three important dates for Lisa, Georgia and Larry would all be on the table.

Day after tomorrow would be the day before Christmas. Larry wanted to take Georgia to Siletz so he could show and tell about that town and the native culture. Lisa wanted to have Georgia see the ship on which she had spent her summers as well as the interesting shops along Newport's waterfront and the beaches and lighthouse to the north. After a short conference it was agreed; Larry would use the next day for taking Georgia to Siletz and Lisa would get an early start the day before Christmas to take Georgia to Newport.

On the way to Siletz Larry spent a large part of the way explaining how different the road was now from the way it used to be. "What is now the highway was a railroad when I was little. The grade over Newton Hill on the old road was steep enough for people to brag if their car could make it to the top in high gear."

As they neared the bridge over the Siletz River Larry pointed out where Camp 12 used to be and that it was there where his dad had worked when he and his mom first came to Oregon from Canada. As they crossed the bridge over the river Larry commented, "Before this bridge was built the old bridge was down stream and you drove a distance before coming into town instead of right into town as we are doing."

As Larry explained a bit about what had been the Siletz Indian Reservation, he was driving to where the government headquarters had been and explained, "It was for that reason this is called Government Hill and now these grounds belong to the Confederated Tribes."

Larry had so many good memories about this area and said so to Georgia as he drove by what had been home when he was real little. He told about his friend Willy who had made a name for himself playing football at Oregon State.

On the way home Georgia said, "I liked what little I saw of the Siletz River which wasn't much." "Sometime in the future I hope to take you to my favorite part of the river that is called 'The Gorge' and that's where the good fly fishing is." "I'll look forward to that," was Georgia's answer to Larry's hope.

Back at the ranch they were in time to ready themselves for the beef stew that Minnie had prepared; the beef and vegetables were all from their farm. Olaf said, "That kind of stew is what we call lopskous in Sweden and Norway."

In Newport the day of Christmas Eve, Lisa was having fun taking Georgia first to the Coast Guard station to meet Charlie her Coast Guard boyfriend and then across the bay to the ship where she worked and studied during her summer vacations. She explained her two goals; one was a degree in Oceanography and the other to graduate as an Officer in the Naval Reserve with enough knowledge of navigation, etc. to make her eligible at least to be a Third Mate in the Merchant Marine.

Next was to Agate Beach where Georgia was able to find an agate and then to the lighthouse on Yaquina Head. When Lisa mentioned rocks that bounced, in order to show Georgia that the story was true she took Georgia on the climb down to the little beach to let Georgia toss a fist sized rock into others of like size. Georgia said, "I didn't think rocks would do that but now I see that these special rocks of volcanic origin really do bounce when they strike another rock of the same material. I'll remember to talk about this in my Science classes when the subject of rocks and minerals comes up."

On the way home Lisa pointed out the spot where barges that had been floated with the tide were unloaded with supplies to be taken by wagon to the Government's Reservation Agency in Siletz. This unloading depot site gave the name Depot Slough to the stream the highway pretty much followed as they continued to the farm. The day spent with Lisa made Georgia understand why Larry was so proud of his sister.

For Christmas Eve dinner the main dish was steelhead that Larry was barbecuing. His dad had caught it on the Siletz River at the Fireplace Hole. Larry explained to Georgia that all the popular steelhead fishing sites had names; this one got its name from the indentation in the rocky bank that someone had carved out like a fireplace years ago. In freezing weather it felt good to stand in front of a fire as one waited for a steelhead to take the bait on the end of the line coming from the rod propped up on a forked stick stuck in the sandy bank. Sometimes a turkey bell hung on the rod tip would signal a bite.

Christmas morning came with everyone enjoying the Swedish Pancakes with butter and Lingonberry jam that Minnie was serving along with their coffee. Then it was time for Olaf as Santa to pass out packages from under the Christmas tree. Georgia was thanking Larry along with a kiss and reading from a note in one of the felt soled wading shoes Larry had given her. The note had references to slippery rocks and sprained ankles. Two framed photographs were being passed around. One was an action picture of Larry fly fishing and the other was a picture of Georgia and Girlie. Girlie's mouth was holding a sign which read WE LOVE LARRY which made Larry comment something to the effect that he should have a sign to hang on his chest saying LARRY LOVES GEORGIA AND GIRLIE.

Christmas was a day of socializing and feasting. For the Christmas dinner the main dish was ham. This ham was from a hog raised on their farm and processed by Ivan. It was fresh from his smokehouse. Olaf had prepared his version of Swedish Grog.

Ada and Ivan of course were eager to meet Larry's fiancé, Georgia. Larry had told her so much about them and their son Willy that it was if she already knew them. Lisa's boyfriend (she was now calling him that) had met Georgia briefly the day before but was now having a chance to converse with her.

Minnie and Olaf mentioned that they wished their friends Jim and Julia were here but they had gone to Eugene for Christmas with their daughter Marie.

Georgia, in bed but not yet asleep, was reliving in her mind the Christmas Day and especially the dinner. This had been the kind of a special occasion dinner she liked with old friends and new discussing current happenings in their lives. Two topics especially had generated considerable conversation; they were Lisa's graduation and plans for her own wedding to Larry in the spring.

Chapter 27

On their way to Salem for their return flight to Fresno Larry drove to the Corvallis home where both he and Lisa had lived while at Oregon State. Larry thought that his folks would probably sell it since Lisa would be graduating in the spring. "However," Larry added, "if Lisa decides to do graduate work at Oregon State that would change the picture."

"There are other schools that offer advanced degrees in her fields of interest. She might learn their take on Oceanography a bit different in some ways from Oregon State," Georgia commented. Larry agreed that Lisa was entirely capable of doing something like that.

In Fresno, Georgia made a call to her folks to let them know that she and Larry were back and as soon as they could pick up their baggage they would be on their way to Firebaugh.

Georgia's dad and mom were ready with a barrage of questions about the trip to Oregon. "We have so much to talk about; it was great to meet Larry's family and I'll tell you all about it this evening," Georgia said as she and Larry were getting their things from her car.

At dinner and after, Georgia's parents were happy to learn that the wedding in the spring would be at Bass Lake. Not at the cabin but at a picnic site on the other side of the lake. Exact time would be shortly after Lisa's graduation from Oregon State and after Larry's and Georgia's schools started their summer vacations.

Learning that Larry's dad would loan Larry and Georgia what they would need for a down payment on Oliver Johnson's business in Oakhurst was of interest to George. He had been planning to help too if necessary.

BB's New Year's Day dinner featured Angus roast beef from the ranch plus veggies from their garden. It was a fine dinner which generated compliments to the chef; but the main topic of conversation always seemed to come back to wedding plans.

Georgia and Larry let it be known that it would be a fairly simple wedding celebrating one of the most important happenings in their lives. Details would be worked out in due time.

Back with his teaching Larry was debating as to when he should let school officials know that he was leaving his teaching position. At the moment his decision was to wait until near ending of the semester. In a way it would be hard to keep his plans to himself.

As the time passed, slowly it seemed to Larry, he did bits and pieces of planning. One item he took care to do was to alert his friend Willy about the wedding and that he wanted him to be the Best Man at the occasion.

Georgia was having similar experiences and feelings. One thing of importance to her, she had contacted her friend Sharon to ask that she be her Bride's Maid. One problem she did not have that Larry did, she was keeping her teaching job.

Many weekends were spent with Georgia at Bass Lake. Together the two went to Oakhurst to visit Oliver's business. They let him know that they were serious about buying the business and they told him about their wedding plans and that she wanted him to be present at the occasion.

Larry as he studied the building was making mental notes as to how the building should be enlarged to fit plans he had in mind. Oliver mentioned ways he had thought would help with space problems, there had been things he wanted to do but couldn't because of space restrictions. He just hadn't felt like doing what he knew should be done. "That's something for young people like you two to do," Oliver said to Georgia and Larry.

There were happenings in Lisa's life; graduation was not far away and she knew that she would be graduating with honors. However, there were some things for her decisions such as looking for a job after graduation. She knew that there would be a change in ranks for ship's officers. First Mate was retiring and the second was taking over that duty. If the Third Mate applied for and took over that position, there would be an opening for a new third officer. Lisa would wait for developments regarding that.

However, Lisa would have qualifications for a position with the Oceanography department. If there was an opening she had made up her mind to apply for that.

Olaf and Minnie were making plans; as soon as a wedding date was known for Larry and Georgia, they would make reservations at a hotel in Oakhurst for a time a week or ten days previous.

A subject that often came up as Larry and Georgia talked was about a honeymoon. Should they right after the wedding just slip away with nobody knowing where they had gone? Perhaps they should delay a honeymoon until some time after the wedding? There were many ideas but as yet no answers.

It was graduation day in mid June. Olaf and Minnie had come to Corvallis to be with Lisa several days before the ceremony at Reset Stadium. It was an exciting day for the family. Larry and Georgia had arrived the day before the event; both their schools had just closed for summer vacation. A month earlier Larry had let his school know that he was leaving the district to take part in a business venture.

Lisa's family and Charlie were proud when honor students were asked to stand and Lisa was standing with the group. Charlie had come from Newport that morning to see his favorite person graduate. Just as after Larry's graduation, feasting would celebrate Lisa's graduation. Minnie had everything organized; all she had to do was get things cooking. The main dish would be a pot roast from beef raised at the farm.

With a wedding in the offing, conversation around the table seemed to wander around a variety of topics but always came back to Larry and Georgia's wedding. It was quite well established that it would be at Bass Lake, but when?

Celebrating the Fourth of July at Bass Lake always included fireworks from a barge out on the lake. Should the wedding be before or after that? Would Sharon be Georgia's Bride's Maid and would Willy be Larry's Best Man?

Larry and Georgia had privately discussed the merits of before or after the

Fourth of July celebrations; Georgia suggested the day before the Fourth and Larry at first agreed with that date but after thinking a bit brought up a question. They had tentatively planned for several days in Monterey immediately after the wedding and just before the Fourth it would probably be difficult to find hotel accommodations.

Fourth of July celebrating was always a big thing at Bass Lake with fireworks; Georgia agreed that after the Fourth would be better. All the friends and family gathering for the wedding would be able to enjoy the festivities. Two days after all the celebrating, the 6th of July was set as the wedding date and that was the date Larry and Georgia passed on to the family gathering.

Chapter 28

Olaf and Minnie were staying at a motel in Oakhurst; they had arrived almost a week before the wedding. Larry and Georgia had taken them to see the business they had been talking about and to meet Oliver Johnson. It was interesting to hear those two Scandinavians getting acquainted with each other; they immediately started comparing Oliver's Norwegian roots to those of Olaf. Olaf had to mention that he was born in Norway because his home was on the Norway side of the line at that time. At the time Olaf migrated to Canada the boundary line between the two countries had been moved to put the Peterson home in Sweden.

It was about a week before the wedding that Georgia said, "Larry, why don't I come with my car to Madera? You give up your apartment and we can move all your stuff into our two vehicles to bring to my house. You already have some things in the room where you've been sleeping and you can put everything there; we can sort things out later." "That all makes sense," Larry said. It had been done; they had brought cold boxes for emptying Larry's fridge. Georgia's fridge and freezer were now quite full.

Georgia's parents were planning to come the morning of the wedding. They would be bringing a long time family friend Judge Smith who would conduct the wedding service.

It was two days before all the Fourth of July celebrations would start that Oliver called Georgia to remind her that he had promised to give her and Larry first chance to buy the business. He had received a cash offer to buy the business and wanted her and Larry to come so he could explain the situation.

This was shocking news for Larry and Georgia who lost no time in coming to talk with Oliver. When they arrived at the business they were surprised to see Olaf there with Oliver. It seems that those two Scandinavians after considerable talk had cooked up a deal.

Olaf said to Larry and Georgia, "Ja, if I buy this business would you two take over the management of it? (Note: 'Ja' in Norwegian means 'yes' and the 'j' is pronounced as if it were a 'y'.) Larry and Georgia looked at each other in surprise. Larry had counted on his dad loaning what they would need to add to their resources in order for them to buy the business.

Olaf and Oliver together went on to explain that Olaf proposed to buy the entire property. Oliver would continue to live in the apartment above the store rent free and in return would be available to help meet customers when needed. Larry and Georgia would be responsible for the day to day operation of the business, details as to sharing profits after expenses would be worked out to the satisfaction of Larry and Georgia. This was an offer that seemed impossible not to accept. To Olaf they could only say, "Yes, we accept the offer and agree to the conditions." Olaf and Oliver would start drawing up necessary papers immediately after the Fourth of July celebrations.

It was midday at a picnic site under the trees on the western shore of Bass Lake. A catering service from Oakhurst, owned by a friend of the Browns, was busy with preparations for the feasting that would follow the marriage service. Georgia's parents were providing the

Angus beef that the caterer would prepare. Georgia's dad and Judge Smith were busy planning their part in the proceedings. Portable tables were already set up; Olaf and Oliver were busy assembling a bower; Lisa was helping Larry and Georgia's moms who were putting together ivy vines with attached assorted flowers for decorating the bower.

Brita Halverson, music teacher at Georgia's Yosemite High School had helped three of her students form a string instrument trio who were hired to provide background music for the party. Among music selections they had been practicing was the traditional Wedding March. Brita and several other teachers were guests as were several teacher friends from Larry's school in Madera.

Everyone was waiting for a car or cars to arrive with the wedding principals when someone called out "Look what's coming in from the lake." Larry and Georgia had rented a pontoon boat from the Lodge Marina and it was slowly coming to rest with the bow sliding up on the sand at waters edge.

With a gangway in place Georgia, Larry, Sharon, Willy and Wilma disembarked to receive multiple welcoming hugs. On schedule Judge Smith with Larry, Willy, and Sharon waiting in front of the bower, Georgia's dad was approaching with Georgia to sounds of the "Wedding March."

After the presentation with Georgia at Larry's right, Best Man Willy on his left and Bridesmaid Sharon beside Georgia, Judge Smith was ready to conduct the wedding ceremony. Of course there would be a pause as the group posed for the taking of formal wedding pictures.

With the exchange of rings and the traditional comment from Judge Smith to Larry, "Now you may kiss your wife," there was heard the sound of popping champagne corks, hand clapping and Big Band music from the trio.

It seemed that just about everyone wanted to kiss the bride or give her a hug. The toasting and chatter was interrupted by the clanging of a triangle. The caterer was announcing that food was ready to serve cafeteria style.

At the head of the line were the newly married Mr. and Mrs. Peterson and the rest of the wedding ceremonial party followed by the many guests,

The trio was playing popular music of the day as everyone at the tables filled their wine glasses and prepared to again toast Georgia and Larry. Good wine and food with friends at a joyous celebration is something to remember and this was one of those that Georgia and Larry would never forget.

Out on the lake, Georgia and Larry had quietly boarded the pontoon boat and they were on their way to Georgia's cabin where Georgia's car was already loaded with what they would need for the next few days they planned to spend in Monterey.

Because of the time of day when they were leaving Bass Lake, Georgia had told her folks they would stop at the home in Firebaugh overnight. At the same time Georgia's folks, Judge Smith and Sharon would spend the night at the Bass Lake cabin. Joining them for an evening get together before returning to Oakhurst were Willy, Wilma and Lisa along with her parents and Oliver. It was an evening of lively conversation mostly concerning the newlyweds and the new business venture along with refreshments and snacking on leftover food the caterer had packaged up for them.

As teenagers in high school Georgia and her best friend Sharon had often talked about the boys they liked and dated. In their discussions they had vowed to resist temptations in order to keep their virginity and graduating from college each was proud and happy that they had kept their vows not only in high school but also in college.

Often though, as Georgia was about to fall asleep she had wondered what it would be like to have someone she loved in bed with her; now in that same bed she was finding what it was like.

At Bass Lake Georgia and Larry always awoke in their separate rooms, but after they were engaged the night didn't always start that way. That was when they were engaged but now it was different; a married couple was sharing a bed at the start of a life together.

All settled in their hotel in Monterey they were planning the next day's activity. There were two things they planned to do; one was go to the Monterey Aquarium and the other was go deep sea fishing. At this time, however it was time to think about dinner.

The specialty of the little sea food restaurant by the docks was sand dabs caught locally and that was what was on their plates. They had debated the merits of white wine versus red. The pundits recommended a white with this type of fish but Larry preferred red and that's why Georgia had a glass of pinot griglio beside her plate and Larry had a glass of zinfandel beside his plate.

The kind of wine to have with their sand dabs was only a side issue. Which of the two things they had come to do in Monterey should they plan for the next day? It wasn't the flip of a coin that decided that the first day should concentrate on the aquarium and the second on deep sea fishing. Larry was confident that they would catch fish of some kind and it would be best to have it on ice nearer the time they would leave for home and Georgia agreed with that. And there was another thing; they would need to make reservations on a charter fishing boat. They would have time for that along with going to the aquarium.

Back at their hotel which was quite near the famed Cannery Row another thing they realized should be on their agenda should be a shopping tour to that well known tourist attraction. As far as Larry and Georgia were concerned weren't they just a couple of young tourists?

The main difference between the Monterey Aquarium and the one at Newport's South Shore Aquarium to Larry was that each had their emphasis on their parts of the Oregon-California coast. Georgia had seen the Monterey Aquarium previously and that was when she was just starting high school; she remarked on attractions that had been added since then.

It was an early morning start on the half day fishing trip and all of the half dozen passengers were betting that they would catch the heaviest fish which could be any of different species they might catch. Each person put five dollars into the pool.

Everyone was assigned a number and when a fish of whatever kind was landed by someone; a tag with their number was attached to it. It had been a great trip all agreed as they approached the boat's docking space. The excitement mounted as weigh time began. Everyone had caught fish and weights and numbers were recorded. When all were weighed the number of the heaviest fish, a halibut, was called out. It was Georgia's number and as she was handed the thirty dollars everyone cheered and clapped their hands. Everyone had learned that this fishing trip was a part of Georgia and Larry's honeymoon. There was a surprise ten dollars from the boat's skipper for the largest variety of fish caught and it was handed to the only other lady aboard to more cheers and hand clapping. It had been Ladies Day on that fishing trip.

All the fish Larry and Georgia had caught the day previous were packed in dry ice and in a cold box. Georgia remarked as they unloaded that cold box back at their Bass Lake cabin, "I think we had better be prepared for a fish diet for a while." "I don't think that'll be a problem; I know a couple people who have no trouble practically living on fish and I think you know who that is," Larry remarked. In discussing the time they had spent in Monterey. Larry and Georgia agreed that it had been only a little fun trip. Their real honeymoon would be what they were planning for sometime in August.

Chapter 29

Events were moving at a fast pace for the Petersons. Minnie and her architect had settled on a plan for the home to be built at the back of the business property. Olaf had made several suggestions that Minnie liked and foundations for the home were already in place.

Olaf and the architect along with Larry and Georgia had settled on the planned additions to the business building. Work had begun and was being done with little interference to regular business.

At the same time Georgia was working with Oliver to set up a book-keeping and account system that would be right for any changes in the business. Both Olaf and Larry had ideas about that for the future which might or might not be considered.

As old customers dropped by with repair jobs or chains to be sharpened Oliver introduced the new owners: Olaf, his son Larry and his wife, Georgia. To loggers Oliver made a point to mention that Olaf was very familiar with the logging industry because he had started out as a timber faller sharpening not only his saw but those belonging to other loggers.

A normal business day would find Georgia greeting a customer. Larry and Olaf would each be renovating a chain saw engine. Oliver with nothing else to do at the moment would be with Georgia in the combination business display and office entry room. With Larry and Olaf at the same time a machine had been programmed to sharpen a chain saw chain and it was doing just that. When it was finished either Larry or Olaf would program it for another chain sharpening job.

But sometimes the day wouldn't be a normal day. Since they advertised small engine repair, and outboard motors were not large, a potential customer asked if they could get his old 9.9 hp. Johnson running again. That turned out to be something Larry was eager to take on and it gave him an idea. He would find what motor brands were sold locally and then find what other manufactures might offer a dealership.

That evening Larry explained his idea to Georgia. She thought it was something worth investigating and they agreed to do that. This talk about outboard motors reminded Larry of something in the past about fishing. Camping near Fish Camp on his way to Yosemite he had met a fellow named Joe who had described the fishing in the upper reaches of Big Creek and a tributary called Rainier Creek.

Looking at Georgia, Larry remarked, "I haven't had a fly rod in my hand for all too long." Then he went on to explain about meeting the guy named Joe who had told him about fishing Big Creek and its tributary Rainier Creek. "Georgia, are you game to go with me to do a little exploring? We can pack a lunch and take a day away from the business. It's really only a short drive up the hill to the road that turns off at the top of the hill this side of Fish Camp." Georgia answered that with, "Larry, I think you knew the answer to that before you asked. Of course I'd like to do that; I've seen where that road turns off, but both when I was with my folks and later alone I've never turned off on it. I'd like to see where it goes."

It was only two days later with engine repair jobs caught up and Olaf and Oliver tending the business, Larry and Georgia were leaving the highway at the top of the hill near Fish Camp.

There was one point where they could look down to their left to see Big Creek and a cluster of buildings. As they drove it became obvious that they were driving on what had previously been a logging railroad roadbed.

Coming to a wide spot beside the road that Larry recognized as the parking place that had been described to him, they parked. They could hear the sound of rushing water and could see the trail leading in that direction. Larry gathered up his fly tackle and with lunch in their day packs they hiked down the trail to Big Creek. They could see close to their left where Rainier Creek joined Big Creek beside a beautiful little waterfall. Here they had a choice; they could cross Big Creek by boulder hopping and taking a chance on getting their feet wet but chose to walk the small log they could see had fallen across the stream just upstream which did require somewhat of a balancing act. As teenagers they had both been good at walking a fair distance on a railroad rail without stepping off,

They could see that this part of Rainier Creek was very brushy and assumed that the trail leading up the hill might bypass what appeared to be a narrow canyon. The trail leading up the hill put them on another old logging railroad roadbed. Looking to the right they could see where a trestle had crossed Big Creek to meet the road just a short way above where they had parked. Larry commented, "This isn't just a fishing trip, we're looking at history." "Yes, I have a mental picture of a steam locomotive crossing that trestle heading up the hill for more logs. The picture is so real that I feel like getting out of its way!"

Suddenly they could see where the little valley flattened out a bit. The stream was brushy in places but at times passing through a grassy little meadow. This was the type of stream that Larry loved to fish, places with brush hanging over a spot where he knew there would be a trout; a spot where it was a challenge for Larry to lay a fly without getting it caught in a branch above or behind.

Where they reached the stream was a wide expanse of smooth bedrock with water only inches deep flowing over it; but for some reason to one side was a pothole about four or five feet across and looking to be several feet deep. Larry pointed it out and said to Georgia, "I'll bet there's a trout in that pothole!" It was on his second cast with his fly swirling around out of sight that a nice eight inch Rainbow thought it looked like some tasty bug and Larry's comment proved to be correct.

With another trout, this time a Brown, at a friendly little spot beside a tree they were having their lunch when something caught Larry's eye. He walked over to see a collection of old rusted cans of various sizes. He realized that this had been the site of the cook shack for a small logging camp. There were signs of digging among the rusty cans and he knew why he saw no bottles. He remembered seeing similar sites in Oregon where bottle collectors had dug through dumps at old logging campsites.

On the way home Larry and Georgia discussed their day of his fishing and her picture taking; how lucky they felt to have places like that almost in their backyard. Larry had kept only four fish between eight and ten inches, just enough for their dinner; he had released a mix of Rainbows and Browns of various sizes.

Georgia had taken a few pictures but they were not planned to be a part of the book she hoped to write; at least for now, that was her thinking.

Olaf was doing what he liked to do; and that was repairing things with no thought as to time taken to complete a job. In Oregon he did things for neighbors for no monetary charge and they responded with gifts of farm produce of various kinds as well as labor when needed. This created a problem for Larry and Georgia; they had to figure out how much should the customer be charged?

This is where Oliver came to their rescue. He had done the same things that Olaf was doing and pretty much knew the time it took and the cost of new parts. Larry and Georgia were getting an education in the management of a fixit and small engine repair business. The customer could be charged the current hourly rate for a particular repair job or in some cases they could estimate the time a particular job would take plus its difficulty and quote a cost to a customer. When selling a new chain saw the dealer mark up was in most cases established and that was not a problem.

Georgia and Larry had to think about their honeymoon or forget it; Georgia would soon be back in the classroom. They had been planning this honeymoon for some time; they only had to finalize the details. A week would give them time to do what they wanted and Olaf and Minnie with Oliver's help could take care of the business with no problem for that length of time.

This honeymoon would not be a cruise to Hawaii or some island in the Caribbean, all popular honeymoon destinations; their honeymoon would take them to a place in the mountains about which they knew little more than what they could see on a map.

Lower Mono Creek was familiar territory but above that it and its tributaries was something new to explore. Before, their packs had been packed with only themselves in mind; now it was different. As an example, each had pots and frying pan to fit his or her needs but now they would need only what they as a couple would need.

That is why the content of their packs was in a pile on the bed in what had been Larry's room and now the packs were ready to be packed with what a couple would need for a week. Girlie was watching and suspecting that she might be involved in an adventure of some sort.

There was a shopping list for supplies that would call for a trip to Fresno. They pretty well knew which dehydrated foods to avoid and what to buy. A goodly share of their meals would of course be freshly caught trout.

Georgia's little one person tent would need to be replaced with a two person tent and they knew there would be many to choose from, each with its special features.

Back home on the deck Larry and Georgia were practicing at setting up the new tent. When they made use of it for the first time at a campsite they wanted to have no unforeseen problems. And yes, Girlie had to make certain that there would be room for her.

In loading their packs Larry said, "I'll make my pack a little heavier than yours because I'm bigger and more muscular than you." "That may be so but I'm tougher than I look," Georgia said, but finally had to admit that what Larry said did make sense. Fully packed and ready for travel his ended up in the vicinity of fifty pounds and hers near forty five. As usual, Girlie's food was in her saddlebags.

Larry wanted to have a conversation with Lisa before leaving on the pack trip but before he could call her, she called him. "Larry, I want you to be the first to know that in answer to Charlie's continued wanting us to become engaged, I finally said yes." This caught Larry a bit by surprise so about all he could think to say at the moment was, "Congratulations, I knew that sooner or later it was going to happen."

They went on to talk about a number of things, among them their parents' future plans. As soon as the cottage was completed and additions to the business finished, Olaf and Minnie were planning to fly to Salem. They would rent a moving van and drive to the Corvallis property. There they would load furniture, kitchen equipment and any personal items into the van; then contact their realtor to put the property on the market for sale before continuing on to the farm.

"I'll arrange to be at the farm when that happens. I'm going to lease an apartment at The Embarcadero and I'll want some furniture and kitchen stuff for that. Mom would want some things from the Corvallis property as well as the farm to furnish the new home in Oakhurst."

A big item for Olaf would be tools, etc. from the garage and importantly his plan was to rent a car hauler for towing behind the van. He wanted to bring the old Model T Ford truck for display at the business. The plan was not to sell the farm but to advertise it for lease partially furnished. After a bit of arm twisting, Lisa had agreed to handle that task for her dad and mom.

There was something Larry wanted to know, "Lisa, I don't hear you saying anything about wedding plans, what about that?" Lisa responded to that with, "No plans for that yet; I still don't know when or if I'll get the job as Third Officer on the ship. You'll be the first to know when I start making plans for a wedding."

Larry went on to explain that they were ready to leave on their real honeymoon. The trip to Monterey they didn't consider a part of their honeymoon. Their real honeymoon destination was a place in the mountains called Pioneer Basin. Since it was an area probably nine to ten thousand feet in elevation surrounded by peaks well over twelve thousand feet in elevation, they would make overnight stops along the way. Making changes in elevation too suddenly sometimes caused headaches and other physical problems. Their first night would be at Edison Lake, elevation a little over seven thousand feet.

Chapter 30

Out on the lake as Larry and Georgia watched, the Lodge's Ferry was returning with passengers on its afternoon trip. When the ferry landed and passengers disembarked, Larry recognized a couple he had met at the campground near Fish Camp at the time of his first trip to Yosemite, Joe and Sarah. They recognized Larry too and after gathering up their packs they found a bench where they could sit and visit a bit.

Before Larry could introduce Georgia, Joe spoke up with, "I see a pair of rings on this lady's finger. Is this the Lucy you spoke of as your fiancé?" This caught Larry a bit by surprise so at the moment he was at a loss for words. Georgia came to Larry's rescue with, "No I'm not Lucy. I am Georgia; Lucy lost her life in a shootout with a poacher gang but before she died she had written a letter to Larry to be opened only if she lost her life. She knew that in her work there was always an element of danger." As Joe and Sarah listened, Georgia went on to explain what was in the letter and when Larry showed her the engagement ring that Lucy had worn and gave her the letter to read before asking if she would wear that ring, the only thing she could say was "Yes." There were tears in Sarah's eyes as she gave Georgia a hug.

Further conversation brought out that Joe and Sarah had come west over Mono Pass. They had exchanged car keys along the way with friends heading east over Mono Pass and now they would have to find where their car had been parked.

Joe and Sarah found it interesting that Larry and Georgia had first met on the Lake Edison ferry and were now celebrating that with their honeymoon in this same area by backpacking to Pioneer Basin. Joe commented, "It's a great place to spend a little time and the fishing is good there too." Sarah added, "You couldn't have picked a better place to enjoy your honeymoon."

Larry mentioned that he had left his teaching job at Madera. His dad had purchased a chain saw and "fixit" business in Oakhurst and he and Georgia would manage it. Georgia planned to continue with her science teaching at the local high school. They parted with the prediction, "We'll probably meet along some trail in the mountains again sometime."

It was the next morning as they were leaving the ferry that Larry said, "Georgia, notice all these bits of obsidian in the sand." The lake was low enough to expose a stretch of sand over which they had to walk a distance before reaching the start of their trail. Larry continued to say, "I've read a little about what this area was like before the lake was here in what was called Vermilion Valley. California natives from the foothills would summer here to hunt and fish. Natives from east of the Sierra would come over Mono Pass to trade obsidian for items plentiful in the west. Vermilion Valley had been the site of an active barter system between natives from opposite sides of the Sierra."

"Fish Camp" was the name on their map near where Larry and Georgia planned to spend their first night of their packing to Pioneer Basin. It was very near where Second Recess met Mono Creek; Larry had seen the camp site the year before when he had fished up

Mono Creek. The camp site was popular with packers who brought groups there to camp with everything including meals furnished by the packer. There was pasture too for the packer's horses and mules. Larry had seen small camp sites nearby and that's where he had in mind for them to spend the night.

It was no surprise to Larry when they reached the group camp site to find a group there. A packer from Rock Creek on the east side of the Sierra had brought them over Mono Pass. Larry and Georgia stopped to talk to several people and the packer at the camp. They told the packer that they planned to camp nearby and were warned that they should be sure to hang their food sacks high out of reach of a bear at night. There was a bear in the vicinity that they had chased out of their camp several times.

Larry had picked up four pan sized trout for their dinner; along with their fried trout they used some of their dehydrated mashed potatoes and a veggie mix which had made for a good dinner. Now, as they sat on a log beside their campfire sipping their hot tea they discussed the days hike. It was all uphill and they had hiked in the vicinity of five miles since leaving the ferry. Their packs were heavy but they had stopped often to rest, drink bottled water and snack on some of their trail mix. In the morning they would boil more water for drinking; no mater how pure the stream water looked it might contain Giardia. They felt just tired enough now to sleep well this night; a night where they slept together in one tent, so much nicer than when they had camped apart beside Mono Creek.

The next morning as they shouldered their packs and started up the trail they spotted fresh bear scat. Once during the night Girlie had growled, she had smelled that bear and the bear probably got a smell of dog and left to raid some other camp.

At a point near Fourth Recess they saw on their map where another trail branched off to the north leading to their destination. The past four miles or so had been covered in good time in spite of the leisurely manner in which they hiked. Now it was time for lunch and a rest, they could see that the trail they would follow for a bit over two miles leading to Pioneer Basin looked to be a little steeper than the trail they had followed along Mono Creek.

Along the stream as they came to where they could have a look at the little basin like valley surrounded on three sides by a range of mountains with their four peaks, Larry couldn't resist putting aside his pack to flip a fly to a little pool he just couldn't pass up. Two pan sized trout tried to catch the fly at the same time so neither got it. Another cast and Larry's fly was taken by a nice fat eight inch trout that looked to be a cross between a Rainbow and Golden trout.

"That's a nice trout and I know it's hard to put that fly rod down but shouldn't we find our camp site and get our camp set up?" Georgia questioned. Larry couldn't disagree with that.

They did find a well used camp site with a fire pit and branches on a tree high enough to hang food sacks out of a bears reach in case they would be out of camp for a time. It was on high enough ground and far enough from the stream and the small lakes that perhaps they wouldn't be troubled much in the evening by mosquitoes. Larry was happy that there was still time in the afternoon for him to hike down to the little stream to catch several more trout for their dinner.

As they ate, they watched a buck deer with probably a four point antler spread, run across the valley as if something was chasing it, but they could see nothing of that sort. Before putting out their little camp fire, plans for the next few days were pretty much finalized. They would be at this camp site for the next two days. After that, a non-stop trek downhill to catch the late afternoon ferry would end their honeymoon except for the champagne they would have aboard the ferry to celebrate where they had first met. They had arranged with the ferry operator to have aboard at that time on ice enough champagne and plastic glasses for all aboard.

The reason this place was called Pioneer Basin was that the four peaks on three sides of it were named after historically important early California pioneers. Their names were, to the west, Mt. Hopkins and Mt. Crocker; and to the east, Mt. Stanford and Mt. Huntington.

Larry and Georgia could see on their map an easy slope to a ridge between Mt. Crocker and Mt. Stanford; from that ridge which was actually a part of the Sierra Crest they would be looking at the east slope of the Sierra. They used the last of their loaf of sour dough bread as part of the lunch they would have in their day packs. Exploring would be the thing to do this first day in the basin. Each would carry equipment for what each liked so much to do; Georgia, her camera and Larry, his fly rod and tackle.

"Georgia, with all these lakes this place could have been named Lakes Basin instead of Pioneer Basin."

"Yea, but Larry some of these seven or eight lakes shown on our map are just wide spots in a stream." "Right, but it does make for the nice pictures we'll see in the Honeymoon Album you talk about putting together." "Correct, but I'll want pictures of you catching fish too, not just of the scenery. Now it's time for you to catch fish."

That's the way the conversation went as Larry and Georgia hiked past lakes and streams. Actually one of the lakes was about a half mile long and there were fish in it, but the best fishing was in the streams. Girlie liked the lakes better for swimming.

"This is really amazing. We're looking almost straight down into a canyon and look at all those lakes." These were the kinds of comments Larry and Georgia were making as they stood at the top of the ridge. The approach to the ridge from the west was an easy slope but to the east it was completely opposite. Standing on the ridge was like being at the top of a cliff as they looked to the east.

Beside a small lake east of Mt. Crocker as they hiked back down, they found a scenic site for lunch and a swim for Girlie.

At the stretch of stream below the largest lake on the return hike to camp was where Larry said, "Georgia, are you getting tired of eating fish for dinner?" Georgia answered that with, "Why do you ask? Are you getting tired of catching fish?" Larry's answer to that was "No." "And my answer to your question is also 'no' so start catching dinner." This was a stretch of stream that Larry was happy to make the source of the most important part of their dinner menu.

The morning of this, the last full day of Larry and Georgia's honeymoon in what seemed like paradise, had been chilly. Only after warming rays from the morning sun struck their tent had they left the warmth of their sleeping bag. One thing that came as no surprise was the difficulty it was to find wood for a camp fire. For most of their cooking a single burner screwed on top of a propane bottle worked quite well. They also found a little fold up sheet metal stove using canned-heat, a form of alcohol jelly in a can to be useful.

As they ate their breakfast of scrambled eggs with bacon bits, reconstituted from their supply of freeze dried foods, they discussed plans for the day. One thing Larry would do was cook enough of what he called bannock bread for this day and on the trail tomorrow, which was made from Bisquick dough cooked in a frying pan. Instead of trout for dinner, he would catch enough for lunch. For dinner they would have a beef and veggie stew that they had used in the past and found to be good. Along the streams they had seen wild onions; they would gather some of that to add to their stew.

Along the streams, Georgia had seen some small willow bushes that looked to be the same variety that were larger along the streams at a lower elevation. She would want photographs of those for her book. For their last evening they really wanted a nice evening campfire. Searching for wood had to be on their agenda.

When Larry and Lisa with their fly tying sessions tried to create new versions of old fly patterns, Lisa had come up with a nondescript looking little nymph that she called a buggy bug. Larry found that the fish in the waters of Pioneer Basin really loved that Buggy Bug. There was no problem with catching what they would need for lunch.

In their search for wood they had noticed a very old juniper on a rocky promontory that didn't look healthy. On closer inspection it had obviously been struck by lightning. The main trunk was split and pieces of wood and broken limbs were scattered about. That is why after dinner as the setting sun was still touching Mt. Stanford and Mt. Huntington with gold, a happening known as the alpenglow, Larry and Georgia were sitting in front of a cheery campfire sipping hot cocoa laced with the last of their brandy.

Among the subjects under discussion were Larry's mom and dad. Larry knew that his dad was not happy with being retired and doing nothing. That is why his neighbors got broken farm equipment repaired by a person who refused money for his work, would only accept as gifts meat or produce from their farms.

Now, Minnie was excited about the new home that was almost ready for their moving into. Olaf was happy doing what he liked best to do with his time and that was fix things that needed fixing. Larry often heard his dad and Oliver conversing in what was either Norwegian or Swedish, perhaps a combination of both. Larry commented to Georgia, "It's as if my dad and mom are starting a whole new life."

Turning to face Larry, Georgia commented, "Larry, it's not only your mom and dad who are starting a new life. You and I are also starting a new life; I'm PREGNANT!"

The Author

Rudy was born October 28, 1912 in Western Oregon, a first generation American. His parents were from Norway. He grew up in a rural environment and was involved at various times with lumber and timber occupations as well as dairy farming, work in Oregon's salmon hatcheries, commercial fishing and merchant marine. For a time he was a clerk in a hardware and sporting goods store.

After serving five years in US Navy during WWII, GI Bill paid for Industrial Arts teacher training at Oregon State. Rudy retired from teaching in California in 1973. He married the love of his life near the end of WWII and has one son. Rudy lost his wife after sixty two years of marriage and now lives in Grass Valley, CA.

Acknowledgements

Friends who don't wish their names mentioned deserve a big thank you for their encouragement and help. Special thanks must go to long time friend Beth McCormick who did the major part of proof reading.

Made in the USA
San Bernardino, CA
03 February 2016